Louise Imogen Guiney, Louis Morvan

The Secret of Fougereuse

A romance of the fifteenth century

Louise Imogen Guiney, Louis Morvan

The Secret of Fougereuse
A romance of the fifteenth century

ISBN/EAN: 9783337344719

Printed in Europe, USA, Canada, Australia, Japan

Cover: Foto ©Andreas Hilbeck / pixelio.de

More available books at **www.hansebooks.com**

THE
SECRET OF FOUGEREUSE

A Romance of the Fifteenth Century

FROM THE FRENCH

BY

LOUISE IMOGEN GUINEY

Tout passe fors aymer Dieu.—OLD DEVICE

BOSTON

MARLIER, CALLANAN & CO.

1898

TO

GRACE CLARKE DENSLOW,

For Auld Lang Syne,

*The translator's share in this book
is dedicated.*

October 20, 1898.

CONTENTS.

THE SECRET OF FOUGEREUSE.

CHAPTER I.

THE DEVIL'S HOUSE.

"A house: but under some prodigious ban
Of excommunication.

. . . .

For over all there hung a cloud of fear:
A sense of mystery the spirit daunted,
And said, as plain as whisper in the ear,
The place is haunted!"

THOMAS HOOD, *The Haunted House.*

IN the reign of good King René, there stood
buried in the forest of Pouillé, not far from Angers, a solitary hunting-lodge. Two graceful tur-
rets shot up from its huge low stretch of roof. The
.dows, heavily barred, were yet a safe defence;
 massive oaken door was firm on its hinges; the
e entrance-steps, sunken now in the ferns and
grass, were neither discolored nor broken; and
er the dark-glistening tapestry which ivy hung
n the walls, there was hidden no gap in the
sonry. The whole place told of neglect, not
ruin. Cobwebs at every casement, brushwood

choking the walks, brambles covering the threshold, were like so many voices, testifying that it
had been some time since a human foot had en-
croached on the lawn, or a human eye tried to
pierce the mysteries of the abandoned dwelling.
The woodman's axe stopped short of those trees;
the fowler never dared pursue his game into the
coppices; and any homeless vagabond would rather
sleep in the open air on the stormiest night, than
seek shelter in so dreaded a spot. What was the
strange curse fallen on a habitation meant for
bright banquets and happy comradeship? What
was the secret charm which spread its thrilling
shadow over once hospitable halls? Curse and
charm summed themselves up in a word: the
house was haunted! A murder had been committed there : a dark, impenetrable, crime whose
victim had received no Christian burial, and whose
authors had eluded royal justice. The popular
imagination, seized with superstitious terror, had
formulated a report which daunted the living from
invading the ghostly precincts; the house, men
said, was haunted, and at the sight of it the boldest among them fled away. As to Sir Bertrand de
Pouillé, he chose rather to give up his hunting-
ground than to remain the owner of the Devil's
property. But no one would buy it, no one would
take it as a gift: for the house was haunted.

One single person stood out against this general
sentiment, and looked upon the hawkers of the
legend as mere chicken-hearted cowards. This

was Martin Bodin, landlord of the Red Rose tavern, which was set at the edge of the woods, on the road to Angers. To hear him talk, by daylight, one would think Martin a gallant sceptic. He grew a little more anxious by even-time, and would mumble *Paternosters*, and glance steathily up and down the road; but if any meddler began to talk about the haunted house, the innkeeper flew into a rage. With a partner and kinsman of his, Jacob Piteux, he would come often to threats and even blows, to avenge this offence against good manners. And for a perfectly simple reason. One turret of the lodge rose in plain view of the tavern windows; and, amid great fantastic boughs, it seemed a sort of challenge to the curious stranger, a lure to the bolder spirits, and a menace to the weak. Nobody could ignore it. Those who rushed to court adventure returned limp and beaten from the hands of some demon backed by Beelzebub, and the others fell into a brown study and departed: two results which broke the innkeeper's heart.

"If only they saw not *that* from their windows!" said he to his cousin Jacob; "I should care no whit were pandemonium let loose. But no! that has to be th very first thing to take my guests' eye. 'O turret is that, Master Bodin? Whose fi that?' And thereupon you cannot arself, but must needs tell them its history embellishments all your own!"

y because I am fain they shall not learn it others, cousin Martin."

"Ah, confound them! I would that the villains who killed the old fellow had killed him somewhere else," sighed Bodin. "For five years long, not a single traveller has passed more than three nights at the Red Rose. And if this sort of thing goes on, I shall take up my ancient trade of soldiering, and leave you to run to ruin alone."

"Tut, tut, mate! You know well, do you not, that in these parts a great coward is a yet greater drinker? Have a care of your cellar, my respected relative, and then the guests will leave their terrors at the bottom of the cask. Of course if you are bound to go" —

"You would be in too great luck, Jacob the Weasel. I shall cling to my duty, to my hostelry. If only they saw not *that* from their windows!"

One day, soon after, it was noised abroad that the Devil's House had found a purchaser. Had this purchaser been an aged, cracked, miserly personage, he would have been set down for a sorcerer. But what could be said against the baron Guy de Fougereuse, a gallant knight in the glory of his youth, the favorite of King René, and the idol of the people for his noble bearing, his good humor, and his liberal almsgivings? Gossip contented itself with murmuring resignedly, "God help the gentle lord!" Nor did the courtiers fail to rally Fougereuse for his latest whim; but he was wont to act for himself, and to pay little heed to outside opinion; and what would seem odd in another seemed in him so much a matter of course that the incident was soon forgotten. Bodin, indeed, with all his heart, invoked a blessing on the baron's head, ·trusting that his very first move would be to raze the lodge, with its accursed turret, to the ground. However, he did nothing of the kind. The old house lived on, in as bad repute as ever, and the new owner appeared not to concern himself about it.

Upon a certain November night, Master Martin came into the great room of the tavern with a very uneasy air. He went about trying the shutters, and carefully examining the bolts of the main door, sliding them to and fro in their staples; then he shut and locked every exit, with a great clinking of iron, and much creaking and banging. He opened a large oaken chest, and began to explore minutely its compartments and corners. The two waiters of the inn stared at their master open-mouthed; Jacob, winking those small sly eyes of his, touched his glass to that of a soldier at table whom he knew, and kept up the song he had already begun :—

> " *A health to Father Noah,*
>   *Pass around !*
> *He planted first the vine*
>   *In the ground.*
> *And to better keep afloat,*
> *He built himself a boat,*
> *For his own, own, own,*
> *For his ben, ben, ben,*
> *For his own, for his ben, for his own benefit,*
> *When the rain rained a bit !* "

"What are you laying out for us, cousin?" he cried, interrupting himself. "All Souls' Day is over and gone."

Without replying, Martin drew forth from an oblong box a taper blessed at Candlemas, such as every Christian household then made it a point of honor to treasure up; and lighting it, he set it before an image of Saint Martin, which was nailed against the shutter. A great fire was crackling on the hearth; two torches, fastened to the wall by iron clamps, threw out their ruddy blaze. The little pale, wavering ray of the candle, seen against the warm glow of fantastic light, made its own impression upon the frequenters of the Red Rose.

"How now, good Master Bodin!" questioned a young nobleman, who was stretched at ease in the leathern armchair of the host; "are we to have High Mass?"

"Master dear," whispered the two waiters, shaking from head to foot, "let us set it to burn in the back kitchen. It freezes one's blood to see it here."

"Surely," said in his deep accents a lusty equerry, who was busy draining a full cup of Angevin wine, "surely you have odd notions. comrade! Is this the illumination befitting a jolly company? Oh, fie!"

"Tease no more, Vincent. And, cousin Jacob, sew up your tongue. Pardon me, Messire de Maulny; but it is just five years, day for day, since the thing happened over there. One cannot be too cautious. Pray allow the candle to remain here."

"It is a small matter to me whether it be here or anywhere else. But I reserve the right to be amazed at such a sudden devotional attitude on the part of a person hitherto supposed to fear neither God nor Devil."

"As my lord of Maulny ought to recall," put in the equerry Vincent, "it is much more usual to lose the fear of God first."

"Have our Martin and the Old Harry had a scrimmage, then?" laughed Walter de Maulny, in the light, mocking tone habitual to him. "I should have believed more readily that the two were sworn cronies."

"Then your wager had been lost, my lord!" answered the sharp voice of Jacob Piteux. "They have been at swords' points ever since Satan strangled our uncle Jasper without allowing him time to make his will."

Walter raised himself on one elbow, his face losing a little of its scornful indifference. "The Devil really strangled your uncle Jasper, did he? How did it happen Martin?"

"It is a fine yarn," muttered Vincent between two bumpers.

"My friend, it is no yarn," said the innkeeper, "but as true a truth as ever was. I love not to tell it, nor to bring it back to mind on a day like this. Jacob would have done better had he held his peace."

"I thought the adventure would interest my lord of Maulny, cousin Martin. It is altogether extraordinary. If I was wrong, I beg absolution of the honorable assembly, and will speak no more unless I am ordered."

"As for me, I do order you!" continued Maulny. "The tale will nourish my sinking soul for a quarter-hour."

"Indeed, I am your lordship's humble servant to command; but I dare not fly in the face of my cousin Martin, who is so proud of the fame of his inn."

"And would you rather offend my lordship, then? Have a care, O clown! But proceed, proceed."

"Shall I do so, cousin?" asked Piteux meekly, turning towards the proprietor of the tavern.

"Yea, ninny, since that gentleman requires it," replied Bodin testily. "But if ever again you dabble in such topics at the Red Rose, you will have had your final bite out of my larder!"

"Then, by his lordship's order," and Jacob bowed towards Maulny. "It is but a sorry thing to offer those ears which are accustomed to the noble entertaining of the troubadours; yet we poor nobodies can give only what we have. You have possibly heard, my lord, of Wolfram, the old physician who lived in the hunting-lodge belonging to the sire de Pouillé?"

"Wolfram the Owl? I had clean forgotten him: an unlovely person, whom Bertrand de

Pouillé brought from Lorraine, without letting us know where he stumbled across the wonder. A bit of a Jew, they said, or a witch. What became of him?"

" He had a tragic fate," said Jacob, lowering his voice. " Wolf was a strange being. He lived alone in his tower like a fox in his hole, asleep by day, awake by night, eating next to nothing, and always aware of the vision no one else could see. Among us he passed for a vampire. It was believed that he had led seven or eight lives in as many different bodies."

Cried Walter: " Too many by half! But these Germans are so immoderate."

" Well, when a man sells his soul to the Devil, the latter is most liberal in his pay, my lord. Some folk declared they had spied Wolf, changed into his namesake, crossing the thickets, by the waning moon. And Martin here, one fine evening, counted six and thirty weasels holding one another by the tail, and wailing, calling on Wolfram's name."

" Are you raving, boldest of liars?" the inn-keeper broke in. " Never in my life did I see such a sight!"

" Peace, peace, cousin. (I would not contradict you in so small a matter.) However it be, my lord, the doctor delved for secrets no Christian man could teach him. Time after time we used to watch the bright lamp begin to gleam in the high turret window, which would burn on till the dawn; and we used to say to one another, 'Wolf is at work with Satan!' We did not know then how truly we spoke. One November evening — it is exactly five years ago to-night — no light appeared. On the morrow, Farmer Huche went to rap at the door of the little house, to get some remedy or other for the quartan ague: for the sorcerer could cure diseases better than any one. There was no answer to his knock. Huche resolved to climb the turret stair. And once there, what should he behold but Master Wolfram stretched before him: dead, beyond the shadow of a doubt! His eyes were wide open; there was a flush on his cheeks; his garments were singed; and a strong smell of sulphur gave witness that the Evil One had passed that way. All about the body fragments of vases, retorts, alembics, blackened manuscripts, strewed the floor. The alarm was given, a judge was called in, and the inquest began. The seneschal, Messire de Beauvau, was determined to find manifold evidence of murder, and he came near hanging some innocent men. But the Devil's claw was plain in that death, so that they gave up trying to fathom it. All the same, the priest at Ponts-de-Cé wished to give old Wolf Christian burial, as he had been to confession not long before. But the people got wind of it, and there was a clatter: a regular riot, so to speak. The grand provost sent the constable around, by night, to my uncle Jasper, who was a gravedigger by trade, ordering him to bury the

German doctor in the forest. I was there myself. When we lowered the coffin into the ditch, it seemed to me as if the body stirred within. No prayer and no benediction were given the departed, which was a pity, because unbaptized earth cannot keep the dead. Wolf did not sleep in peace. He rose many a time from his grave, to go back to his scrolls, and handle his alembics again. Neighbors saw him flying over the tree-tops, all aflame, or crossing the Loire, draped in his shroud, and gliding barefooted over the water, without leaving a ripple on the surface. And a storm of complaints and reproaches showered on the gravedigger, for no fault of his at all. 'You did not half bury him!' they cried. 'You do not know your business!' All the souls in Purgatory will soon be wandering up and down the roads, if they keep you in office!' So the good man got somewhat angry at last, and swore he would plant a cross over Wolfram's grave, to force him to lie quiet. Martin and I then accompanied him to the edge of the wood. He plunged into the bushes, singing the penitential psalm, *Languentibus*, to appease the doctor's spirit. But when he reached the grave, lo! it was open and empty. Peels of laughter filled all the air about. Now, on looking up, he noticed the turret window was agleam, and he rushed thither. The door was ajar; he climbed the stair, and entered the laboratory. There was Wolf, in a scarlet gown, his white hair in a sort of bluish smoke from hell, and his eyes like fiery coals. Two scapegrace imps were blowing the flames in the kiln; a tall demon was mixing a potion, another held a phial; and Wolfram, in the middle of all this, stood issuing commands. Any other man except my uncle would have fled. His avocation had toughened him a good deal against the supernatural. 'Hail, Master Wolf!' said he. 'Would it be an offence to inquire whether I address the living or the dead?' The other never looked at him at all; but kept turning over the leaves of a manuscript, and repeating, 'I cannot find it! I shall never find it!'—'You old miscreant!' continued my uncle, 'do you know that I am in danger of losing my place, all on your account? They say I did not bury you properly. Tell me how it is.' Wolfman never heard him. Throwing down his manuscript, he cried, fetching a deep sigh, 'I cannot find it! I shall never find it!' At that very moment a smiling, sinister figure appeared at the doctor's elbow, offering him, with one hand, a parchment lettered in strange characters, and with the other, a pen dipped in some red fluid. Wolf uttered a cry of joy, and snatched greedily at the precious script; but the sneering demon shot away from him, uplifting himself in air, and floating there, with a horrible laugh. Wolfram used every effort to obtain the magic parchment; and at last, worn-out and panting, he exclaimed: 'Thou hast conquered, Satan! Give me knowledge, and I give myself to thee.' The smile of the diabolic spirit was enough to freeze

one's blood, as he passed to the doctor the bloody
pen. 'Sign the contract,' so he spoke, in a voice
which had not a human tone in it: 'sign, and
knowledge shall be yours!' Wolfram seized the
pen, and traced his name. My uncle Jasper could
hold in no longer. 'Whelp of Germany!' he
shouted, 'go damn thyself somewhere else than
in our village!' And throwing himself between
the Devil and the doctor, he tore the document
from them. A throng of hideous demons surged
about him with angry shrieks and imprecations,
and over all arose this lamentation of Wolf. 'I
burn, O my friend the gravedigger, I burn! Why
did you not have my grave blessed?' My uncle
tried to make the sign of the Cross, and to say
Vade retro. But an iron hand was at his throat,
and he knew his hour had come. Overcome by
the diabolic creatures, he fainted away, and fell
half dead to the floor. Well, there we found him,
the next morning, stretched out, quite unconscious,
on the planking of the turret chamber. When we
threw a bucketful of water over him, he opened his
eyes. Then for three days he had the fever, and
shook with it till he died. He received the Last
Sacraments very devoutly. Nobody had time to
think of sending up the notary. It is a terrible
foolish business for men to neglect making their
wills while they are alive and well! If my uncle
Jasper had but taken due precaution, Martin and
I would be this day among the richest burghers of
Angers."

"A pretty figure you would cut!" cried Walter. "Over and above all this, Master Jacob, whence did you get the details of the story? From your uncle? From Wolfram? Or from the Devil?"

"From my uncle, my lord; from my worthy uncle, God rest his soul! He told me the whole thing during those last nights when I sat up with him; and pitiful it was to hear."

"He was delirious, in short," said Martin. "The truth is, he died of a good old-fashioned pleurisy, and his grandnephew Roger inherited the entire fortune, which the old fellow had saved penny by penny. Jacob and I never saw a red cent of it."

"If he had pleurisy, brother Martin," remarked Vincent, "it would appear that the aforesaid bucketful of fresh water was clearly intended to restore the health of your money-bagged uncle!"

"A good hit, Master Govier! Irony has come to you with years!" laughed Walter, bringing up his hand in a satirical salute to the honest Vincent. "Whether true or false, Jacob, it is a well-invented tale. I notice that the tramps and other gentry who scour the woods are very careful to nourish this sense of popular terror: it secures them from interference. Come, now, are you not a little more partial to them than is reasonable? You may own it to me, you know, quite safely."

"My lord," protested Piteux, drawing himself up to his lank height, and lending to his yellow,

crafty person as much offended dignity· as his
sorry figure could bear, "my lord, your sojourn in
Sicily must have familiarized you with brigands,
or you could not talk like that."

"Though one brigand is as good as another,"
answered Walter, with a sarcastic, habitual shrug
of the shoulders. "Do you think you can persuade me that your tale is true? If you do, *per
Bacco!* you lack not enterprise."

"Mayhap your lordship disbelieves in the
Devil?" Jacob put both elbows on the table, and
looked across at Maulny. "There are those who
consider him a more useful patron than the saints!"

"One would say you have put him to the test.
But his client is small credit to him. Ah, well,
enough of heathenish chatter, my prudent Jacob.
You and I know each other by heart; and my six
years of absence have not made me forget. Tell
me, does Wolfram's ghost still pursue its nocturnal
travels?"

"No, indeed, sir; not that I know of. Since
the accursed house changed owners, the old sorcerer has been seen no more. My lord of Pouillé
was his friend and his dupe. But this one is able
to hold his own against him and keep him quiet,
whether he will or no."

Walter's eyes were eagerly questioning Piteux.

"He is a wealthy and powerful nobleman," Jacob went on; "Vincent will give you his name."

Vincent made a gesture of vexed refusal ; but
. controlling himself, he rose, crossing his arms.

"Why not name him yourself, Jacob Piteux? My master, the baron de Fougereuse, makes no secret of his transaction with the lord of Pouillé. These lands are now ours; we hunt here every week."

The name of Fougereuse gave Walter de Maulny a thrill; he turned his head quickly. "Is that so, Vincent Govier? Has my dear cousin Guy become the happy ruler of the Devil's House? I knew he had courage, but I hardly expected so much of him. To have the Old Harry for vassal and tenant would scarcely delight me."

Vincent shrugged his shoulders with an air of superior disdain. "Can it be, my lord, that you lend any credit to old women's tales, bred in the brain of that white-livered Jacob? A man has a fine chance to lie, who talks of things that nobody can dispute from personal knowledge! The fact is that the house is haunted neither by the wretched alchemist himself, nor by the Devil. All that is the merest trash, concocted by idiots."

"Would to God it were!" murmured Martin.

"But, friend Vincent," Jacob sweetly expostulated, "you would not deny that Wolfram died there, or that my uncle Jasper" —

"Plague take your uncle Jasper! He was the biggest liar and boaster on the earth; worthily did he claim relationship with you."

"Hold, Master Vincent!" cried Bodin. "Remember that Jacob and I are of the same blood. Respect our family; else you and I will have it out between us, some fine morning. By the bull's horn, I have not forgotten how to fight!"

"Simpleton!" growled Vincent for his sole reply. And he turned his back on the inn-keeper.

Martin was only too anxious to further the quarrel, so glad was he of the opportunity to talk of something other than the dangerous proximity of Satan, and to vent upon any one his long-accumulating wrath. Walter de Maulny, both elbows on the arms of his chair, regarded the two champions with such a smile as might be worn by a bored spectator who begins to take interest in the play. Jacob drew in closer to the high chimney-piece, and crouched there like a hunted quarry. At this moment re-entered the two waiters, carrying jugs filled with wine. Shaking and bewildered, clinging close together, they rolled unsteadily into the middle of the room, and stopped there, transfixed with fright, babbling words of no meaning or sequence.

"On my word!" said Walter, as coolly as ever; "what has come over the rascals? To see their wan noses, one would suppose they had encountered old Wolf's ghost."

" Boobies, what have you done?" cried the inn-keeper, taking the swishing jugs from their hand. "I vow, you have let my best wine run to waste, as you did the other day. If I catch you in the act."—

One of the servants made a negative sign ; the

other, somewhat less terrified, managed to articulate a few words.

"Master, master! It is . . . it is . . . the Thing! Woe is me!"

"What?" roared the landlord, "what thing?"

"O master! It is shining again!"

"Shining, ye bibbers?"   .

"Yes, master. The light . . . the light over there . . . high up in the turret. You know."

"How now!" laughed Maulny. "This is getting to be quite absorbing."

"My lord, the report is simply incredible," said Martin, not without agitation. "The blockheads are full of wine, and crazed with fear."

"Open the window, comrade! It will settle our minds." Thus spoke Vincent.

Bodin hesitated; but at an imperative sign from Maulny he pushed back, sighing regretfully, the heavy wooden shutters. Nor could he help murmuring once more to himself: "If only they could not see *that* from here!"

The waiters had told the truth. Across the sombre mass of oak and chestnut boughs rose the slender contour of the eastern turret. A light burned at the narrow, grated opening which was called the window of Master Wolfram. The gust of wind which swayed the tree-tops set creaking the ancient weathercock of the inn, and rattled on its iron rod the sign of the Red Rose. Clouds were heaped about the moon, whose pale, sad face, obscured every now and then, reappeared abruptly, and newly vanished. But nothing darkened or disturbed the mysterious ray which sparkled on in the dark, like a star forgotten between earth and heaven. There it was, inexplicable; and Bodin and his guests were mute for a moment, while the waiters, kneeling close to the blessed candle, mumbled their awe-stricken prayers.

"God help us all!" Jacob murmured in the accents of contrition. "Will you consider me a chicken-hearted idiot after this, Vincent Govier? Will you call my accurate testimony old women's tales? Behold the lamp of old Wolf, re-lit. Whether he be man or demon, the eastern turret has at least one occupant to-night."

"Some tramp or some madman," scornfully answered the equerry. "I wonder what has come over the gamekeeper!"

Jacob obstinately resumed. "There is nothing human about that light. It burned just so the evening of the murder, the same day, the same hour, as this. Do you remember, cousin Martin? We were seated near the casement when those pitiful groans " —

"Go hang, with your pitiful groans!" cried the master of the house. "Never did I hear any in this place but your own. Did I, I, bear part in Wolf's murder? Does his shade parade the corridors of my inn? I defy any man, whosoever he be, to say that this is not an honest Christian dwelling, with blessed candles in it, where travellers sleep sound. It is nothing to me if the demons are holding carnival in the depth of the woods. Thank God, there is peace at the Red Rose."

"Landlord," said Maulny, who up to now had been scanning in silence the mysterious glare, "landlord, do not play the braggart. You are shaking in your skin, like the servants. And, indeed, it is an odd incident. Are you perfectly sure that for five years there has been no glimmer from that accursed house?"

"As sure as that I am alive, my lord! I never went to bed without looking at it from this side; because, unluckily, you can always see *it* from the windows."

"Yes, the turret is plain enough, Martin, but the foliage conceals the lodge; and if men, or ghosts either, had chosen to light up the lower hall every evening of the five years, who would have been the wiser?"

"In that case, Messire Walter," replied Vincent, "the neighborhood would not have lacked eyes to see, and tongues to tattle. But the feat is quite impossible, for mortals at least, thanks to the solid bars which defend the casement, and the stout locks which my master, the baron, has provided for the doors."

"I recognize the admirable prudence of my cousin," said Walter, withdrawing from the window. "If, then, we agree that it is the Evil One, that does not look well for your master, does it, Vincent?"

"What are you saying, my lord of Maulny?

Do you mean to hint that the baron de Fougereuse " —

"I mean nothing, my friend. The Lord preserve me from casting suspicion on a kinsman,
whose honor is so close to mine! But I did say,
and I repeat it, that I am not pleased to see this
sort of thing at his house. Guy has enemies at
court; and a misstep on his part might have grave
consequences for a King's favorite, even if that
King be the trusting, easy-going René of Anjou!"

"If the King's favorite were Walter de Maulny
instead of Guy de Fougereuse, I could then name
various missteps which might have grave consequences!"

"Impudent varlet!" cried Maulny hotly, touching the hilt of his poniard. "Were you a noble,
my sword would have made you pay already for
that speech. But one deals out justice to your
sort with a stick. I am foolish to lose my temper
over a creature who does not belong to me, and
whose master I would fain not offend."

"Your sword could never be dishonored by contact with mine, sir knight! Rude though it be,
it has met upon the battlefield more than one
blade as proud as yours. But I must not vex my
master. You are his kinsman; therefore let us
have a truce. What were you aiming at, in expressing your displeasure at the fact that the
Devil's House and his window are now in the
power of the baron de Fougereuse?"

"What was I aiming at?" echoed Walter, turning around in the chair where he had reseated himself. "Do you not perceive, my threefold idiot, that if the mystery of this evening be not solved, all Angers by to-morrow will be crying magic and witchcraft, calling for exorcism, piling up fagots, and burning down that reprobate house, — the house your master bought, and was so careful to furnish with big locks? They will say that there are ghosts in it, and hidden treasures ; they will say that my cousin Guy deals with the former in order to secure the latter. Perhaps it is nothing to you, to have them speak so of your master; but Guy is my cousin, and . . . in short, Vincent Govier, it goes against me to have such things connected with him. Understand if you can! "

"I understand you, sir," said the equerry in a laconic tone, rising up. "Our acquaintanceship does not date from an hour ago. When you were a child at the manor of Fougereuse, I taught you to throw the lance and to run at tilt. Your heart and character have not changed, nor mine either. I forewarn you. Now, as then, you will find me standing between my young master and his enemies. 'A word to the wise is enough!'"

" Vincent, what are you doing?" Bodin spoke in astonishment, seeing the equerry buckle on his sword, wrap himself in his cloak, and draw down the hood over his forehead. "What are you doing, friend? Hey! . . . you would start out? At this hour? In the middle of the night? Do you want to be bewitched? Whither would you go?"

"I am going to the Devil," replied Vincent; "and I advise none of you to follow me. Good-evening."

Jacob threw himself energetically against the tavern door. "O cousin Martin, keep him in! keep him in! He will meet uncle Jasper's fate; and the baron will hold us responsible. Vincent, my old friend, do not try to get strangled!"

Vincent, with one sweep of his arm, brushed the meagre Jacob aside. and busied himself with the bolts of the heavy door.

"Let me alone! Do you not see how impatient my lord Walter is growing? I should have been thither and back by this time."

"What ails you?" said Maulny, turning his head. "What right have you to mix up my name with this sudden whim of yours? Did I ask anything of you?"

"You did not, sir; and that is why I must hasten. I see your thoughts. Before an hour passes you will know all."

As he spoke, the last bolt gave way under his resolute fingers. The door creaked on its hinges, opening wide, and letting in a gust of wind and rain. Vincent Govier gathered his cloak about him, and descended the first of the gray stone steps.

"But, really, where would you go?" cried Martin, springing after him. "Can you commit the folly of going . . . going . . . over there?"

The equerry stopped an instant on the road, and

faced about. "I commit that folly, good friend Bodin, for I must reassure my lord of Maulny on a point of family honor. Tell him that I shall arrive presently at the Devil's House, for the purpose of inquiring of Satan whether by any chance he is not slighting his pet, the lord of Maulny, in giving his confidence to the baron de Fougereuse. I shall return with his answer."

"If you never return?"

"In that case, I shall have died; and do you notify my master. Good-night, good fellows!" and the equerry swung down the road, at a great pace, toward the haunted house, and was soon lost in the darkness. Bodin re-entered, shaking his head.

"I'll be hanged if I know his object! There must be a fatality in that infernal light, to attract a man to it at midnight, in the teeth of a storm. Vincent is brave enough in his dealings with other men, but I never would have believed him so rash as to collar the Devil in person, and ask him to give an account of himself."

"Govier was drinking to-night, was he not?" asked Maulny superciliously. His blazing eyes belied his affectation of calm.

"Not a fourth part of what he can take without moving a hair, my lord. If he be drunk with anything, it is with anger."

"Such a fool was never in a nobleman's service before! But Guy de Fougereuse has the knack of fascinating his retainers; they are tame greyhounds to him, and to other people snarling wolves. Vincent's is a case in point. . . . Do you think he will come back, Bodin?"

"He promised he would, my lord; and I have never known him to break his word."

"But," interrupted Jacob, "he may find yonder some one to hinder him, cousin Martin. The best soldier on earth has his moments of ill luck. If the ghost of Wolf" —

"Stuff and nonsense, cousin Jacob! Tell that to babes."

"Very well, then. If the Devil" —

"Vincent went to confession at All Saints'."

"If scoundrels, thieves, cutthroats" —

"There will be a lively dance, and little left of them for the' law to deal with. I assure you, Govier could skewer a dozen without exerting himself at all, and two dozen by exerting himself just a trifle. I wager that he will have returned within three hours."

"Cousin Martin, replied Jacob, "I take up the wager, because Vincent Govier will not return to-night. What are the stakes? Will you risk ten crowns?"

Bodin protested, but Jacob constrained him. The bet was agreed upon, and the ten crowns were placed upon the table for the winner. The two established themselves there with a pint of wine between them, meaning to beguile the weariness of waiting by sipping the nectar of the Red Rose. Meanwhile, in apparent indifference to the talk being exchanged, Walter de Maulny, his eyes fixed on the fitful hearth-fire, sank into a revery.

Though he was barely thirty, he might have been ten years older. He looked prematurely aged, with his melancholy face, his sated air, his listless attitude. Analyzing this man, one felt that his youth was long ago over and done, and past reclaiming. Generous illusions, the heart hot for action, chivalrous ideals, were not for him; and he could barely remember that he had ever known them. His eyes, flashing with sombre fires, indicated, nevertheless, an ardent, obstinate, passionate nature. The close, finely chiselled lips denoted energy and will, and the low but intelligent forehead seemed formed for philosophic thought. Above all, a certain innate elegance characterized his whole person and his every motion, and bespoke noble breeding. How was it that such brilliant gifts had so poorly served their possessor? or that, after having dazzled the court of Anjou, and basked in the royal favor, Walter de Maulny should be now a cheated dreamer, tired of life, and forsaken by fortune? He seemed to read his own history in the fantastic volumes of flame and smoke before him. He dwelt upon his childhood, passed at the castle of Fougereuse with his cousin Guy and little Isabelle; of his first riding-lessons; his first attempts to wield arms: his first hunt through the woodland; the instructions of the master equerry; and the instructions of the chaplain.

He thought of all that manly and soldierly training which his youth had received under the eye
of the austere Baron Amaury, and of all his in-
tellectual labors encouraged by his godmother,
Yvette, the mother of Guy and Isabelle. And
as he thought, he frowned, and his eyebrows
puckered. Like a far echo, he seemed to hear
the voice of Vincent Govier, and that of the venerable chaplain of Fougereuse, repeating together
a word which was a challenge: "Master Walter,
you do well indeed, yet your cousin Guy does
better than you." Another picture came up before him. King René's court, gracious, animated,
attractive; the paradise of troubadours, the father-
land of artists; the King, himself an artist and a
troubadour, open and sweet of nature, and busied
rather with the enriching of his lovely city than
with the defence of his duchy against the greed
of Louis XI.

For a brief while, Walter had played a leading
part on that brilliant stage. A friend to poetry
and the arts, a skilful diplomat, an exquisite
courtier, he knew how to please the credulous René,
how to enter into intimate relations with him,
and secure his good-will. Maulny's counsel was
acceptable, and his policy was able to checkmate
that of the King of France. Fortune smiled
upon him; but one day (as if to show upon how
slight a thread hangs the friendship of the great!),
one inauspicious day, the favorite awoke to find
that he had no influence, the dictator was without

power; the ready adviser had no advice to give. René of Anjou turned suddenly against his loyal minion of the evening before, and reproached him with having served two masters, Louis XI. and René I. And to whom did the old King pledge his wounded faith? To a young knight newly arrived at court: to the baron Guy de Fougereuse. This time Walter's hand clinched itself angrily over his sword-hilt, while Vincent's parting words came back to him: "I shall inquire of Satan whether he is not slighting his pet, the lord of Maulny, by giving his confidence to the baron de Fougereuse!" And he added, in his own mind: "If I were indeed the object of Satan's partiality, Guy would be there to supplant me!"

Nor was this all. Walter recalled his six years' sojourn in Sicily. Deep in a certain conspiracy, and one of its leading spirits, preparing to seize the government, and overthrow public order, the lord of Maulny was hiding at Palermo, in disguise, and passing under a borrowed name. But one day, in the street, a gentleman came upon him with a "Good-morrow, cousin Walter!" bewildered him with a vehement embrace, carried him off, by main force, to sup with ten or a dozen Angevin knights, old playfellows of Walter's, questioned him closely, and tendered him many offers of service. The next day, thanks to this excellent relative, all Palermo knew of Maulny's presence, and the plot was discovered. The zealous friend was, of course, Guy de Fougereuse

Walter, entreated by him to leave Italy and return to Anjou, and being pardoned by the good King René at the request of his favorite, consented, in the hope of retrieving his fortune and starting upon a new career. But it was ordained that everything should go against him. When he came back to Maulny, he found his affairs in a very bad state; his debts unpaid; his estate, mortgaged before his departure, on the point of being sold: ruin, in short, at his doors. A splendid inheritance, on which his last hope was staked, fell to a happier rival: that is to say, again and always, to his cousin, the baron de Fougereuse. It was maddening! For a moment, it seemed to Walter as if all the powers of darkness had taken possession of the great room of the inn, and were dancing a crazy saraband around him, shouting the name of Guy de Fougereuse.

"Who defeated you in such and such a joust or tourney?—Guy de Fougereuse."

"Who captured from you the affections of the King?—Guy de Fougereuse."

"Who blocked your way in Italy, and made your projects come to nothing?—Guy de Fougereuse."

"Who secured the inheritance which was yours by right?—Guy de Fougereuse."

"Who now accords to you a sort of scornful protection, and spares you neither advice nor reproof?—Guy de Fougereuse."

"He has taken my sunshine from me," thought

Walter, "and he owes me some reparation. What is there about that fopling courtier that he should succeed so, when all my efforts fail? Is he handsome? I was handsomer than he. Intelligent? Not so intelligent as I. Brave? We were both that. A clever politician? One far inferior to me. His birth was not nobler than mine; his fortune was ordinary. He is not diligent; he has an air of jesting and unconcern. Yet I waste myself in labor and speculation, I use up my energy, I fight with the strength of despair, and it is he who wins! Everybody seems to be under an obligation to him because he took the trouble to be born. Everything smiles upon him, and makes his life a holiday. Fickle fortune is constant enough to him. For six years past, his standing has been unassailable. What special talisman has Heaven given to him?"

"He is *happy!*" a tempting voice seemed to murmur at his ear. "And happy you will never be."

"We shall see!" Walter hissed between his clenched teeth. "I am not a player who throws away the dice because he loses at the first few throws. This is the very hour for a sweeping retaliation. Guy has taken my all from me; Guy shall now restore it. Choose, haughty Fougereuse! Take me for brother, or take me for deadly foe: give me the hand of Isabelle and her dowry, in restitution for a confiscated heritage, or let us have war to the knife. I will drag you from your high places, and make your disgrace serve me as mine served you: as a stepping-stone to further advancement. If Heaven refuse to watch over me, at least hell will help me on. Lucifer! I can say to you what Wolfram said: ' I cede myself to you, in exchange for my own victory, and the ruin of Guy de Fougereuse!' "

Even as Walter de Maulny conceived this impious defiance to the future and to the Most High, he caught the glance, sharp and saturnine, of Jacob Piteux's eye. It seemed to answer him like a voice: "We play the same game, my lord." A rap at the door woke him from his musing, and brought the two startled drinkers to their feet.

" Vincent! " they cried together.

" Or the Devil rather," Jacob added; " since our poor Vincent " —

A second knock, more vigorous than the other, shook the tavern walls, and an imperious voice, half drowned in a squall of wind, shouted forth, —

" Are you ever going to open, landlord? Bad luck to you ! "

" H'm ! " murmured Walter. " This is a demon of some social importance."

Bodin, not anxious to see the whole structure tumble about his ears, did not wait for a third summons. The door, which he cautiously set ajar, was shoved vehemently from without, and the newcomer, dripping with rain, and wrapped in a huge cloak which concealed his face, stood before them.

"See to my horse, innkeeper. Let him have plenty of oats. The poor beast is exhausted."

Then, without a greeting to any one, he went over to the chimneypiece, and took a comfortable posture in an easy-chair, facing Walter de Maulny. From beneath his cloak he drew an oddly shaped cage, where wild creatures were moving about confusedly.

"There now, my beauties, warm yourselves!" he said, placing the cage on the hearthstone. "The journey was a hard one, but here we are at home. Show your pretty selves a little to the gentleman, my darlings!" And teasing his feathered prisoners with the tip of his switch, he won in answer a frightened beating of wings and some hoarse croaks.

Bodin, who had thought to see Vincent enter, stared at the stranger with open mouth. Jacob muttered, " I told you so. It is the Devil ! "

Walter, half smiling, seemed amused at the scene, though not surprised.

" Wake up, innkeeper ! Has your cellar run dry ? " continued the unknown, " or what has come over your larder ? Do you think that a gentleman rides hither in a storm, past midnight, for the mere privilege of gazing upon the chimney-piece of your establishment ? "

" But . . . but " . . . stammered Bodin, " who are you, sir ? "

" What now ? Who am I, clown ? " cried the stranger with mock fury. " Does that concern you? My name is too patrician for your long ears. Bring me something for supper, and bring it quickly."

"I will, Messire Loïc," replied the innkeeper, who had just recognized the voice of his guest. "I do not know what got into me, that I should make such a mistake!"

Messire Loïc burst out laughing. Presently he cast aside his cloak, drenched in rain, and appeared before the others as a young page of a graceful figure.

"Well, well!" said Walter; "I believe it is little Kernis! . . . grown a bit, to be sure, and with a larger stock of impudence. Are you not in singular company, my boy?"

"Jacob, why are you prowling about that cage?" exclaimed Loïc, without paying the slightest attention to Walter's presence. "Those innocents are under my care, and I have to answer for them to the keeper of the king's aviary. Do not plague them! They object to your Jewish aspect."

"Jewish! Oh, sir," mumbled Jacob indignantly, "you know that is not true."

"I know nothing of the sort, nor do these ladies. Ask them. Do you take him for a Christian, my loves?"

"By my soul!" cried Walter in disgust; "how can you be smitten with the charms of such outrageous objects! What do I see? Instead of falcons to train for the chase, as I supposed, here are vulgar screech-owls! A pretty business for an aspirant to knighthood : to set up as body-guard for vermin ! At your age, Kernis, I should have wept for shame and anger, if my uncle, the baron de Fougereuse, had given me such game to carry ! ”

“ Then I am less sensitive than you, Messire Walter, for I should not waste my tears on so small a matter. When I receive a command, I obey it. For the rest, I see no reason why I should disdain to travel in company with screech-owls which the King wishes to put in his aviary, and which I myself caught for him. They are growing tame. Wait ! . . . suppose I open the door of the cage ? ”

“ No, no ! ” cried Walter, pushing back his chair. “ Nothing is lacking now but to set loose here that brood of horrors. You are an incorrigible wag ! Take them away, my pretty tutor of screech-owls, and explain ” —

“ Allow me to eat first, my lord, as I am famished. Behold Martin, who has decided to produce his viands. I drink to your very good health.”

While the page appeased his hunger on a venison steak, Walter silently inspected him. Loïc de Kernis appeared to be fifteen or sixteen. His gay, mobile face ; his candid brows, shadowed with thick blond hair ; his dark blue eyes, with their trustful and trustworthy glance ; his frank smile and mischievous air, belonged to the schoolboy and the child. But his height and bearing, his physical vigor, his proud, firm step, his ringing voice and decisive speech, proclaimed the future soldier, as his independent conduct proclaimed him a Breton. Though his dress was that of a royal page, and exceedingly elegant, his silver dagger-sheath being a wonder of Italian chiselling, and the hilt of his sword beautifully wrought, yet Loïc seemed no more concerned than if he had been clad in burlap. He never once turned his eyes upon himself, to survey the state of his costume.

"Explain, my child," Maulny resumed, after some moments of private observation, "how it happens that a lad of fifteen, not on his own responsibility" —

"By your leave, I was sixteen years old at Candlemas," interrupted Loïc.

"Very well. How does it happen that Master Loïc, page and ward of my dear cousin Fougereuse, Loïc, who is known to be an arrant featherbrain, is out on the high road at this time of night alone" —

."That proves how he can be depended upon, despite his arrant featherbrainishness."

"At this time of night alone, as I was saying, escorting a nestful of birds of prey, which he is ready to scatter without warning on the heads of a peaceful assembly?"

"You are precious uncivil to my fair friends, Messire Walter. They behave as sedately as dowagers. See. . . . Come here, pretty, pretty! Is it not provoking, when I would show them off to you, not one will turn its head?"

"To which birds of prey aforesaid," continued

Walter imperturbably, " he is much more attentive than he is to his lord's blood-relations."

" Ah, that is why you are so hard, then, upon my little owls ! And, indeed, you are right. I did not salute you when I came in. Pardon my neglect, Messire de Maulny. I never dreamed you did me the honor to be jealous of my attentions, and I am quite ready to atone for my discourtesy." Rising from table, the page bowed very low, bringing his cap over his heart with a sweeping gesture. " Your humble servant, my sweet lord ! . . . And now you are, I believe, properly saluted."

" Beautifully, count of Kernis !" answered Walter gallantly. " I consider that I have received satisfaction."

" May I hope," continued Loïc, still cap in hand, " that your estate of Maulny is in good condition ? "

" In wretched condition, alas ! I intend to sell it. And you — where did you leave your master ? "

" In wretched company, at Précigné: that is, in the society of those Englishmen Madame Margaret has with her. If you love not night-birds, Messire Walter, meddle not with them. The hoarsest of my screech-owls is delightful by comparison. I could no longer put up with them ; and if my master had not despatched me with these princesses to the man who is to keep them, I believe that I and the Saxons would have ended by reciprocal assassination !"

" You are a stiff-necked Breton, and to the race-hatreds of a Breton there is no truce. . . . You say, then, that your guardian, humoring your dread of the English, sent you out alone, with four miserable bipeds, on a stormy night? It does not seem of a piece with the habitual prudence of my cousin Guy. Own up. You have broken bounds, and are in full flight. I will respect your secret."

"Secret!" cried Loïc, with another peal of laughter. "A thousand thanks; but it would be so very useless! I make it a point of honor that my master shall know of all my goings-on, and shall know of them from my own lips. You see, in that way I forestall all slander and misrepresentation."

"The candor of it is certainly edifying; yet it must secure you some good round sermons as part of the day's work."

" What of that, Messire Walter? It is my nature to prefer my master's scolding to a stranger's flattery. Fergus does the same."

"Fergus! Is that the hound who nearly ate me up? I compliment you on the tastes you share in common, Kernis! . . . When shall I see Guy?"

"To-morrow, I think; for I am charged to tell the major-domo to prepare the lodge at once. The baron will come hither, preceding the King by a few hours, in order to welcome to the palace of Fougereuse, the lord Robert de Villepreux."

" Villepreux!" Walter raised his voice a little. "They told us he was dead in Palestine."

" He may be, in Palestine; but in Anjou he is

as alive as he can possibly be, and Messire Guy is happy enough over his resurrection. Their affection is closer than that of Roland and Oliver. We shall hear now, I fancy, some fine tales of prowess, and of exploits against the Saracens!"

"Villepreux!" murmured Maulny. "Robert the Lion, the Knight of the Round Table, the flower of chivalry, without blame or fear; brave to madness, loyal up to the point of — sincerity! as devoted to his prince as a dog to his master, heroically faithful to his friend and to his word: a Crusader of old, who believes no Christian false. Villepreux, once the foe of Fougereuse, now his friend; the one man in the world to whom Guy could offer his hand, and ask of him at the same time the forgetfulness of a hereditary feud. And now they are brothers-in-arms, Oliver and Roland! This is more of the chronic good luck of your master, Loïc."

"My master deserves just such a friend," replied the page with animation; "and I do not see that he need envy any of his qualities. For he, like my lord of Villepreux, is without blame or fear, brave, loyal, devoted, faithful, and all the rest."

"Is it news to me, my dear child?" broke in Walter, with an accent of ironic conviction. "Before you arrived in this world, I knew all my cousin's perfections by heart. They merit a disciple like you; prompt to admire them, and eager to cry them up even in the desert, if needs be. I tell you, Guy is fortunate in everything. I could never catch a retainer of this enthusiastic temper! I am amazed that he does not rely more thoroughly upon you. If I were he, I would withhold nothing from you."

"Nothing in my master's career is kept secret from me," said Loïc, straightening himself proudly.

"Really? Then you can tell what he conceals in that mysterious retreat, that little apartment over against his chamber, where, they say, he shuts himself up for hours at a stretch."

"They say wrongly, my lord. The baron never shuts himself up for hours at a stretch in that little apartment. I am aware that he alone can open it, as the door has neither lock nor key. But there is no mystery about the place: it is a storeroom. . . . What are you laughing at, Master Walter?"

"Take no offence, my pellucid youth. You contradict the expression, 'As malicious as a page.' Vincent knows better than you; be sure of that."

"Vincent? What can he know that I am ignorant of, I who keep close to my master as his own shadow? . . . But Govier has always been jealous to seem the only one in my lord's confidence. He may have told you something silly, to give you a sense of his own importance. I who know "—

"You who know? You divert me. They have not initiated you yet, poor fellow, and Guy will not answer for your discretion. In fact," Maulny went on, as if to himself, "this child is a paragon of heedlessness. He could see his master stand at the stake without dreaming that the flames would burn him."

" What are you saying, sir? "

" Nothing, nothing at all. Finish your supper, and take care of your screech-owls. The suspected spot is a storeroom. I believe it, on your word of honor. And if there be any sorcerer at my cousin's, at least, my believing Breton, it is not you.".

" A sorcerer!" Loïc cried out. surprised and in-dignant. " Are you growing crazy, Maulny?"

" It would appear that you are growing imperti-nent, Kernis. There! do not feel provoked; I was not in earnest. According to you, then, Guy does not give himself up, in private, to studies hidden from the common herd. Have you ever been in the place we are speaking of, Loïc? "

" Never. Now that you remind me of it, I have seen my master come forth from it, twice or thrice, very early in the morning, looking pale, as if he had not slept. And he was by no means overjoyed to see me in the way, for he knit his eyebrows. I gave him no reason to distrust me, however," con-tinued the ingenuous lad, "and I can keep his secrets as close as Vincent can."

"Guy has never been wise in his choice of con-fidants," said Walter, in his most sympathetic tone. " But to drop the subject, have you any court news to give me? "

" Yes. Antonio Blandini, the King's learned physician, has left us, and gone back to Italy."

" Is that so? All the worse for the King; since Antonio is a clever man, a genuine doctor, versed in all sorts of science; and I have seen him work some wonderful cures. The King never seemed to wish him out of his sight. What was the cause of his sudden disgrace?"

" Please observe, Messire de Maulny, that it was the doctor who disgraced his illustrious patient, and not the King who exiled his Æsculapius. The misunderstanding between them began when a certain Master Cornelius, a physician from Tours, given out to be the best pupil of the famous Coictier, was sent hither by King Louis. You know how much professional jealousy Antonio has! Well, the medical advice of the stranger from Touraine contradicted his own. Antonio had kept the King under a strict regimen, and forbade late hours. protracted feasting, imported wines, and all that. Now Master Cornelius, who is a courtier, and does nothing by halves, changed the whole order of things, removed the restrictions, allowed his Majesty to follow his own whims, and to multiply his entertainments and festivities. Antonio's emphatic protests went for nothing. So it befell, in due time, that the King came down with quartan ague, thanks to his sailing all one evening among the mists of the river Maine. The two doctors met beside his pillow, each advocating a different system, and refusing to yield an inch. Cornelius was very arrogant in his manner. And Antonio, seeing the King hesitate between them, and endeavor to harmonize their hostile theories, turned about indignantly. 'During the fifty years that I have followed the practice of medicine,' he said, 'I have always held and taught that a physician should be the sovereign authority over his patient. Since my right is contested, I abdicate.' 'Hear my haughty doctor!' rejoined the King. *Abdicate,* indeed; it is a royal word. What then?' And that ended it. Despite the opposition of my master, Antonio left the palace that same night; and never once since has he been seen in Angers, or anywhere in the neighborhood. Master Cornelius meanwhile regulates the health of our lord the King, and has succeeded in changing his quartan ague into tertian ague."

"Until it becomes quotidian and malignant, all to the greater glory and advantage of Louis, King of France. Does our gracious liege miss Antonio?"

"He is inconsolable over his departure. They say he would give his right arm to get him back. But Antonio will never return."

"Do you think so? The forfeit of a prince's favor is a thing to be regretted."

Loïc shook his head. "No, messire; at least, not by that man. He lived for nothing but science; he cared no whit for wealth or advancement. In his eyes there was neither rich nor poor, neither old nor young: only the sick, or, rather, only sicknesses. 'I have a fever to allay here, I have a pleurisy to look out for there'—that was his manner of speech. He scarcely ever mentioned a

name. He judged of a man's worth by the gravity
of his disease : and he preferred a thousand-fold a
peasant with the plague, to a gouty lord. As to
healthy folk, they are a breed which he ruled out
of his universe, and despised heartily."

"A strange character," sighed Walter thoughtfully. He was silent for a few minutes, gazing
dreamily at the burning logs. The clock of the
great room chimed sonorously, one, two, three ; and
Jacob spanned with his hand the ten crown pieces,
the sum at stake.

"I have won!" he announced energetically, "for
Vincent has not returned."

"One moment," cried Bodin, covering the coins
with his big hand, "one moment! Be the um-
pire, Messire de Maulny. Vincent never said he
would return at three o'clock."

"He said he would return before three o'clock!"
contradicted Jacob; "and that if he did not, he
would be dead. So"—

"Vincent! of what Vincent are you talking?"
asked Loïc, lifting his head. "Was Vincent
Govier here, waiting for me?"

"Govier is the person in question," answered
Walter. "He was here some hours ago, but
seized with a fit of ill-nature. he left us behind,
and posted off to Pouillé woods to find the gamekeeper, whom he thought to be in need of correc-
tion. And these merry-andrews laid a wager upon
his return. That is all."

"That is all, is it? Why did you not tell me

sooner? What is the real trouble? Vincent beating the woods, past midnight, to surprise old Faribault! Vincent stipulating his own death, in case he does not come back at the time agreed upon! ... What is at the bottom of this? ... You are deceiving me. Bodin, you are an old soldier: tell me the truth!"

"I can tell you nothing, my young lord, except that there is a light in Wolfram's turret to-night, and that this miserable Jacob has been relating stories which give one the shivers. Messire de Maulny made fun of them; and then Vincent swore he would go over to catch the Devil at his orgies. He promised to return promptly. I begin to believe that something may have happened to him."

But Loïc demanded further explanations; and, importuned by the eager page, Bodin had to repeat in detail all that had passed. As soon as he understood the situation, Loïc de Kernis broke out into reproaches and angry invective : —

"What notion did Vincent have, think you? Is it not a shame for men to take alarm because old Wolf comes back to ask for prayers? ... It is just like these Angevins! In Brittany everybody has seen signs and wonders, and understands how to deal with the spirit-world. Piteux is a coward, and he spreads around him a contagion of fear. And Master Walter, with all his philosophy, allowing such folly under his very eyes! And keeping me here more than an hour, making me talk nonsense, instead of telling me that Vincent was over yonder. Bodin, you will have to answer on your life for whatever comes of it!"

"Hush, hush, firebrand!" exclaimed Walter sharply. "You will wear out our patience with this gabble. Am I to control the actions of equerries belonging to my cousin Guy, and render an account of them to his pages? . . . Vincent has gone of his own free will to pick up a quarrel with Satan, and if he succeeds, why, by my soul, that is his own affair."

"And my affair too!" cried Loïc in exasperation. "Govier is a retainer of the house of Fougereuse, and the baron would never be reconciled to lose him. Give me a lantern, Martin!"

"What would you do, Messire Loïc? Would you also"—

"I also. Precisely. I am going to Vincent's rescue; and if you have any feeling for an old comrade, you will come along with me."

"Of a certainty you are mad!" said Walter.

"I would to Heaven I were the only one here who is mad. But I intend to be as mad as I like, mad to the hilt. Though all the demons strangle me, and the sorcerers weave spells over me, and the night-hags wring my neck, and the other sprites drag me into their dance, and the lost souls singe me with their fires, I must discover what has become of my master's equerry! Now, are you ready, innkeeper? For if you are afraid, I will go alone."

"I am with you, messire," answered Bodin, moved by the boy's resolute spirit, and secretly rejoiced to be able to succor a former fellow-soldier. "I am with you. Only let me take a stout cudgel, and the blessed candle!"

And so armed with weapons spiritual and temporal, Loïc and Bodin departed from the Red Rose, reckless of the torrent of rain, and the roaring of the furious wind. Walter, face to face with Jacob, made a sign for him to open the window. Piteux obeyed silently, and leaned out.

"The light burns on just the same, my lord."

"Very well."

"The page and my good cousin are headed straight for Pouillé wood."

"That is their business."

"Would you like to see me follow them, my lord?"

"If you have any reason for doing so, do so."

"I have no reason, save the desire of serving you."

"I would not take it ill of you. Be prudent."

"Depend upon me, messire!"

Jacob disappeared. Walter de Maulny was left alone with his thoughts. Time passed in the great room, where the silence was unbroken save by the regular tick-tick of the clock, and the mournful hoot of the screech-owls abandoned by Loïc. Maulny, disagreeably impressed by these birds of ill omen, turned his back to them, and placed his elbows on the sill of the yet open window. At last, he heard the sound of footsteps and of voices from the road. A moment later a key grated in the lock, and Bodin entered, supporting Loïc, who was pale and overcome.

"What has happened?" asked Walter anxiously.

"Very little," replied the weak voice of the page. "I fell from a tree; but I had seen nothing."

Martin assisted him to the armchair, bathed his bruised forehead with fresh water, and gave him a cordial to drink: all this with a tender solicitude which one would not have looked for in a man of his sort. To Maulny's questioning, Loïc answered in disjointed phrases, repeating stubbornly, "I had seen nothing."

Bodin shook his head, murmuring:

"It was by an accident, messire, a mere accident. And for all our efforts, we have no tidings of Vincent."

Walter saw plainly that the innkeeper knew no more. Awaiting the return of his spy, he resigned himself to act as nurse to the wounded, and lavish his attentions on him. Loïc was moved to the best room in the Red Rose, and laid upon the best bed. The lord of Maulny himself offered to examine his injuries. This was no easy task. The page complained that his every limb was broken, screamed if Walter tried to touch him, and grew half delirious when there was talk of informing his master. Incoherent words, causeless laughter, snatches of song, now sad, now jovial, streamed from Loïc's lips, all night long.

"A bad business, a bad business!" growled Martin. "A fate has overtaken this poor lad. May it never fall upon me!"

Towards morning Loïc seemed more calm. He asked for his screech-owls, and the cage was brought to him. He then declared his wish to sleep, and complained so loudly of the din which, according to him, Walter and Bodin were making, that they finally retired, and left their patient by himself. A half-hour later, the innkeeper came down the staircase, unmanned.

"My lord, it is diabolical! I shall sell the Red Rose."

"What is up?" cried Walter.

"The page's chamber is empty. His horse is no longer in the stable! Yet nobody has seen him, nor heard him leave."

Thought Walter: "He was playing upon us with his mock hysterics. I will get at the meaning of this."

The first rays of the dawn were breaking, when Jacob Piteux arrived at the door of the Red Rose, and knocked softly. Walter, alone in the lower room, let him in noiselessly.

"You are late, rogue. Did you find Vincent?"

"Indeed, my lord, I found no Vincent. He has vanished, evaporated, leaving not a trace behind. And as for the page" —

"That page is a sly one! What has he done

but gone off without a word of warning, after having kept us on our feet the entire night, pretending to be suffering agonies?"

"He, he, he! That is not an ill move for a novice. The lad knew no other means of getting out of it, my lord."

"But what came to pass?" asked Maulny abruptly. "Are you presuming to play upon my credulity? Speak! or if not"—

"Eh, my good lord, do not push a man too hard! A little patience, and you will learn. I reached the accursed house just in time to see that madcap of a Loïc tumble from a tree which stands over against the lighted window. It amazed me, because he is nimble as a wildcat; and I was still more amazed to hear him wail and moan like a six-months-old baby. Martin hoisted him on his shoulders, and carried him from the wood, while I remained to ferret the thing out. Having examined the vicinity of the house, and discovered, sheltered under a shed made of boughs, a horse, saddled and bridled, I made up my mind to await the rider. I had to wait long, crouched in the shrubbery. At last, a figure glided from the foot of the turret, and came straight to the faithful horse; it was the figure of a richly clad gentleman. He carried a lantern, as if to show me his face the more clearly, and he spoke to the animal, so that I could not fail to recognize his voice.

"And he was —?" added Walter eagerly.

"Your beloved kinsman, the baron Guy de Fougereuse."

"Guy!" cried Maulny. "Guy de Fougereuse! Guy!"

"Yes, my lord; himself in person," Jacob repeated dryly; "and to speak truth, I have suspected as much for a long while."

Maulny hardly seemed to hear these last words. Absorbed in his own train of thought, he reflected for a moment, his forehead supported on his hand. Then, lifting his head with an imperious gesture, he murmured between his shut teeth:

"It shall be between us two. Fougereuse, I will know your secret yet!"

CHAPTER II.

DISGRACE.

KENT.   "Royal Lear,
        Whom I have ever honored as my King.
        Loved as my father, as my master followed,
        As my great patron thought on in my prayers!

            .   .   .   .

LEAR.   Kent! on thy life, no more."
                            SHAKESPEARE, *King Lear, Act I.*

IF there be any country where Saint Martin's summer is at once sweet as spring and melancholy as autumn, it is surely the province of Anjou. On the 15th of November, in the year 1470, the sun rose brilliantly on a pure sky, and the transparent air gave an ideal glory to the distant landscape across the Maine. The meadows of Reculée were sparkling under the morning dew; the leaves of the poplars which encircled the grotto and the tiny convent of Baumette were yet of the clear golden tint which follows the green of the year's prime. The imposing ducal castle, defended by seventeen towers, and surrounded by deep moats, had a festal mien. At the very top of the ramparts, where the banners of Anjou, Aragon, and Sicily were floating free, was a group of soldiers,

squires, and attendants, wearing the royal liveries
The gardens and terraces were overrun by a motley
crowd. Moors, Jews, Italians, Spaniards, men of
Provence and of Lorraine, called one another in
as many languages. Famous painters, courteous
poets, wise doctors and astronomers, dignified
magistrates, rich merchants, grotesque jesters,
some in bright scarlet, some in the duke's sober
colors, white, gray, and black, moved about, in-
termingled in picturesque disorder. The people
choked the narrow ways in the neighborhood of the
castle, crying, "*Noël!*" to each nobleman, as he
clattered past with his train. In the courtyard of
the palace all was stir and bustle and merry uproar.
Steeds were pawing and neighing; the streamers
on the lances, the knights' pennons, the armorial
ensigns, were fluttering on the breeze; beautifully embossed armor glittered on every hand;
pages and equerries gathered here and there about
their lords: for the radiant chivalry of Anjou and
Provence was assembling under the eye of its
prince. Before Queen Margaret of England and
her young son Edward, Prince of Wales, they
were preparing to rehearse the " passage-at-arms of
Joyous Garde." Margaret of Anjou, the daughter
of René, the wife of Henry the Sixth of England,
still a comely woman, and as full as ever of that
indomitable pride which the defeats of the Wars
of the Roses had not been able to quench, leaned
against a sculptured balcony. She smiled upon
her son, who was leading up and down, under the

window, a blooded courser; and in her motherly
pride, she seemed already to behold the crown of
England on his boyish head. Alas, that dream
was to cost him dear! But for the moment no
sinister forecast overhung the serenity of the blue
skies of Anjou; nothing darkened the splendid
holiday. The laughing pasture-land made one
forget sorrow, and charmed away all premonition
and regret. Margaret felt the universal beguile-
ment; those near her remarked a softened expression in her heroic features. Close to her sat
the young winsome queen, Joan of Laval, King
René's second wife, the loyal companion of his
declining years. Around the two queens was a
bevy of maids of honor, dark-eyed damsels from
Provence, and the blond heads of Anjou. In the
very last row stood a young girl, with a serious
even pensive air: Isabelle de Fougereuse, sister
of the baron Guy. Reared in the saintly shades
of the monastery of Our Lady of Ronceray, and
chosen but two months before to be among the
personal followers of Queen Joan, Isabelle felt
a little aloof from her gay associates and their
light, unreserved prattle. The new world on
which she had entered surprised her without winning her over. She, who was the flower of purity
and truth, had great unconscious beauty; but a
glance of admiration disconcerted her, and made
her hide behind her laughing comrades. One
might truly apply to her what Dante said of his
Beatrice: —

" She walks with humbleness for her array.

.   .   .   .   .   .

Merely the sight of her makes all things bow."

"Isabelle!" It was the lively Yolande de Beauvau, daughter of the seneschal, who whispered in her ear. "The King is growing uneasy because your brother is not here. What has happened to him? Nothing goes well when he is away. The tourney is not opening as it should; the English lords are tossing their heads. Is not the honor of Anjou in danger?"

"Guy has been delayed by the arrival of his friend, the lord of Villepreux," answered Isabelle. "He has just come out of Palestine with the strangest company: baptized Saracens, converted renegades, and Christians rescued from slavery, all of whom the King wished to appear in the jousts to-day. Guy is staying at the manse to see that they are properly accoutred, despite the protest of my lord Robert, who is not very eager to show off in public his 'Society of the Penitent Thief,' as he calls it. I left them contending over it. But I hope the King may soon have his wish."

"I am so glad he expressed the wish!" cried Yolande. "Do you hear that, Bertha, Lucy, Clotilde? We are to have negroes and Christian Paynims in the tilt-yard! Villepreux the Lion caught them, and brought them into the Church; and some day he will help them to found a monastery in memory of the Penitent Thief, where the priest will sing Mass in a turban and a coat-of-mail, with a scimitar at his side!"

And the news, flying from lip to lip, made a great sensation, and reached the ear of Joan the Queen, who smiled approvingly. Thenceforth all eyes were fixed impatiently on the great door, and were no longer interested in present preparations for the festivities.

While the baron Guy and his famous friend Villepreux were thus expected, the town house of Fougereuse was all astir, as well as the ducal castle. The unforeseen command of King René, his express request that the "Society of the Penitent Thief" should figure in the tournament, had turned everything upside down. Horses had to be provided for these numerous riders; and the fierce, tawny men, wearing their old raiment of the East, had to be arrayed so that they should not be put to shame by the luxurious attire of the court. Time was pressing. Meanwhile two persons, one a big, burly individual already growing awkwardly fat, the other slight and insignificant, with a cringing, sullen aspect, burst into the court through the folding doors, and insisted that they must have speech with the master of Fougereuse. Nobody listened to them; there was too much business on hand, of a verity! Men and horses, Christians and Saracens, French and Orientals, were inextricably mixed up, beckoning, calling, working, running, as busily and confusedly as an army under fire. But, nothing daunted, the thin stranger, who was none other than Jacob, accompanied by his cousin Martin, accosted a groom hurrying by.

"Good sir, we must see your master on important business. Two of his household have been abducted."

"What nonsense! We are here in our full strength; not one response is lacking when the roll is called. See my lord, would you? It is easy to talk. Run off, run off."

"Consider, my friend," said Martin, "the matter relates to Master Vincent Govier, the baron's chief equerry, and " —

"Consult him about it, then, and worry me no more."

"Consult him!" repeated Martin in dismay. "What an ill-conducted house is this, that they have not even informed themselves whether poor Vincent be in Heaven or worse!"

A deep voice, roundly scolding some negligent lackeys, became audible a few feet away. Jacob drew back with a cry of amazement, while Martin Bodin sprang forward. Vincent Govier, in complete armor, with a cap of chain mail, steel-pointed, stood below the entrance steps, issuing orders, and supervising the preparations.

"O my friend Vincent! Living! living!" shrieked Jacob, throwing up his arms. "May Our Lady and Saint Eloy, and the great Saint Maurice and his companions be blessed!"

"Tra-la-la! Go on with your litany!" was the

rude reply of the equerry, as he avoided the embraces of honest Bodin. "What is the cause of your lamentations and thanksgivings? Have I not a right to be living? What put you up to coming here at all?"

" We thought you were dead!" gasped Martin.

"I am not dead; and that is all there is to it. And if I were dead, how would it concern you? Did I ask you to bury my remains? Begone, with your blanched gills, and eyes bulging out of your heads, and leave me in peace!"

" But, Vincent, man," wailed Jacob, "will you not at least tell us how you escaped the Devil's claws, on your excursion to the haunted house?"

"I did not visit the haunted house." Govier answered. "What have you to say to that? If I chose to return to my duty instead of coursing after goblins and ghosts, am I not my own master? Clear out! You are wasting my time for me."

"You yourself declared, 'If I do not come back, it will be because I am killed.'" continued Jacob. "We took you at your word."

The equerry burst into a ringing laugh, though it sounded a little forced; and he gripped Piteux's bony arm. "Look at the manikin!" he cried, shaking him vigorously. "Was there ever such insolence? Summoning me to die at his beck, on the ground that I gave him my promise to do so, over the wine-cup, and disputing the liberty which I take to remain overground! Martin, my old crony, persuade your relative to go hang himself, that I may encounter him no more forever."

He loosened his hold on Jacob, who tottered and nearly fell; and he turned his back on Bodin, with a decisive movement which plainly meant, "You two imbeciles, you!"

"Master Govier, Master Govier!" It was a page who called thus, coming out upon the steps. "Where are you? Hurry! 'My lord is in need of you."

The equerry went quickly towards him. Bodin, stiffening with his astonishment, recognized Loïc de Kernis as he stood talking with Vincent. The youth was in a superb costume of silver and blue, the Fougereuse colors. He had resumed his usual brisk and easy carriage, evidently not remembering how moribund was his state, some hours before, at the Red Rose.

"Perdition!" murmured Martin. "The two of them! For a resuscitated creature, yonder lad is sufficiently jolly. And there was I, carrying him on my back like the good Samaritan, and caring for him as piously as if he had been my own father! If ever I saw the like!". . .

"Come along, then, cousin!" said Jacob, pulling the innkeeper by the sleeve. "We are better out of this." And the couple slipped through the courtyard, and were lost in the crowd.

A flourish of trumpets meantime announced the beginning of the jousts. The heralds-at-arms were giving the signals to enter the lists, "Let

"Noël to the Crusaders! God wills it."

the champions advance !" when sudden cries of, "*Noël* to the Crusaders !" "God wills it !" drowned every other sound. A thrill of impatience and curiosity swept through the noble assembly ; with acclamations they greeted the welcome arrival of Robert de Villepreux and his Penitent Thieves. Fougereuse had succeeded wonderfully in his equipment of the *cortège*. That group of men bronzed by the Eastern sun, with their strange array, their fierce, haughty faces ; that leader, easily carrying a suit of armor of Richard Lionheart's time, the antique helmet pierced only with two holes for the eyes ; that banner of the triumphant Cross, with its device, " *Diex vult*," — all this was a living vision of the bygone Crusades. The popular imagination, especially that of the knights, felt the enchantment of the past ; and a spontaneous shout, " Hail to Jerusalem ! Hail to the Cross !" uprose from a thousand hearts. The ensign of Villepreux, raising the visor of his casque and revealing the well-known features of Guy de Fougereuse, saluted gallantly with his sword, as he passed under the balcony of Joan the Queen, while Villepreux himself slowly lowered the tip of his lance. King René, standing on the platform erected for the judges of the day's prowess, received the homage of the new-comers.

" Sire," said Fougereuse, reining in his charger in front of the royal box, " your Majesty's leal subject, Messire Robert de Villepreux, humbly begs pardon for so great a delay. But Palestine is a far land, and he was unable to return so speedily as he desired. He brings with him captive Arabs, baptized heathen, Christian men ransomed from slavery; and with these does he desire to do fealty unto his sovereign and gracious lord. What is your Majesty's will in his regard?"

"Our good pleasure is that our trusty Villepreux shall come forward, sir standard-bearer, and salute us. Let him hear from our own mouth the praise due to his prowess, and the expression of our joy at his return."

Villepreux dismounted, tossing the bridle to Loïc, and ascended the steps of the scaffolding where René had seated himself. "With raised visor, Robert," whispered Fougereuse. "You are forgetting."

Robert obeyed; and his proud eyes, his soldierly, austere face, framed in the helmet of burnished steel, towered up among the throng of nobles gathered around the King. To him he bent the knee, with the profound respect and glad fidelity of the subject vassal, and renewed his oath of homage. René raised him kindly, and with fatherly affection pressed him in his arms.

"I longed to have you back among us, my brave knight! I know that over yonder you have rivalled the feats of Richard Lionheart, working for the freedom of Christians in Jerusalem. And I think the golden collar of our Order of the Crescent could not be in a better place than over against your breastplate." Then, detaching the precious

chain which hung from his neck, the King fastened
it, with his own hands, around Villepreux's. The
lords applauded; the crowd again cried, "*Noël!*"

Walter de Maulny grew pale with smothered
rage and jealousy. The honor so lightly granted
to Villepreux, in open tournament, had been refused to him. Among the courtiers, he was almost the only one who wore no insignia of any of
the numerous orders of knighthood instituted by
the Duke of Anjou. His evil star shone for him
in all the events of the day; he made a most luck-
less choice of adversaries. Unhorsed at the very
first encounter by Villepreux, whose charge was
worthy of his fame in the Holy Land, and defeated,
after a trial of skill and agility, by Fougereuse,
Maulny determined to revenge himself on a rider
whose shield bore no device. His victory was
only too quick and easy. The young knight,
thrown to the ground under his mount, was picked
up unconscious; and on a wave of general consternation, the rumor of the death of Prince Edward of Lancaster ran about among the crowd.
Queen Margaret withdrew in haste from the balcony, and did not return, although the prince
himself, recovering from his faint, assured her
that he had suffered no harm.

The award of the day was decreed to Guy
de Fougereuse, whose courage and capacity distanced all rivals. Robert de Villepreux, unwilling
to make parade of his extraordinary strength in a
passage-at-arms, had not sought to wrest from his

friend the glory of being first in the jousts. The
"good luck of Fougereuse" held in all things.
The young favorite saw his fortune and influence
increase day after day. Life smiled upon him.
His happy nature, wonderfully dowered with va-
ried aptitudes, lent itself without effort to the
exercise of each. Be it to break a lance, to rhyme
a virelay, to organize a festival, to lead an assault,
to chase the wild boar, to dance the pavane, to confer with an ambassador, — Fougereuse was perfect
at it. He spoke several languages well, and he
was a student of such sciences as were known at
that time. A good singer, a minstrel-poet, Guy
possessed, with all his agreeable worldly graces, a
very keen knowledge of men. His policy proved
a check to the ambitious designs of Louis XI. over
Anjou, and held René, in his old age, to a firm and
cautious line of conduct. He bore his sovereign
an all but filial veneration, and was devoted to him
for better or worse: it was to this true attachment,
and its absolute disinterestedness, that Fougereuse
owed the favor of the king. Besides, his natural
good humor and sweetness of character endeared
him to all. But though his manner was evenly
gracious to every one, he was at heart, under a gay
and serene exterior, inaccessible; and he was chary
of his intimacies. Villepreux was his one and
only familiar friend; despite their marked contrast
of temperament, they lived in undivided love.
Villepreux, so independent as to be almost rude,
bluntly sincere, happiest on the battlefield, and a

despiser of pleasures, was more feared than loved
at court. Yet even there he was generally es-
teemed. Meanness, cowardice. falsehood, dared
not show themselves to those loyal eyes which no
danger had ever clouded; to that open brow which
had never inclined itself before the might of injustice. The most cunning slander fell powerless in
presence of honor so spotless, and of such a shining
name. Maulny had spoken truly when he had
compared Robert to the paladins of the olden time.
What now excited his rage was to see his foe safe-
guarded by the friendship of Villepreux.

The evening hours of the festival were as brilliant as the passage-at-arms had been. Southern
dances, the slow stately steps of Spain and of Provence, gave full play to the grace of girlhood, and
the elegance of the younger nobles. Then the company broke into groups, and followed their individual whims. At one end of the hall, the King
leaned over a table, surrounded with his architects,
looking at sketches and plans. Both Queens, with
their ladies of honor, seated near a window, were
amusing themselves with the wit of the dwarfs
Phélipot and Tuybelin, and the tales of a troubadour. Not far away, Isabelle de Fougereuse was
softly singing, at the request of some English
dames, a simple Christmas hymn which she had
learned at her convent school. Elsewhere a min-
strel accompanied with the chords of his guitar the
voice of a young page, who was trolling a roundel
of Charles of Orleans: —

> *" Scatter, scatter, run to cover,*
> *Worry, Care, and Melancholy !*
> *Though ye ruled me, in my folly,*
> *Slave am I no more, nor lover.*
> *Scatter, scatter, run to cover,*
> *Worry, Care, and Melancholy ! "*

Laughter was on every lip, joy in every eye. In that gay palace, one's sole concern seemed to be to pass the time gently away, as if there were nothing in the world, save pleasure, which was worth pursuing. Villepreux, withdrawn into a deep alcove, looked out thoughtfully over the radiant company. He saw his friend Guy, the hero of the day, stepping smilingly among the eager courtiers. He saw Isabelle, frankly happy at her brother's success, glowing with natural lightness of heart. He saw Maulny, who, grave, proud, conventional, appeared absorbed in a political conversation with Lord Rous. To an ordinary spectator, indeed, the picture would have suggested no lurking shadow. But it gave Robert a painful impression; his eyebrows contracted. He seemed to be aware in a moment that whispers were exchanged wherever Fougereuse passed, and that gossip broke off at Isabelle's approach. Malicious glances from behind a fan, a mocking nod of the head, a murmured but emphatic confidential word, lent him a foretaste of distant but certain calamity. And all too soon Villepreux heard voices close by which gave him a pang, and changed his causeless anxiety into open wrath.

"What is this rumor about Fougereuse?" It was Yolande de Beauvau who questioned Cornelius, the King's new physician. "You, who know everything, should know what is at the bottom of it. They talk, do they not, of enchanted arms, and of a fairy lance which can overturn every combatant it touches?"

"Not quite that, Yolande," answered other feminine accents. "It concerns a haunted house given in fief to the Devil by Guy de Fougereuse. If ever the baron requires anything of his vassal, he goes thither to issue orders; and they are always obeyed. I heard that he has been there this very night."

"Oh!" exclaimed several bystanders. "Fougereuse! Who would have believed it?"

"Everybody says so," was the authoritative answer of the last speaker. Protests were silenced by this assurance.

"Here, then, is the secret of Fougereuse's astounding good luck!" said the young Geoffrey d'Anglure.

"But what do you think, master?" insisted Yolande de Beauvau, addressing Cornelius. "I should like to ascertain the truth."

"My noble ladies," the doctor began, in his most important tone, "the exact truth in such matters is by no means easy to ascertain. Nevertheless, I must say that the singular influence of Fougereuse over our sire the King, the prolonged period for which he holds the King's favor, the success which in all comes as easily to him as if he were playing with it, — these things hardly seem to be the work of nature alone. It may be, that abetted by the powers of the air, that is, by the infernal legions of whom we read in Holy Writ (*ab insidiis diabolis*, by the insidious demons), it may be, I allow, that the baron de Fougereuse is possessed of some occult powers. Since his intimate friend and my predecessor, Antonio Blandini, went away, have you not noticed that my illustrious patient and liege lord, King René of Anjou, whom may God preserve! is failing and growing weaker, despite all my care? The baron's dearest wish is to undervalue my skill, in order to secure Antonio's return. . . . Draw your own conclusions."

" A spell cast?" said Geoffrey.

" The evil eye?" said a Neapolitan knight.

"Perchance, gentlemen; perchance downright sorcery, forbidden arts, witchcraft, a murder in effigy."

"Viper!" cried Villepreux, coming suddenly between the young d'Anglure and the startled physician. "Viper! repeat but that calumny, and I will crush you beneath my heel. And what are you doing here, sir knights? A contemptible liar and parvenu, a man with an end to gain by it, drags in the dust the reputation of one of your brothers-in-arms — and you endure it! Nay, worse: you listen, you smile at his wretched inventions! By Heaven, my lords, your laughter has a ready flow. If this sort of amusement is considered so choice, it would be more loyal in you not to forbid him to share it on whose good name you batten. It is such fair play, attacking the absent! But if you would injure Fougereuse, and would do it with impunity, be careful not to attempt it before me."

The prompt intervention of Robert had its effect upon the few who were tearing to tatters between them the repute of Fougereuse: it threw them into consternation and disorder. The rash maids drew back affrighted from the indignant flash in the eyes of the enraged soldier; the leech Cornelius, as if struck by a thunderbolt, glided away like a shadow, up the length of the tapestried wall; the Neapolitan also disappeared at Villepreux's vehement opening speech; Geoffrey d'Anglure, and certain youths, who were drawn into the altercation without thoroughly understanding what it was about, were the only ones of the group to hear Robert de Villepreux close his arraignment with an intended challenge.

"How is this?" cried the bystanders, as soon as the chevalier had spoken; "a quarrel in the King's presence?"

"What is the matter, Villepreux?" asked Walter de Maulny, approaching the alcove. "Do you fancy yourselves still among the Paynims? Would you slaughter in the very ballroom the hope of the chivalry of Anjou?"

"If the Lion must roar," some one added sarcastically, "let him return to his desert lair."

"Enough, gentlemen!" Villepreux replied, in a

steady and controlled voice. " I was defending the honor of my friend. Those to whom I addressed myself will find me prepared at any time to maintain my words."

A hand laid upon his arm restrained him, as he touched his sword-hilt in defiance. Turning quickly, with a motion to shake himself free, he came face to face with Guy de Fougereuse.

" It is all folly, Robert," said the young favorite, in his authoritative way. " Have you not forgotten where you are? . . . And you, my dear d'Anglure, when next you would malign me, let me be the sole audience. I have such dangerously warm friends! . . . Pardon the too great vivacity of this particular one, my lords. I think his wars in foreign lands have driven out of his mind the golden rule of life at court: —

> ' *To see all things, and notice naught;*
> *To hear, but show not; nor, untaught,*
> *Say ever a word of the known and thought.*'

My cousin Maulny, do you come to my aid in making peace between these two noble champions who have vowed to stand upon their dignity. Is it not a hard, hard vow to keep in this world, Master Cornelius?" Then, passing his arm through Robert's, the speaker led him away, leaving Geoffrey d'Anglure and Cornelius bewildered at the turn the event had taken, and persuaded, more strongly than ever, of the mesmeric power of Guy de Fougereuse.

"Guy, this is no place for me," began Villepreux, as soon as they had reached a great porch which overlooked the gardens. "You will only craze me by requiring me to stay. Let me go back to the house."

"Go then, Lion of mine," answered Fougereuse. "It is hardly the time for explanations. I dare not disclaim your generous defence of me; and yet nothing is more likely to harm me."

"Harm you, Guy! Have you grown to be so much of a courtier that you would sacrifice your friends to uphold your enemies? If I believed that" —

"Good-night, Robert!" exclaimed the young baron, with a sweetly whimsical smile. "I take to heart what Walter once said of you, 'Never be cross with Villepreux, whatever he does: he is newly come from Palestine.'" And with this Guy wrung his comrade's hand, and returned to the festal hall.

Villepreux, on leaving the palace, crossed the court of honor and the gardens, without much thought of whither he was walking, strayed aimlessly awhile along the terraces, and ended by throwing himself on a stone bench sheltered by a hedge of holly. The solitude, the quiet, the pure fresh air of the beautiful starry night, breathed peace, little by little, into the wounded spirit of the loyal knight. He had been wroth with Cornelius, and vexed with Geoffrey d'Anglure and the others; but he had ached at hearing Fougereuse blame him for his conduct, and he comforted himself with the thought of a frank understanding to be had with him. A great many things might have come to pass while he was away. And, after all, was the quicksand of any court the right ground for him, a man in love with war and glory?

"It matters little," he reflected. "But for a choice of foes, give me a Saracen rather than a courtier. At least, with the former one can play an open game, and strike straight ahead!"

"What under the moon are you doing here, Villepreux?" The voice of Walter de Maulny was close to his ear. "Were you not able to go out by the main door? Come with me: I shall have the eastern postern-gate thrown open, and you can profit by it."

Robert followed him, asking himself how it was that Maulny's presence invariably woke in him a sense of repugnance and hostility. As soon as the two were side by side, in the narrow, crooked streets of the town, Walter, with his cat-like stealth, came close to his companion and took his arm, as if to make Villepreux lean a little towards him. "Do you know, Lion," he began in confidential tones, "you wasted all your fine anger just now. They were but contending to see who could exasperate you best. It was a pity to spoil the scene, for it was pretty enough to have gone bodily into some troubadour's tale. It makes me laugh now, to think of those prattlers falling into a blue fright at the sight of your tall figure and your angry countenance! Before you had uttered four words, there was a general rout; and it took every atom of courage he had to keep Geoffrey firm on his feet. Another time, my dear Crusader, make a better choice of foes! It is hardly worthy of you to vent such fury upon a flock of girls, gentlemen of tender age, and an old leech very fond of his personal safety; and the worst of it is, Fougereuse will not be in the least grateful for your services. Your aggressiveness has compromised him, up to the neck, as we say. What was only a rumor this evening will be cried from the housetops to-morrow, thanks to you."

"What ought to be cried on the housetops, thanks to me," Robert replied, disengaging his arm from Walter's pressure, "is that to permit one's fellow-soldier to be insulted before one's face, is an action which calls for degradation from the rank of knighthood!"

"Ah, yes: you are from Palestine, my noble friend. If everybody were of your mind, merit would have no detractors, and royal partisanships would breed no jealousy. But who dreams of putting a stop to the slander and evil-speaking of courts? As soon build dikes against the ocean. I admit that Guy uses no caution. They may boast that he has wisdom; and yet his very gayety of heart gives a pretext for all sorts of absurd stories which are current about him."

"Pretexts! What pretexts?" cried Robert, subduing a strong desire of his own to smash his companion's head. "Are you aware that Cornelius accused him of sorcery and witchcraft?"

"That is going too far. Nevertheless, we must acknowledge that Guy gives some provocation to common talk, by his eccentric habits. Does he not ride down to Pouillé wood at midnight, to visit his haunted lodge, the terror of the neighborhood, and to set up his telltale light in the window? And in the evening, at his own house, he shuts himself up in a closet with neither lock nor key, and forbids his servants to enter, and so clear up the mystery. In short, what can be said about it? Simply that Guy de Fougereuse has *something to conceal.* That explains all."

"If Fougereuse has a secret, it is an honorable secret, my lord of Maulny. Is it not a fair employment for gentlemen to spread far and wide the gossip of the vulgar? How can suspicions cling for an instant to a knight of noble blood, whose allegiance cannot be called in question?"

"Calm yourself, Villepreux. Far be it from me to throw suspicion on the honor and good faith of my own kinsman, the friend of my childhood! If I am thus frank with you, it is because you are the sole person who has sufficient influence over Guy to draw him away from these practices which so endanger his reputation. . . . Why that indignant gesture? Will you never cure yourself of the notion that the others here are like you? The King, to you, is infallible: a friend of yours cannot deceive. All the better, if this be so. Perhaps you know what Fougereuse was after last night at Wolfram's house? . . . Though he does not exempt you, any more than the next one, from his teasings, I believe Guy is sincerely attached to you: as much as he can be to any one. I have never shared the opinion of those who look upon him as a hypocrite and trick comedian. I know him to be ambitious, an able diplomat, an accomplished courtier, but—"

Villepreux stopped short, in the middle of the Rue Saint Aignan. "Maulny," he said, with a quietude which masked his passionate temper, "if you prefer that we two should survive and reach our homes to-night, then let us separate. Choose your road, and I will take the contrary one. Say not a word more! You never were so near to death in all your life."

A few minutes later, Robert de Villepreux returned alone to the palace of Fougereuse, and sank wearily into a chair, murmuring: "I ought never to have come back from the Holy Land!" If it had been given to Walter to read Villepreux's candid soul, he might have shuddered at the storm he had created there. All who have suffered under the errors and disillusions of life will agree that the moment hardest to bear is not that in which one feels the cruel blow fall, but that in which the presentiment of it is clear and sure: the moment when the heart, till then serene and trustful, hears a whispered, *Beware!* or when doubt first glides in between a man and his dearest beliefs. That moment abides in memory as one of unique anguish. Robert's nature, being generous and lofty, gave him, by so much, the sharper torment. He blushed at his own misgivings, he hated himself for his sceptic fears; yet he could not escape them. He, who would have taken his oath before God and men that Guy was incapable of the least disloyalty, heard the words of Maulny echo implacably in his ears: "*Guy de Fougereuse has something to conceal.*" He remembered how his friend had evaded certain queries, and he remembered some curious circumstances which he had not noticed at the time. A growing unrest crept over his thoughts, and weighed down his spirits; hours passed by, and he was unconscious of their passing. Very late, Guy came home. His friend could hear him scolding Vincent and Loïc, with an unwonted severity which surprised him.

"My fault, my fault, is it?" grumbled the equerry. "My lord holds me responsible, forsooth! Am I supposed to dog the footsteps of a young good-for-nothing who never knows his place, and rides over every rule? Was I able to foresee that those two simpletons would try to slice each other, in the public courtyard of the ducal palace? On my word, there are no children nowadays!"

"A gentleman, however young, is old enough to resent an insult!" Loïc's voice was shrill with exasperation. "I take no orders from any one, on such a matter."

" You will take orders from me, now and here, Messire de Kernis," said Guy, in cold, peremptory tones which admitted of no reply. " I commission you to confine yourself to this house until I give you leave to quit it; and I dispense you from all personal service to me, until your repentance shall have proved itself genuine."

"I repent nothing. I shall stand by what I said, and by what I did. If I had to begin again, I should do the same thing, and that is the long and the short of it!"

"You heard me, Loïc. I will be obeyed. Go to your room and meditate, and do not approach me again, unless I send for you. I have pardoned a great deal in you, but this latest folly exceeds all bounds, and such impertinence no indulgence ought to cover. Go."

The page went hurriedly. Guy walked down the long corridor to his own apartment. As he opened his door, he sighed: " There must have been a wager on it to-night!"

Disturbed by this novel incident, Robert determined to let nothing interfere with his desire to question his friend. He entered his room without difficulty, and then he had a shock of surprise. It was empty! The only evidences that Guy had been there, were his rich cloak and his dress sword thrown across his chair. Not knowing what to think, and recalling Maulny's hints, Villepreux retreated, sadly puzzled. Loïc's little room, in the tower, was next his own. Robert approached the door between, and knocked softly, calling the page in an undertone. Not receiving an answer, he let himself in, torch in hand. Loïc, still in his tournament costume, was lying on the bed, his head buried in his folded arms, sobbing with all the hot hopelessness of a child unjustly punished. Robert laid his hand gently on the boy's shoulder. He sprang up instantly, excused himself, dried his tears with an impatient hand, and seemed greatly chagrined that his grief had found a spectator.

"Loïc, I heard it all," Villepreux began. "What happened to your master after I left the palace?"

"This, my lord. One of the King's pages, that coxcomb of a Paul de Fleurenville, cast an aspersion upon the baron in my presence. So"—

"What did he say?"

"He said that my master used amulets and talismans to make him win in the jousts, and that he had woven a spell around King René, in order to get his confidence. Do you suppose I could abide that? We went down into the courtyard and drew upon each other, and Master Paul got a good slash of my sword. Unluckily, the King's doctor, Cornelius, whose old eyes let nothing escape them, passed by just then, and he began shouting for help, and crying that I was slaughtering one of his Majesty's household. They all rushed in upon us, and had it not been for Vincent, who dragged me out of the scrimmage at the very first moment, I should have been imprisoned without further trial. And I should have liked it better. I would rather be buried alive in a dungeon by my master's enemies, than to see myself disgraced by him, simply because I defended him bravely."

" And because you answered him impudently," Villepreux remarked.

" Ah, that is too hard on me," the page protested, in an altered tone. " Messire Robert, I leave you to judge. Has the baron any right to treat me so, after all he has done for me? See! he found me a young child, an orphan, in Brittany, left in charge of a miserly guardian who used to send me out into the fields to tend his sheep. He took me away from that tyrant: I dare say he bought me from him with good gold. He brought me to Fougereuse, treated me as one of his family, had me reared like his own son, became to me father, mother, sister, brother; and now he refuses me the privilege of drawing a blade in his defence. I, it seems, must allow him to be lied about, and called a sorcerer and a reprobate, without lifting my finger! Now, if it be my duty to hold my tongue while my master is maligned, I prefer to go back to Brittany. Why was I not left with my scamp of a relative? I should have no temptation to fight in that person's quarrels."

" Be quiet, child," Villepreux answered kindly. " This will all be cleared up. To-morrow I will speak to Guy, and make your peace with him."

" Not that; never!" Loïc, whose pride had reasserted itself, cried out with animation. " I beseech you, most earnestly, not to come between

us, in the hope of any reconciliation. My master
wishes my services no longer, and I shall not
impose them upon him. But whether dismissed or
not, I am able to watch his foes, and unmask them.
I can devote myself to my lord despite him, away
from him, in the shadows; so that one day he
will be forced to proclaim: ' It is Loïc who saved
me.' Then, perchance, he will regret having cast
off a friend who would shed his life-blood for his
sake."

The hectic fervor of the page impressed Villepreux, and he surmised that the reprimand which
he had received was not the only reason for it.
He was anxious to learn the true cause.

"What is all this, Loïc, about saving your master despite himself? Does some great danger menace him? Do you know of any?"

"I know what I know," Loïc replied laconically.
"The baron of Fougereuse may do what he likes,
and go whither he pleases: that is his own affair.
It may be that he takes pleasure in being dubbed
a magician: if so, that is his own affair too. But
morbleu! any one who accuses him while I am there
to hear, will not be likely to repeat his words to
any second pair of ears, unless it be Satan's. I
mean to keep guard over the honor of Fougereuse!" As Loïc ended, he swayed to and fro,
and sank down upon a seat, with a look of sudden
agony.

"My poor child!" cried Robert; "you are
wounded. There is blood on your sleeve. Stretch

out your arm, and let me bathe it. Why did you
not speak of it?"

" Probably because I thought nothing about it.
A cut in the left arm, a mere scratch! Bah! I
was awkward at it. Another time I shall take
pains to get killed."

Robert left the boy only after he had dressed
the wound, which was not deep, and endeavored
to calm his excitement. But Loïc was in the
melodramatic mood, and persisted in regarding
himself as a wronged and magnanimous hero. The
next day Guy was summoned early to the castle, and was absent until afternoon. Villepreux
awaited him, in much anxiety.

" Well, Robert," the baron said, on accosting his
friend, "I find you already famous at court, and
the place divided into opposite camps, all on your
account. Cornelius is sore at having been saluted
as an intriguer, a parvenu, a contemptible creature : you did not spare him such compliments!
He has complained to the agents of King Louis,
who uphold him; he has complained to d'Anglure
and the other fops, who make common cause with
him, having been as badly treated by you as he
was himself; he complained to the good King, our
own liege lord, who sent me to soothe him. In
short, the question agitating all minds at present
seems to be: Is it expedient for the Lion to roar
anywhere outside Palestine? One party says yea,
another nay. As for me, being too nearly concerned, I remain neutral; but you have a strong

champion in my sister Isabelle.   Poor little one!
she is inconsolable not to have had an opportunity
to thank you for waging war on my detractors.
But, as a dutiful brother, I express her gratitude
for her."

" What tidings are these you bring !" exclaimed
Robert, bewildered at the unexpected results of
the affair of the preceding evening.   " What!
Has that Cornelius the effrontery to complain, and
to complain to the King?   You make me regret
that I did not wring his neck."

" How could it be otherwise?   Audacity is the
path to success, and the first to appeal is the first
to win his cause.   I could say nothing after that.
I did my best to exonerate you, on the known plea
that you come from Palestine."

" And so," said Villepreux indignantly, " it
is the aggressor who complains, it is the defender who is apologized for, and it is the injured
person who holds his tongue!   Where is the
right ? "

" That, my friend, is what no one worries about.
The right!   Ask Louis XI. if he cares to know.
What rights has he over this duchy of Anjou?
Nevertheless, he will give himself no repose until
he has wrested it, willy-nilly, from the hands of his
uncle René.   I notice that our gentle sovereign
tires of contention, and makes concession after
concession,in order to have peace.   He is mistaken
if he thinks to disarm his affectionate nephew by
such compromises.   Louis of France covets every-

thing, and will not let go his hold until he has obtained everything."

"One can have no peace with him except at the point of the lance, as Joan the Maid said to the Duke of Burgundy. Now, if I were the King, I "—

"If you were king, Robert, you would have royal theories instead of military notions. The right, in this generation, has few supporters."

"Guy, is it indeed you who say such a thing?" asked Villepreux gravely. "Are you so much changed? Must I set up as chief mourner for our friendship over and gone?"

"No, if you please," Fougereuse answered quickly; "for I mean to keep it alive. My dear Robert, you take whatever you hear in so tragic a sense! Your Penitent Thieves have corrupted you with their fanatical admirations and their blind obedience. You have made them over into your own image. But consider: I am not on their level, having been neither a Saracen, nor a renegade, nor a captive, nor anything else which enlists your enthusiasm. Show me, then, a little indulgence."

"Can you give me any news of the page whom Loïc hurt yesterday evening?" Robert made his serious inquiry without lowering his eyes from the mobile, playful face of his friend.

Guy frowned. "Forbear mentioning Loïc to me. He is a rebel, an ungovernable firebrand. I have spoiled him: he goes too far. He deserved a severe lesson, and he has received it. Do not take his part."

" You are severe. He was acting in your behalf. I do not see why a naughty prick of the sword " —

" If it had been only a prick of the sword! But it was a prick of the tongue as well, and one past cure. . . . Are you astonished? I warrant Loïc does not brag of it. One of the King's pages, repeating, like a parrot, the gossip of the day, accuses me of having bewitched his Majesty, in order to win and retain his favor. And my discreet lad finds nothing better to do than to respond, with the boldness quite characteristic of him : 'You are hard put to it, my poor Fleurenville, if you hope to persuade us that one has to be a sorcerer, before he can over-rule your master's mind! If it were King Louis, now, it would be quite otherwise.' "

" The madcap! The little fool!" cried Ville-preux. " His anger must have made him forget himself."

" Anyhow, it came off, did it not, in plain hear-ing of the royal household ; of pages, equerries, guards of the palace, and all the rest? Of course the sarcasm will be laid to me. A master of the house is always measured by the language his sub-ordinates use."

" And as King René is extremely anxious to seem possessed of the qualities he lacks, it will offend him mortally," Robert continued.

" You have hit it precisely. Had Loïc only

taxed his Majesty with avarice, or perfidy, or igno-
rance, my royal master would have laughed at it;
but a hint that he is weak and indecisive can never
be forgiven. After all, it is truly our gracious
liege's only fault: this too easy good-nature.
One could nowhere find a heart more generous, a
more upright soul, a more cultivated intellect,
more thorough goodness of character. It pains me
deeply to see him struck by a dart aimed from
my threshold, though not by my hand. Well, the
thing is done! I must try to atone for it as I
can."

"I sympathize with your trouble, Guy; but I
must say, I do not consider Loïc very guilty. How
can you expect that child, whose one affection is
for you, to hear you abused without protesting,
when I myself " —

"It is true you cannot act impartially, Villepreux," answered Guy, with gayety; "and I read
it in your face that you are not over and above
pleased with me. You find me affable with my
enemies, rude with my friends. thankless to my defenders, and lenient to my detractors. You have
a grudge against me for interfering with you yesterday, just as you were on the point of impaling
half a dozen striplings ; and your blood boils at
this moment to hear me laugh and jest. You say
to yourself that I have softened, degenerated ; that
the court has vitiated my heart and mind ; that the
chase for pleasure is my sole occupation in life,
and that I imperil the salvation of my soul. Do

you not think me a bit of a sorcerer, yourself? Come, own it."

"God forbid, Guy! I do not see how you can speak so lightly of such grave matters. In the funeral pile of Giles de Retz, the ashes yet smoulder, and such rumors as those of yesterday may yet rekindle them."

"Receive my thanks for the comparison with that strangler of little children! Have I tried to rival him? You humiliate me indeed, Villepreux, when you set Bluebeard's name over against that of your best friend. Fie upon you! Ah, you shake your head. Then let us be calmer. One must be Robert the Lion, to believe that any one topic can hold the interest of the court of Anjou for two consecutive days. Every morrow's news blots out the memory of the news of the evening before. After having shuddered at the idea of Guy de Fougereuse dealing in the Black Art, they will seek the next sensation in the morality of *The Worldly Man,* which is to be given this week. It is just what you will approve, Sir Ascetic; and I will have one of the front seats set by for you, at the side of my cousin Walter de Maulny, who will explain to you all the local allusions."

"I object to my proposed neighbor," said Robert fiercely. "If you inflict him upon me, and there should be consequences, you are responsible. Have you sworn to drive me to something desperate, Guy?"

"There: what a puzzling, inconsistent fellow you

are! You bring home from the ends of the earth a tribe of reformed brigands, on whom you lavish infinite kindness and forbearance; yet you cannot endure Maulny, who, after all, has nothing in his disfavor except that he has squandered his patrimony. Frankly, I must ask you to let me place my cousin on a different plane from that of your jailbirds."

"I, too, should put him on a different plane. My thieves are on the right side of the Cross, while Maulny dwells always on the other side, with a mighty small chance of conversion. There is no more arrant trickster in this world than your cousin Walter. As a choice between thief and thief, I prefer the penitent sort to the impenitent!"

"You are unjust towards Maulny, Villepreux. He has been embittered by his failure in life, or discouraged by the reverses of fortune: experiences such as his do not sweeten one's disposition. You never liked him, and you are too hard upon him. But remember how fate has always gone against him, until now he is on the very brink of ruin. I realize what you would add: that Walter has no love for me. Would it not rather be a marvel, Robert, if he liked me ever so little? I have been, at every turn, his rival, and, without meaning it, his successful rival. I have unconsciously blocked his way to preferment, and distanced him in the King's favor; besides, I have refused him my sister's hand, and her dowry. His resentment is natural enough. I know not"—

"Isabelle's hand!" literally roared Villepreux, as he sprang straight up. "The felon! The traitor! How dared he?"

"And why not? Walter's own birth is as noble. Isabelle's dowry would have allowed him to re-purchase Maulny. The alliance commended itself to a great many members of my family. I would not consent to it, because Isabelle's happiness must be confided to no man in whom I have not absolute trust. Still, there is no cause to cry felony and treachery. If you were in Walter's place, would you not act in the same way?"

"Never!" Villepreux indignantly answered. "It is infamous!"

"Infamous, is it, to sue for the honor of becoming my brother-in-law? My poor, dear Robert, it is certain that the atmosphere of Palestine"—

"Guy, you are pretending to misunderstand me. The infamy would be to marry an angel like Isabelle to a being like Maulny! Even to name them together is sacrilege."

"I told you I would not hear of it. Do not blaze up so! It makes dealings with a caged Lion extra difficult. Go· and exhort your Penitent Thieves: it will quiet you."

"Guy, I shall not go, nor exhort my Penitent Thieves," replied Villepreux, slowly mastering his temper. "I exact of you, for the sake of our sworn friendship, an honest explanation. What part am I expected to play here? Am I a stuffed figure in the games, a butt for every man's lance?

Do you imagine you can blind me, as if I were a
child, by your perpetual small talk, and your affectation of frivolity? I have not lost (and I thank
God for it) my skill to read you through ; and I
know you are, at bottom, the same old noble heart.
But this court-like trifling is worthy neither of
you nor of me. I challenge you, Guy de Fougereuse, to throw your mask aside, and at last to let
me see your face. I weary of being maltreated by
my dearest friend, one who will always be that,
whatever fault I have to find with him."

The baron listened without interrupting, and
in an attitude of great seriousness. His eyes fell
gradually under that steady, direct glance which
sought to penetrate his soul, and his gay, careless
expression changed to one of ever-deepening gravity. Another man sat there : Guy, unknown to
himself, was obeying Villepreux, was showing
him his true lineaments, without disguise. It
would have been impossible for any spectator not
to have been struck just then by the contrast
between the two. Villepreux's uncommon stat-
ure, his austere garb, the firm lines of his mouth
and cheek, his dominant air, as of a chief accustomed to command, made the other appear shorter
and frailer than he really was ; and Fougereuse,
with his graceful, well-turned figure, in his doublet of bright blue satin, with his delicate smile,
his blond hair, his youthful look, his quick speech
and gesture, was like a mere boy beside a warrior.
Yet the dignity and nobility of his whole person

were such that they bred respect in his most boorish inferior, as well as in his most critical equal. Villepreux, on his part, acknowledged the power of what he called "Guy's grand air." After a short silence, Guy raised his head and met his friend's eyes.

"What fault have I committed against you, Robert?" he asked gently. "Tell me: and if I have given offence, I shall be eager to repair it."

"What fault against me, Guy? This: that you withhold your confidence from a brother who has nothing apart from you; that you treat me like a babe whom one hushes at bedtime with stories, or entertains by day with words, words, words; that I have to stand by and behold you running light-heartedly into imminent danger, and risking your good name, not to speak of your position and fortune, with the recklessness of a young blade who will take no advice. Has our ancient promise of fealty to each other come to this, that I must fold my arms and close my ears, when your enemies are about you? Is it my duty, in this battle, never to succor you? I may have been a very, very long time in Palestine; but I have not come back so deaf and so blind that I can take calumny for a proof of personal interest, the enviers of a person for his loving friends, nor Walter de Maulny for a good man."

Fougereuse smiled and nodded his head; but Villepreux was unwilling to let him speak. "Listen," he said, laying his heavy hand on his comrade's arm, "I shall set you an example of candor which I trust you will follow." And leaning towards Guy, lowering his voice so that no one else could overhear him, he related to him, in detail, all that he had witnessed or apprehended since the previous evening. He omitted no one circumstance: neither the conversation at the ball, the accusations of Cornelius, the stinging aspersions of Maulny, Loïc's despairing state and his reference to undiscovered perils, nor even the narrator's own visit to Guy's chamber, when he perceived it to be empty, a few seconds after Guy had been heard to enter it.

Fougereuse was attentive, but not impressed. At the last specification he shrugged his shoulders. "How like you that is, my big Lion! You must have adventures at any price. Not finding me in, you conclude that I had gone to join some witches at their orgies, or to race through the city streets in the form of a werewolf! Or I have the secret art of making myself invisible, have I not? How should I be able to satisfy you on this point, when for my own part, I hardly comprehend for what the populace are ready to arraign me? They strike hard enough, plague upon it! What with nocturnal travels, necromancy, murders in effigy, and dark deeds done in mysterious cubby-holes which have neither lock nor key, I should have to be two men to have achieved the half of it! Now I see nothing worth notice in all this, except Walter's malice. He is evidently seeking to establish bad blood between us, and to estrange us; and here you are mistrusting me already! Be sure, too, that he has turned Loïc's head. In regard to that child, if you would do me a service, take him with you to Villepreux, and keep him awhile. His independent nature needs some firm discipline. You see, I could not, in decency, allow him to appear at court again, after his escapade of yesterday."

"As for taking Loïc, I will do it gladly. But you try my patience, Guy. Have you nothing else to say to me?"

"Nothing, Robert, save that I thank you for having forewarned me. That is the act of a true friend."

Villepreux had a thrill of vexation. He went close to the baron, put a hand on his either shoulder, and looked at him, face to face. "Have you no shame, that you treat me thus?" he said, in a bitter and mournful tone which startled Fougereuse. "Am I your dupe? I see it all now, Guy. Walter was no liar: you have something to conceal."

"Yes, Robert," was the grave reply, "I have something to conceal. Do not seek to discover it."

"Very well." Robert turned away, in wounded pride. He advanced several steps towards the door, but a hand closed around his own, and retained it; and the sight of Guy's pleading eyes softened his rising anger. "Let me go," he continued. "You do not know what I have to bear.

Have you altered so, within two years, that you cannot pity a friend? Can you not open your heart to me yet?"

"Robert, I ask your pardon," replied Fougereuse, with sadness and tenderness. "I did what I could to postpone this moment, and to evade explanations. I wished to spare you the chagrin of it. Your friendship is my chief treasure: I could not bear the thought of forfeiting it. I could brave the opinion of the court, of the whole world, but I could not bear to have you suspect me. Yet let me unbosom myself, and stake my hopes upon your generosity. As I admitted to you, I have a secret, and a secret which no one, not even you, ought to know before the allotted hour. I have sworn to keep it, and I must observe my vow. I will say to you only that my conscience is clean, that there is no stain on my shield. The test of our affection is at hand. I have not changed towards you, Robert: I never ceased to love you and believe in you. Were I guilty of a crime, I should confess it to you by choice; were I cast off by every one else, I should confidently claim shelter from you. And to-day I ask you to give me your blind credence. Are you fond enough of me to grant it? Do you esteem me enough to trust me, notwithstanding all evidence against me? Could you consent to follow me without question or debate, and be without resentment when matters become more and more entangled, and I shall be powerless to right them in your eyes? If you will go with me on this new track, you must walk in darkness. It would be madness to ask such allegiance from another man: but you, Villepreux, are equal to it, equal to that heroic exercise of faith in humankind. In case you feel you cannot accord it to me, let us part. Leave me to my fate. I can endure to suffer alone; I shall never be so unjust as to hold a grudge against you. Now give me your verdict. I am at your mercy."

With an impulsive motion, Villepreux stretched out his loyal hand to his friend. "I have faith in you, Guy; I would follow you to the ends of the earth. Keep your secret, and keep your resolution: I mean to respect both. Here is my hand, offered frankly, as on the day of our reconciliation long ago. . . . All the same, confound your reticence and your everlasting circumlocutions! Could you not have begun by saying this, instead of tormenting me so? I shall have hard work to forgive you for my last twenty-four hours."

Guy came towards him with open arms. A fraternal embrace sealed their mutual exoneration for the past, and their promise for the time to be.

So the time wore on in peace. Not that Robert lacked a cause of disquietude. Although he was certain of the honorable nature of Guy's secret, he was ill at ease in regard to its accompanying circumstances. The rumors at court grew in volume and in importance, clinging always to the selfsame subject, and varying only in their manifestations. Maulny, who had allied himself promptly with

Cornelius, beheld his own influence on the increase. A little group began to gather about him. It was composed of those interested for Louis XI., those jealous of Fougereuse, certain aspiring wretches who had all to gain and nothing to lose, and a few prim old ladies with long tongues, easily disedified, and quick to bewail the sins of some one else.

"My dear," said the marchioness of Thibault to the dowager-duchess of Bouchemaine, "I have always deplored, in that young Fougereuse, his excessive frivolity and his zest for worldly pastimes; but I never dreamed they would lead him so early to destruction. How melancholy it is to think that our lord the King should ever have given his affection to such an impostor! For that matter, the whole Fougereuse family are full of pride and hypocrisy. The late baron and his spouse" —

"That goose! Mention her not to me," interrupted Madame de Bouchemaine. "When she came to court, you would think nothing existed except for her benefit. If her son be vain and conceited, we know from whom he gets his qualities. And that little Isabelle seems to me to be taking after her mother, too. It is enough to make one tremble for one's own salvation, cousin, when one sees what the unchecked love of idle pleasure can lead to. May the saints keep us from it! To think that all those splendid coaches and horses are gifts from the Devil!" And the two good Christians crossed themselves in holy horror, and went off to whisper from ear to ear the *They say* and the *It looks as though*, which are the final evidence in the world of tittle-tattle.

Little by little the young aristocrats, who were at first among Fougereuse's allies, went over to the other side: for it was agreeable to disparage one whom they had tried in vain to excel. What a rare morsel for human malice to fall upon, even in our own day, is a spotless reputation! Aristides was ostracized by men who were tired of hearing him named the Just. So with Fougereuse. Slander did her best to destroy him, because society was tired of seeing him always happy. A loss or discomfort brought into his private life, a smirch set upon his character, was a cause of public triumph. As soon as hostility to him became fashionable, the crowd of courtiers abandoned him in a body, after the irrational, sheep-like instinct of crowds, who follow their ringleader. Doubts then hardened into certitude, report changed to confirmation, exaggerations set up for simple fact, and lies announced themselves as true and authentic, before any one could tell how it happened. Eight days after the first hint of the charge, it was duly and fully understood that the baron Guy de Fougereuse practised magic; and woe be unto him who would dispute it! "Everybody says so," was urged upon the incredulous, and to that argument they had to submit. Had the Pope himself taken pains to deny the aspersion, there would have been a general chorus: "But, Holy Father! what are you dreaming of? Everybody says so." And no

censure or excommunication launched against
" Everybody " would have abated the ardor of his
disciples.

King René, meanwhile, had not abandoned
Fougereuse. He had shut his ears, in the beginning, to the chatter around him. But two things
succeeded in introducing distrust into his generous
mind : one was the able, crafty, persistent attitude
of Walter de Maulny, who conducted his campaign
with finished art; the other was the importunity of
Cornelius, who could never forgive Guy for having
befriended Antonio Blandini. The King's relations with his favorite became less whole-hearted,
and eventually touched with a new coldness. The
young baron eluded or avoided the avowals which
he was tacitly invited to make, and the ill success
of these appeals was an irritating matter to René
of Anjou. Moreover, the imprudent taunt which
Loïc had flung at Fleurenville had been carried
to the royal ears. Guy was not held responsible,
and yet it had the unhappy effect of leading the
King to ask himself whether Guy's feudal reverence was strong enough to make him always spare
his sovereign, when the mocking mood came upon
him. Thus the strained situation lasted from week
to week, and every hour widened the abyss of disgrace into which it seemed that Guy must inevi-
tably fall.

By the side of his friend stood Villepreux, faithful to him as his sword, steadfastly devoted, a firm
believer, absolutely docile to his instructions. He

had agreed to press on in darkness, and he was scrupulously mindful of it. He could. in truth, have repeated the words of Saint Peter to Our Saviour: " *Though all shall be scandalized in thee, yet not I!* " The patience and moderation exacted by Guy from his impetuous champion were difficult to observe; but the Lion knew how to curb his natural fury, and yet keep his justice-loving arm ready to strike in behalf of the oppressed. As to Fougereuse himself, his conduct was a source of general wonder. Ever animated, smiling, serene, he took his trial as a matter of course, and examined all its bearings with a fine indifference. He seemed to live in a conscious scorn of danger, deaf to threat or prophecy, unconcerned at his own defeat, and perfectly heedless of public opinion. This last trait was exasperating beyond any of the others. He unravelled intrigues, listened to accusations, and let every man say and do as he liked, without offering a single protest or denial. No one could run to ruin more merrily, or at a more even pace! Villepreux also was constrained to notice it.

"You are a living enigma," he said once to his friend. "If your object be not to retain the King's favor, why do you remain with him? Why not be free, and hunt deer again in the woods about Fougereuse?"

"Why, Robert? First, because since it was my sovereign who called me into his service, it becomes my duty not to desert him before he signifies to me that he needs me no longer. I shall never, of my own choice, expose him to the counsels of Maulny, and of those lost souls who belong to King Louis. Discredited as I am, I am useful to him yet. I need not recall to you something in the *Chanson de Roland:*—

' To suffer for one's liege lord is good :
For him, be heat and cold withstood ;
For him be given my flesh, my blood.'

Rather will I sigh, like your 'Ibrahim, *'Allah Kerim!'* which is, as I understand, 'God hath written it.'"

"Excellent, Guy! But Ibrahim was quoting the Koran, not the Gospel."

"Well, the Gospel covers it: *'Sufficient to the day is the evil thereof.'* And again, what would you have me do? Up to this, my will has meddled very little with the trend of my life. I have clung to God's hand, going whither it led me, or staying where it would have me stay, docile to that directing. I leave it to Him to achieve my destiny. I did not seek for the post I occupy; and I shall not seek for another. A soldier does not pick and choose: he obeys. His captain says to him: *' Go, and he goeth; come, and he cometh; do this, and he doeth it.'* There, Robert, is all my statecraft. Now you know why I remain at court." Villepreux pressed Guy's hand in silence. His knightly and religious soul understood a language which was its own also.

But another heart, affectionate, delicate, and pure, had to suffer without consolation or assurance. Isabelle de Fougereuse was the real victim of the envenomed shafts showered on her brother. The sweet face was overcast, and the dear blue eyes filled very often with tears. She fled from society to quiet places; she passed every free moment at prayers in the chapel, and her fingers were ever upon the beads of her rosary. Her companions pitied her, inasmuch as she was the sister of the godless Fougereuse; but their pity did not so far incommode them that they felt obliged to suppress an epigram, or a bit of personal news. In their conscienceless cruelty, they failed to see that they were martyring this poor child, no longer safe from the world's spite behind the gratings of her cloister.

At the town-house of Fougereuse, general uneasiness reigned. Vincent, morose and taciturn, spoke now, when he spoke at all, in monosyllables, and seemed ever on the defensive against an imaginary foe. Loïc, whose wound was healing, was very intractable, and kept sullenly to his dark mood. Sometimes in open revolt against every one near him, sometimes plunged in fierce melancholy, unwilling to walk a step by the side of his master, whom he scarcely seemed to know, the once merry page was hardly to be identified as the same Loïc.

"Villepreux," said Guy on coming home one evening, "I beg of you to advise your *protégé* to be more prudent about it when he sets out to disobey. I have just seen him outside, though he slid away adroitly at his first glimpse of me. You can fancy that I am not disposed to tolerate such a breach of my formal orders. Here is a scapegrace whom the King thinks is lying half dead from young Fleurenville's sword-thrust; and lo! he pervades the streets of Angers, and has access to them by every door, obvious or otherwise, in this house. A stop must be put to it. If I should catch Loïc again, I shall send him down to Fougereuse at once, under Vincent's charge."

Robert undertook to reprimand the lad. At the first word he was interrupted. "You will excuse me, sir knight, for saying so, but you are judging me without understanding the case. If I act as I do, it is for the baron's good, and not without excellent reason."

"Hey! my mad little Breton! do you pretend that playing truant is a means to 'safeguard the honor of Fougereuse'? Your whims and freaks are incomprehensible."

"I am not playing truant," the page answered vehemently, cut to the quick at being treated like a child. "I am baffling spies! That is my business, messire. The baron is always awaited, every night, by an individual who hides himself in an angle of the wall. One fine evening I set forth by way of the narrow gate in the garden, draping my cloak about me in just my lord's own fashion. You know we are the same height. Well, the rascal was taken in by it, and he followed me like my shadow wherever I went. Since then I give him a walk time after time, and I show him considerable territory, too. You cannot tire him out; and nothing discourages him. I have led him into the turbulent part of the town, lost him in the passage-ways, misled him among alleys, got him into the round-house. I once kept him racing for miles along the river, when I took the notion to seize a boat and have a row. He is raging for his prey, he is! During these proceedings, the baron is free to travel where he pleases, unobserved. My master can snub me, but he cannot hinder me from getting killed in his stead if I choose; and it is exactly what I do choose at present."

When Guy was informed by his friend of this eccentric proof of attachment, he burst out laughing. "One never, never knows what to expect with that imp of a Loïc. Who could have foreseen such a contrivance? I swear, I would give something to watch the grotesque chase on the part of a cheated spy, and that young hobgoblin of a page leading him a march. But it is a dangerous game: it must come to an end instantly."

"I have tried to reorganize it," replied Villepreux. "My Penitent Thieves will identify and arrest the pursuer. As to the page, my eloquence is thrown away on him. He is likely to break somebody's head, or get his own broken, and that shortly. Can you not lay by your severity towards him?"

"Dear old Lion, he has worked upon your feelings! I cannot very well go to him, and say, 'Loïc, do me the charity to forget and forgive your misdeeds.' Extract from that hardened rebel one word of remorse, and I will absolve him in all haste. I dislike to be stern; and I am weary at seeing around me only hostile faces."

 . . . .

A day had been long fixed upon for a hunt in the forest of Avrillé. The horns of the outriders, the baying of dogs, the noise and stir of the start, the galloping horses, carrying squires and dames into the openings of the yellowing wood over a carpet of fallen leaves, drove dull care away, and blotted out the present hour in the intoxication of free motion in the open air. Isabelle de Fougereuse had suffered her vivacious companions to pass her by; they pressed on, inhaling the fresh keen breeze, and eager to enjoy the excitement of the chase. But she, guiding her palfrey into a lonely path, ended by throwing the bridle over the neck of the gentle and intelligent animal. Lost in thought, she began to form a fervent prayer. Down her blanched cheeks ran silent tears, which she sought neither to repress nor to conceal. God, the Virgin Mother in Heaven, and the angles,— were they the only witnesses of her sisterly sorrow? At the foot of the path, under the shade of giant oaks, arose a Cross over against a hermitage. Isabelle, who turned her horse towards this solitary retreat, came abruptly upon the stone steps worn by the feet and the knees of pious pilgrims. As she looked around in hesitation, to find some object which should help her in dismounting, the thump of hoofs struck the soft moss, and a cavalier spurred into the glade. Isabelle, in her surprise, had made a slight movement as if to withdraw; but on recognizing Robert de Villepreux, kept her saddle, and gave the new-comer a welcoming smile.

"It is a friend, Lady Isabelle!" said Villepreux, standing bareheaded, with respectful courtesy.

"It is indeed," answered Isabelle, bowing gracefully, "a fast and faithful friend; and I am glad of this chance to thank him for his noble zeal for my brother. May Heaven reward you, sir knight!"

"There is nothing to thank me for, for Guy is my brother too. Did I not swear, when we became friends, to defend his honor as if it were my own? You find me on a pilgrimage to Our Lady of Pity, and looking for the good hermit, who will throw the chapel open. Would it please you to visit it, and offer up a prayer?"

"I came with that very intention, Messire Robert," replied the girl, accepting Villepreux's aid as she alighted on the ground. "Our Lady can assist us in this dark hour, and I have a firm hope that she will do so."

"She is one who never fails, daughter," said a grave voice near the Cross. "No votary of hers goes away with a heart unsatisfied."

Isabelle and Robert turned about, and perceived, at the foot of the Calvary, a venerable man with a long white beard, dressed in a brown robe, and leaning on a knotty stick. Between his fingers he held a large well-worn rosary, and on his breast was a wooden crucifix of rude workmanship. "Peace be to you, my children!" he said, in response to the deferent greeting of the young people. "What would you ask of Our Lady of Pity, and of me her servant?"

"Of Our Lady, her protection for a being very dear to us both," answered Robert. "And of her servant, some good advice."

"Father, pray for an innocent person whose life and reputation are at stake, and who is left to suffer alone," murmured Isabelle. "Pray for my brother, Guy de Fougereuse."

The solitary opened the door of the rustic oratory. "Our Lady's image is here, my daughter. Enter, and weep and pray in peace at her feet. And you, my son, stay a moment with me. Were you not a pilgrim in the Holy Land, and did I not meet you there?"

Villepreux looked keenly at him. "To be sure!" he cried. "Was it not you, Father, who baptized my bandit of an Ibrahim in mid-desert, using the very last drops of water you had in your flask? Blessed be God, who brings us again together!"

The hermit smiled, and seating himself on the steps of the Cross, he motioned Villepreux to take his place beside him. "Now tell me, my son, in what way I can give you counsel." And between him and the knight began a conversation carried on in a low tone, which was almost as confidential as a confession.

During this time, Isabelle, prostrate before the shrine of Our Lady of Pity, prayed with fervor. An air of faith and sincerity pervaded the humble sanctuary, hung with the votive offerings of the poor, and with no adornment save the boughs of green holly. The heart of the young girl, aching from too long repression, filled with hope and comfort in the felt presence of the Mother of the Afflicted, whom the Church salutes as "our life, our comfort, and our hope" in Christ. When she raised her eyes, Robert de Villepreux was kneeling beside her, his forehead bent to the ground: a picture of that manly piety which had not then ceased to burn in knightly breasts. Next to his bowed figure was the good hermit's, and there fell over his cheeks the thin hair whitened in many a holy vigil.

"I beg you to offer this, in my name, to Our Lady's chapel," Isabelle said afterwards, loosening from her wrist a bracelet of ornate gold, and handing it to the old man. "I promise, if my petition be heard, to crown this statue with a diadem of all my jewels. Be you the witness of the promise, Father."

"I have one also to make," added Villepreux. "If my friend be delivered from his present difficulties, I vow to Our Lady that I will dedicate to her all my Penitent Thieves."

"What is this you say, Messire Robert?" exclaimed Isabelle, surprised and amused at the singular proffer.

"The reverend Father understands, my lady. I have a cure of souls! Here is a troop of men whom I redeemed from slavery, or cut off from sin: I am responsible for them before God. So long as we were among the Moslems, there was enough fighting to keep them busy and out of mischief. But it will never do to let them pick a quarrel with the Christians of France. The King would not accept them for soldiery; then I wished some Abbey to employ them; but the trouble is that they will obey no living creature save myself! Now I shall pledge their service to Our Lady of Pity. They will build her chapel on my estate, with a hospice for pilgrims, travellers, and the sick. They will protect the weak, and guard the neighboring hamlets from robbery and pillage. They will provide an escort for strangers, to guide them across the country, and preserve them from mishap, like the archangel Raphael befriending the son of Tobias. It will be their salvation, and it will promote the common good. Our Lady will assist Guy de Fougereuse, and I shall attend promptly to the rest, and spare no pains to make a perfect work of it."

"An excellent inspiration, my dear son," said the monk earnestly, "and I bless it in the name of the Lord. Hope and believe. It may be **that** you will see the realization of your dream sooner than you think, and find more helpers than you look for. Question me not; but leave me now, and may Heaven protect you!"

A little later Robert and Isabelle, having departed from the hermitage, were ambling through the forest. They heard the peal of the horns and the tally-ho; and about them in the autumn wind eddied the golden leaves, which smothered on the ground the even beat of their horses' hoofs. Isabelle was pensive yet, but her winsome face had taken on a new serenity. Prayer, and the loyal constancy of Villepreux, had strengthened her heart. Between the Lion and Guy's sister was a tender bond, formed in the latter's early childhood; and after a separation of some years, she had found in him again the protector of long ago. Though he had an austere manner, even as a boy, his ear was always attentive to her little voice, and the young inflexible will knew not how to refuse any desire of hers. Isabelle was the sort of person whose nature disarmed the harshness of humankind. The poacher, the rebel, the criminal condemned to the gallows. were sure to obtain some degree of pardon, should the sweet lady of Fougereuse intercede for him. A popular saying, then more than a century old, ran thus : —

" No Fougereuse ye find
Unmerciful, unkind.

> *The Villepreux has a soul*
> *Still generous, great, and whole."*

And at no time was it better borne out. The Fougereuse gentleness attained in Guy a height of passionate consideration for others, and of Christian forgiveness; and the "great and whole" spirit of Villepreux stood forth in Robert's heroic fidelity to the pact he had made with one descended from the enemies of his race. His vow to Our Lady of Pity, though it stirred Isabelle's sense of humor, brought the tears to her eyes, and flooded the very depth of her heart with thankfulness. For she knew how attached to his men was the leader of the Penitent Thieves, and how utterly devoted they were to him. To break the association formed in the Holy Land, to sever himself from his own soldiers, and the glory they reflected upon their captain's name, — was it not the supreme sacrifice for Robert to make? Was he not giving up, for the weal of Fougereuse, what he held dearest on earth?

The young damsel and the knight rode towards the hunting-party, and were in sound of their joyous voices. As they advanced, a royal page, bareheaded, bewildered, mounted on a swift courser covered with foam, appeared behind them on the path, and dashed between Isabelle and Robert, crying: "Give way! the King is dying!" Stricken with distress and horror, they spurred their horses on, reached the clearing, and found before them a scene of indescribable grief and confusion. René of Anjou was stretched upon the sod, motionless and senseless. The Queen, Joan, who was weeping, busied herself vainly to arouse her husband. Fougereuse held him in his arms, assisted by several gentlemen ; Cornelius was tendering every possible medical aid. There was great disorder on all sides, much loud lamenting, calling, running hither and thither. The rumor of foul play was in the air: no one knew with whom it had originated.

"Stand back, Isabelle!" commanded Maulny, at sight of his cousin. Approaching Villepreux, he added in low tones, "The King lost consciousness, after having drained a glass of wine offered by Fougereuse."

Isabelle started, and grew very pale. Robert leaped from his saddle, and rushed into the crowd. A commotion arose in the little group around René. Cornelius said a few decisive words in an undertone ; Guy was pushed aside ; the seneschal Beauvau, who had been leaning over the lifeless sovereign, stood up, an avenging figure.

"The King is dying, gentlemen," he announced solemnly, "and he is dying of poison. Treason has done .this. Guards, arrest at once the baron Guy de Fougereuse!"

Had a thunderbolt fallen upon Guy, it could scarcely have affected him so much. His face changed color. He flung out his arms as if to resist the accusation, and he cried in a powerful voice :

"I swear to God that so terrible a crime never entered into my thoughts. Though I submit to-day, to-morrow I shall appeal to the royal justice."

His protestation was received with icy hostility. Villepreux, who had reached his friend, seized his left hand, and faced the seneschal. "I would have you know, Philip de Beauvau, that while I stand here living, that order will not be carried out. You commit an infamy!"

"I am but doing my duty. Baron de Fougereuse, yield up your sword."

Villepreux strode forward menacingly, but Guy deterred him with a sign. Then he handed his sword, in silence, to the captain of the guard, and suffered himself to be led unresistingly away. He saw his sister fall into the arms of some court ladies. His only farewell to Robert was: "Care for Isabelle."

"To the tower!" commanded the seneschal. "You will answer to me with your lives for the prisoner's safety."

But Walter de Maulny's lips were wreathed in a victorious smile as he said to himself: "At last, at last!"

CHAPTER III.

THE PRISONER.

> " 'He dies to-day,' said the jailer grim,
>   Whilst a tear was in his eye:
> 'But why should I feel so grieved for him?
>   Sure, I've seen many die!
>
> .   .   .   .
>
> 'He looked so mild, with his pale, pale face,
>   And he spoke in so kind a way,
> That my old breast heaved with a smothering feel,
>   And I knew not what to say.' "
>
> *The Ballad of Emmet's Death.*

GUY DE FOUGEREUSE was imprisoned in a tower which rose over against the dungeons for convicts, and looked down upon the Maine. A bed of straw, a stone table, one rude stool, a pitcher of water, and the scant prison fare, became the portion of the man who was but now the favorite of fortune and the King. A ray of sunlight could scarcely reach him, for the only openings were a few narrow loopholes cut in a wall twelve feet thick. No living creature entered there, except a clumsy, morose jailer, very sparing of speech, from whom Guy with difficulty wrung the one word of news he wished for: "King René is not dead." A mournful silence reigned in those dark precincts, unpenetrated by any sound from without. The captive's one diversion was to place himself against a loophole and gaze upon a patch of blue sky, or a silver line of water flowing by the foot of the keep. Escape was impossible: it was folly to dream of it. Guy knew he could go forth from that lofty cell only to death or to liberty with honor; and the latter alternative was less than probable. He knew whither the accusation of poisoning and of high treason, and the suspicion of sorcery, were likely to lead him : to the scaffold or the stake; to the rack; to deposition from knighthood ; to public shame for him and his ; to an everlasting stigma on an immaculate name. He knew: and in his long hours of meditation he confronted and measured the horrible perspective of a cruel, ignominious end. Yet no fear came to trouble that brave, calm spirit. Danger did not abate his courage, nor tribulation weaken the faith of the noble Christian whose trust was in God alone. In his confinement, he maintained the very same sweet dignity and good cheer, the same evenness of mind and temper, which marked him in his happier days. The rigors of his captivity increased, nevertheless, and the glimmer of human hope lessened and faded away. Guy had been left free, at first, from shackles. But on the morrow of his incarceration, the jailer received orders to chain his hands and feet, like those of any common criminal.

" They might have spared me that ! " Fougereuse

could not help saying, when he was apprised of
these orders. Then, rising resignedly, he added,
"Our Lord Himself was bound as a malefactor.
'*The servant is not greater than the master.*' Carry
out your instructions, Artauld."

Leon Artauld, the jailer, obeyed without a word,
but he went away full of admiration for his prisoner. "I never saw one of that sort before!" he
exclaimed that evening, to his assistants. "The
others rebel, shout, and curse, or else they whim-
per, and give in like hares. Nothing seems to
move him. He took to wearing those irons as
quietly as if it were a new doublet I had brought
him to try on. 'I thank you, Artauld,' he said to
me, when it was over. I could not answer him.
Be sure he is either a great magician or a great
saint."

The next day, while Guy was profiting by his
modicum of the sunset light to read a page further
in the little book of Psalms which was always
about him, Artauld came in, shaking his bunch of
keys, and swearing furiously between his teeth.

"What news is there?" asked Guy, closing his
book. "Is the King worse?"

"Not so, my lord. His Majesty is much better;
they begin to say he never was poisoned at all.
I had thought that your condition would change
at once for the better. And now I have orders . . .
more orders . . . orders to . . . deuce take the
orders! I have to do as my superiors tell me."

"Would they shut me in an iron cage, like the

victims of Louis XI.? That would certainly be unpleasant."

" No, my lord, not that. We have none of those engines hereabouts. But I am charged to keep you under scrutiny night and day, and to place here in your cell a companion who " —

" Will be a spy, and make it his business to misrepresent my motives, and distort the meaning of my words and my least gestures," continued Guy, rising to his feet. " In short, my good Artauld, you could not possibly have brought me more disagreeable tidings. I had hoped to keep my privacy. Whence comes this order? Who gave it ? "

" I do not know, messire. It was passed on to me by the captain of the guards, who seemed as averse to it as I am. I can do nothing to change it ; to-night I must bring you the man in question."

" Well," sighed Fougereuse, " the chalice must be drunk, and to the dregs. Who has been elected to this honorable office ? "

" They named no particular person for it, and so I hastened to choose for myself. The day before yesterday, a sixth cousin of my own, as he claims, arrived here from Brittany. He is a stubborn young fellow, and not very clever, and he speaks next to no French. I do not know what else to do with him. It struck me, that in any event, he would be less dangerous to you than a shrewder head."

" Follow your own lead, Artauld, but do not

compromise yourself on my account. You know my star is fallen forever."

"I shall not be compromised, my lord. And after all, what of it? A jailer may have a heart, only he must not show it. It will never be you who will inform upon me!"

As night gathered, Fougereuse submissively awaited the room-mate foretold by Artauld. It had cost him a severe inward struggle to accept this new aggravation of the sorrow he had to bear: an unjust advantage taken, which evidently meant that he should be indicted, willingly or unwillingly, for the crime of sorcery. What mysterious enemy was so hot for his ruin ? What irrevocable hatred had Fougereuse aroused in his former career, that now in his adversity he should be pursued with these vile vexations? "Never consciously," he said to himself, "have I wronged anyone, howsoever lightly. I have sought always to oblige those who loved me least: I have had such indulgence for my enemies that I have almost estranged my best friends. What can I have done to men, that they are so bitter against me?"

What, indeed, had he done to men? He had put them to shame with his goodness, and made them ill at ease under the shower of his favors. Gratitude is a virtue not attained by common natures: great souls sweeten with the sense of it, but meanness grows embittered. A benefactor is a creditor: more than one debtor, at a crisis, does his best to escape the debt. Thanklessness is a reason for avoiding payment, and insolvent spirits throw themselves eagerly into oblivion of good received. The magnanimous Fougereuse had excused jealousies, ignored slanders, scorned silly gossip and prattle; but this obstinacy of cruelty, this premeditated perfidy, pierced him to the heart.

The voice of the jailer, growling along the passage leading to the tower, was the signal to Guy that his final hour of welcome solitude was over. The door grated on its rusty hinges, and revealed Leon Artauld, preceding a young peasant dressed in the Breton costume. The face of the newcomer was partly hidden under his long locks, black as the raven's wing, and a wide-brimmed hat, which it did not occur to him to remove in the presence of the baron de Fougereuse.

"Here is the lad Alan, my lord," began Artauld, introducing him. "So long as he eats and sleeps, he is content. If he cannot amuse you, I hope at least that he will not annoy you. You, Alanik! hear what I say. You are here to serve this gentleman: if you do well, I will reward you, Do you understand?"

"*N'intand Ket*," replied Alan, with a stupid yawn.

"*N'intand Ket! N'intand Ket!* That is all the idiot knows enough to say. Well, I wash my hands of him! I have obeyed orders, and no man can deny it. I give you good-night, my lord."

As soon as Fougereuse stood alone with his singular companion, he looked him over from head to foot. Such extreme doltishness awoke his suspicion, and made him think it hid a snare of some sort. As if to aid in his own examination, Alanik took the lantern which Artauld had left behind him, and held it up as high as his ears. Guy then saw a countenance excessively tanned by the hot sun of the plains, and two big blue eyes which contrasted oddly with the gypsy complexion.

"Does not my lord of Fougereuse recognize me?" asked the Breton, breaking without difficulty into the purest French imaginable.

"Recognize you? Where could I ever have seen you? Who are you? . . . Heavenly powers!" cried the baron suddenly, in the most intense surprise; "those are the eyes of Loïc de Kernis!"

"It is Loïc all over," answered the boy, who came, panting with emotion, to kneel close against his master. "It is your poor page, my lord. Have pity: do not betray me!"

"Loïc, Loïc!" Fougereuse pressed hard, in his own manacled hands, the hands of his young votary. "Dear, dear child! is it indeed you? I am not in a dream, am I? Tell me by what miracle" —

"Speak lower, my lord; the walls have ears. I bring you liberty!"

"Escape?" asked Guy eagerly.

"Yes." Kernis drew a file from his bosom, and showed it triumphantly. "Do you see this? In one little half-hour your chains will fall. You must change clothes with me; and I have the ingredients to dye your hair and darken your skin, my lord. Then you will be Alanik, and I the prisoner. To-morrow it will be a simple matter for you to ask to speak to the captain of the guard, and tell him that Fougereuse is planning to break away. And there in the yard below will be a crowd of students inquiring for news from the King : just let them abduct you. They will have a boat ready to cross the river, and saddled horses on the farther bank. In a few minutes you will be free, and sure of a safe refuge. . . . Let us hasten, master dear! The Breton frontier will befriend you."

"Wait a moment," said Fougereuse, interrupting Loïc, who had already begun to file the irons on his feet. "Wait a moment; the scheme is worthy of consideration. . . . Who told you, however, that I wished to escape?"

The page looked up in blank astonishment. "Ah, but you must, my lord. That court breed have sworn upon your destruction; they prefer you defamed and dead. Flight to Brittany is your only remaining hope. My duke is not like your King, praised be the Lord! And our Breton chivalry would revenge you upon the ingrates of Anjou."

"We will think it over, child. Lay down the file, for we have plenty of time for consultation before we act. From whom does this suggestion come? From Villepreux?"

"No," answered Loïc hesitatingly. "It was

not possible to communicate with him. I arranged
the whole thing myself, with some University
friends of mine — fine honest fellows they are!
Their lives are at your service."

Guy smiled, without replying, and reflected
a while. "And you — what is your part in the
clever plot?"

"I repeat that I should take your place here, let
come what may. What could they do to worthless
me?"

"Let me tell you, if you do not know. They
could condemn you to the scaffold for the crime of
high treason. I should say, rather, were you not
noble, that they would string you up, dry and high,
on the gallows. And the very best fate possible
to you would be a lodging for life in a cell like
this, or, indeed, in the dungeon below."

"What of it?" asked Loïc, shrugging his shoulders. "A great compensation that would be for
those gallant lords! They are welcome to pay
themselves, however, as they can. For my part, I
have been to confession; I have made my peace
with God: I am not afraid of the prospect. Let
me go on filing."

"You shall not go on. Do you think I am the
sort of man who would pledge his friend to death
in order to save himself? Fie, Messire de Kernis!
Have you not a flattering opinion of your lord? I
shall never give you such an example of selfish-
ness and cowardice." And stooping quickly, Guy
caught up the file and tossed it out of the nearest

loophole. "'*Get thee behind me, Satan!*' There is the temptation in a fathom of water. *Amen* to it, and a pleasant voyage."

"What have you done?" cried Loïc, bounding up, with a face full of distress. "I, who came . . . who hoped . . . ah! it is more than I can bear. You are . . . you are" . . . Words failed him; a great sob heaved his breast. He stood looking wrathfully at his master, stamping his foot, and muttering to himself.

"Hush now, my poor boy!" Fougereuse said conciliatingly. "Your plan was useless, and would only have sacrificed both our lives. I am touched none the less by your devotion," he added in a serious tone, offering his hands to Loïc.

"I do not deserve thanks." The lad spoke very low, and drew back slowly. "It was I who ruined you."

"You! What folly is this?"

"It is no folly. It was I who ruined you by my imprudence, and I wanted to atone. . . . Walter de Maulny . . . he made me talk over there at the Red Rose. I never suspected. . . . The little room without lock or key . . . it was I who told him that you shut yourself up there at night. . . . And I went to Wolfram's house when the light was burning. Maulny sent that wretch Piteux after me. . . . He tried to play the spy on you in the interest of his foxy patron; and I gave him a lively fifteen days of it, so I did! Then I kept quiet, just because I was abominably proud, when

one word would have given you light. . . . You
see, I ached to serve you in some important way,
so you could no longer be offended. . . . I would
have saved you . . . I was so hurt to have you
severe with me because of my duel . . . and . . .
and . . . can you never forgive me? " wailed Loïc
in despair.

"I shall forgive you when I discover what your
fault is, scatterbrain. Never before was there a
penitent with such a foggy conscience. Come
nearer, draw a deep breath, and tell me, all over
again, that tangled story of which as yet I understand nothing. . . . What were you saying about
Wolfram's house?"

Somewhat relieved by his own outburst, Loïc
now could afford to wonder at the serenity of Fougereuse at such a critical moment. He related
candidly everything which had passed at the Red
Rose. With one knee on the stone bench, and his
spread fingers against the wall, he leaned over the
captive, and murmured his whole confession in the
latter's ear, without venturing to face him. Guy
heard him uninterruptedly, save for a few brief
questions. He gazed at the floor meanwhile ; he
did not lift his head, nor look in the boy's beseeching eyes.

"I should like to clear up one circumstance
here," he began, when the page had ended. "In
the interior of Wolf's turret, did you see anything
unusual?"

"Yes, my lord."

"What?"

"Two men . . . or two demons."

"Did you know who they were?"

"One had his back to me : I could not see him.'

"The other?"

"My lord!" . . .

"Who was the other?" the baron repeated, raising his voice.

"The other . . . some one I knew."

"And it was —?"

"You," answered Loïc in a choked voice, yet distinct and steady.

"Really! Are you sure?"

"I thought so; I think so yet. But if you say I was deceived, I will believe your word rather than my own senses."

"You were not deceived. Your · senses were right."

"I felt it, my lord."

"Did you tell Govier of your adventure and your discovery?"

"No, on my honor! I was aware that I had the key to an important secret : I did not open my lips to any living soul."

"That is well." Guy rose; and this time he turned upon his companion that glance of profound penetration which was characteristic of King René's minister. "That is well: And now, Loïc, answer me frankly, what did you think of your master?"

"To speak truly, my lord, I was puzzled, and I

searched for an explanation. I inferred that you were sheltering some poor outlaw pursued by Louis XI. or his bloodhounds, until such time as you could obtain papers of pardon for him through the duke of Anjou. Hence my anxiety and my silence ; for I dared not question you. I should have disclosed everything to you ; and this I was on the very point of doing, when my quarrel with Paul de Fleurenville estranged you and me. I was mortally hurt by your coldness, to which I was unaccustomed, and I vowed I would achieve some glorious action, and make you repent. So I threw that spy Jacob off the track; I risked my life a dozen times coping with Walter de Maulny's secret measures, and . . . my presumption recoils on me alone, for you do not consider me even good enough for the hangman's rope."

"Less good there than somewhere else, let us hope. But how is this? You saw me, with your own eyes, in the haunted house ; you know that I visit by stealth the famous little room at home which has neither lock nor key ; you have heard me accused of sorcery and diabolic dealings ; and yet would you lay to my charge only the good deed of befriending a fugitive? Was there not some suspicion of me at the bottom of your soul, Loïc? Come, I demand the truth."

"Oh!" exclaimed the page straightening himself, his forehead flushing red : "did you think me capable of that, my lord?" His accent of indignant surprise carried its own conviction to Guy's mind. He blessed God, who had placed on the road to his Calvary this noble heart of a child. "How could you imagine anything so infamous? I may be wrong-headed, quarrelsome, wild, rebellious — and I am sorry to acknowledge that I am all of that. But to doubt my master's honor! To suspect him of commerce with the powers of darkness, and of disloyalty to his sovereign! . . . For what low creature do you take me, baron de Fougereuse?"

"Pardon me, my faithful one!" cried Guy, clasping him, despite the weight of his chains, in his arms. "May God love you for your generous faith and bravery, your nobleness and craziness, my incorrigible little fool! You were given me to exercise my patience in prosperity, and to be my comfort in adversity. What . . . tears? Are you deploring your glorious actions achieved? . . . And what is this you are trying to say? That you wish absolution for your faults? Yes, yes, with all my heart. '*Go in peace, and sin no more.*' Were Villepreux here, I do believe he would offer you, with no dissenting voice, a lieutenancy in his Society of the Penitent Thief!"

"And oh, my dear lord," sighed Loïc, "why did you throw away the file?"

"Chiefly, I think, because I meant to. Had you never considered that to flee would be to admit my guilt? . . . Let us forget this beautiful conspiracy of rescue hatched in very young brains, and have a sensible talk, if you are equal to it.

How does my darling Isabelle get on? What has become of the good Lion? What of the King?"

"The Lion defends you on every side, messire. He is an army of a man. My lady Isabelle, on her part, is a legion of angels: she will yet mollify tigers, and melt the rocks in your behalf. On my sword, I should never have dreamed there was such courage and control in her, though I knew well enough

> *'No Fougereuse ye find*
> *Unmerciful, unkind!'*

Queen Margaret has taken her under her special care; and those two will bring that mad faction to their senses. For all of her haughtiness, Queen Margaret has a fine, true heart. I can pardon her now for having married the King of England."

"She is loyal as any chevalier," replied Guy. "It relieves me of a heavy load of anxiety to know that Isabelle is with her. Margaret of Anjou has suffered too much from unjust aspersions, and betrayals too, not to compassionate others who suffer in like manner. Heaven guard her for her tenderness to my orphan sister, who is far from her only protector! The King, my venerated master — can you tell me nothing of him? Do they still say his life is in danger?"

"The King? Ah, the King, my lord, the King would be certainly, so far as I can make out, exactly as well as we are, were it not for this disturbing affair. He is out of danger, nor would he ever have been in it, if that plague of a Cornelius had not raised the cry of poison. All his illness amounted to, was a faint caused by the cold, and a subsequent attack of fever brought on him by the remedies of his illustrious doctor. And if Antonio had been there, instead of that illiterate fraud from Touraine, there would have been no question of sickness at all."

"Then why am I here?" exclaimed the other. "If I be exonerated from the charge of poison, on what pretext do they hold me a prisoner?"

"Ah, that is the point! *They* are caught in the net they spread for you; they would have you bear the penalty of their folly! After such a brilliant stroke, an arbitrary arrest, and all the uproar following on a pretended treason, you can conceive that they will not brand themselves before the public as liars, by declaring your innocence. No: they are bound to maintain appearances. So Cornelius closets the King (when the only thing the matter with him is just Cornelius), and upsets him by making him believe that he is at the gates of death. Nobody can approach his Majesty, and everybody acts according to his own whim. The mind of your godly relative Walter is set on finding you guilty, in any event. The traitor has removed his mask."

"Eh? Maulny declaring publicly against me?" Guy broke in. "Very prompt of you, my cousin Walter!"

"My lord, you have no worse enemy. This whole

campaign is his work. It is he who set Piteux to watch you; it is he who spreads calumnies in your path; it is he who now renounces and oppresses you. On his line of argument, if you are not an assassin, you are a sorcerer. It is possible you did not actually poison the King, but you certainly did bewitch and mesmerize him; and if you be unconvicted of crime, yet you are strongly suspected of it. That is enough to make them keep you in prison. The honorable aldermen find it entirely expedient, and vote blindly for it. People have spoken ill of you for too long a time: there must be some truth to bear them out! '*No smoke without fire!*' they quote gleefully. Each and all say that. It never enters any one's head to believe you blameless. I did not dream there were so many imbeciles alive."

"Alas, Loïc! a crowd of fools led by a handful of knaves: that is the pageant of the majority. But I do not see that the situation is as desperate as you, in your inexperience, fear. When the King is restored to health, I shall receive justice. ... Why do you shake your head?"

"Once upon a time, my gentle lord, I displeased you, because I cast a slur upon the firmness of character of your beloved monarch. But please allow me to say that he would pardon ten guilty persons, before he would justify one who is innocent. He would have to overturn too many opinions, and defy too many of his friends. Walter de Maulny has newly secured the King's confidence, and he

will never let it be forfeited again. God is our
only hope, since unfortunately "—

"Since unfortunately," Guy repeated laugh-
ingly, " I threw away the file, and declined the aid
of your unique and precious allies, the students.
Well, enough of that! But explain to me to what
providential chance, or masterly strategy, I owe
the pleasure of sharing my jail with you masquerading as an official spy? I cannot account for it,
I own."

It was now Loïc's turn to laugh: a frank laugh,
which rang against the stone vaultings, an unwonted echo there. " The very neatest trick that
ever I played in all my life, my lord! Consider how
I stand in Jacob Piteux's place, and how Maulny
believes, in good faith, that he is shut up with
you! Why, I should have to laugh at the memory of it, were I under the headsman's axe! And
to think that it was Villepreux who outwitted that
arch-hypocrite! . . . I must make up some rhymes
about it when we get safely out of this."

"Awaiting the hour when you can sing your
adventures, tell them to me at once in prose, instead of rousing the owls, and perhaps Artauld
himself. You were saying that Piteux " . . .

" Here is the whole story," began the page,
cautiously lowering his voice. " When that luck-
less hunting-party broke up, the very first care of
Messire Robert was to look to the security of those
of your household, fearing that they might be
arrested as accomplices of your imaginary crime

of poisoning. He sent Vincent down to Fougereuse, escorted by four stout Penitent Thieves, in order to forewarn your vassals, and prepare them for anything which might happen. Hardly had he set out, when Dismas, the sergeant, brought in to us a bundle of rags, upon which one of the horses had inadvertently walked. Well, this bundle of rags, when examined, turned out to be nothing else than my old acquaintance Jacob. Messire Robert began to question him, and under the Lion's paw that miserable weasel confessed a good deal. He informed us that Maulny paid him, or rather promised him payment, to give him a daily account of your proceedings, and to circulate among the peasantry the same falsehoods which Walter was busy circulating at court. His Argus-like offices were to extend even to your cell ; so Master Piteux was on his way accordingly to the turnkey, to offer himself as valet. Maulny was going to take care of the rest. You will guess that we modified the business to suit our own fancy. Jacob, a wee bit damaged by the horse's shoe, was charitably put in a good bed, with two new-baptized Penitent Thieves to nurse him. We locked the door on him so as to insure him proper rest, and then Dismas stained my face and my hair, as you see. They know a wonderful number of things, those Saracens !   I remembered that I was a shepherd once, and I put on the shepherd dress and behavior, and cousined it with Artauld, who received me with open arms. For two long days I watched in vain for an occasion to get near you. Two Bretons, kinsmen of mine, Trédaniel and Keranflech, University students, recognized me when they came in to obtain court news, and we concocted together the plan of escape which you rejected."

" Yes, yes: what then ? "

" Then came the order to place a spy at this post; and Artauld did not hunt for any one else. I was there: now I am here, and here I stay."

" You risked your life, and you risk it still, my boldest of Bretons! Are you quite sure that Artauld " —

"How often I ask myself that ! Is Artauld my dupe, or am I his ? I cannot tell ; but he seems to me to be full of good will towards you. You have friends yet, my lord ; and chief among them, Villepreux, who is gathering your vassals and his own, to re-enforce the Penitent Thieves."

" That is the Lion again, with his Palestine ideas ! " cried Fougereuse in alarm. " What folly ! It means that he is leading the poor creatures straight to the gibbet, and himself to the scaffold. I cannot bear " —

" You can never prevent the Lion from acting after his own fashion, dearest master. Let him alone ! Nobody will be very eager to interfere with the captain of the Penitent Thieves. And as to your own people, do not worry. Is it not a vassal's first duty to proffer his life in his lord's service? You will find that they will not fail you. Never will those lads at Fougereuse have a finer chance to die gloriously."

"God forbid," answered Guy, in deep dejection, "that only for my sake, and not for the King's, I should risk one hair of the head of any servant of mine! I am held accountable by God for those He has confided to me, and I would rather die a thousand deaths than draw them into the sin of unjust rebellion. May Our Lady give me her assistance!" he added, and he made the sign of the Cross. For some moments he remained in profound thought. Loïc, disconcerted, placed himself silently at one of the loopholes.

The chimes of Saint Maurice rang for eight o'clock. Deep night enwrapped the town and the fields beyond, as for many previous hours it had fallen on the two in the tower. A sound, rhythmic and melodious, arose faintly from the river below, and seemed to float nearer and nearer. Loïc leaned over the stone sill in the thick wall, holding his breath that he might hear the better. Fougereuse lifted his head in surprise. " What can that be, so late as this ? "

"Hush, my lord! Do you not catch the plash of oars, as well as the song? They are pilgrims from Saint Magdalen's shrine, returning from Baumette on the Maine boats, and hurrying to reach home before curfew-time. Let me listen to their music."

The voices were so distinct that it was easy to follow the words of the choral. What the prisoners heard was a sweet, melancholy air, a sort of barcarolle brought from Sicily, to which a number of minstrels of that day had fitted their own poetic conceptions. But these particular strophes were on no imaginary theme.

> " *Against a turret stone*
> *Darkly laid,*
> *King Richard, when his own*
> *Him betrayed,*
> *Sad to himself could sing : —*
> *' Hapless King,*
> *Aloof from all that live !*
> *Lord, of Thy mercy give*
> *To me,*
> *To die, or else be free.' "*

"Do you recall it, master?" the page whispered. "It is the poem you made for Queen Margaret, whose husband is yet imprisoned by his subjects."

Guy nodded his head, for he recalled it well. The chorus began again : —

> " ' *Rise, ye whom England bore,*
> *Soldier lords !*
> *Where is the faith ye swore*
> *On your swords ?*
> *Friends fain to perish too,*
> *How of you*
> *Your Richard is forgot !*
> *Lord, grant another lot*
> *To me :*
> *To die, or else be free.' "*

The captive baron rose up mechanically, and sang with the pilgrims the next stanza : —

> " ' *If any dared enchain*
> *In such dole,*
> *Some knight of my domain,*
> *Ere his soul*
> *One added pang should bear,*
> *I were there!*
> *But Richard waits, unheard.*
> *Lord, speak that better word*
> *To me:*
> *Die thou! or else, Be free!* ' "

"Not a word now, my lord, I beg of you!" continued Loïc, very much agitated. "I must not lose what is to follow."

The foremost wherries had reached the base of the tower, and the harmonies welled up, beautifully clear.

> " *Hurt Lion caged within,*
> *Hush: and hear*
> *The answering tune begin,*
> *Hopeful, dear,*
> *Which on the midnight cast*
> *Mounts at last: —*
> ' *Richard, forlorn indeed!*
> *God sends thee in thy need.*
> *(Ah, see!)*
> *Love quickly come to free.*
>
> ' *In service to thy great*
> *Sorrowing,*
> *True zeal I dedicate,*
> *O my King!*
> *My blood is at thy call.*
> *Blondel, remembering all,*
> *Must be*
> *Thy fate, to set thee free.*' "

For an instant the voices were still, and falling oars made the only sound in the evening air. Before Fougereuse could foresee his intention, the other had seized the lantern and passed it quickly, several times in succession, across one of the openings.

"Rash boy, what are you doing?" exclaimed his companion. "Have you determined on your own destruction? Stop instantly!"

"Six . . . seven," counted the page. "Be not alarmed, my lord. It was pre-arranged. Now sing on, my brave fellows!"

From the succeeding boats, rowed close beneath, came the plaintive continuation : —

> "' *Those bonds in victor strife*
>   *Shall dispart ;*
> *Or let the riven life*
>   *From my heart*
> *Be prayer and blessing shed*
>   *On thy head!*
> *To him whom men forsook,*
> *Our Lord of Armies look :*
>   *That he*
> *Go glorious yet, and free!'* "

Then the music commenced to die away, and it was only with difficulty that Kernis was able to distinguish the last verse : —

> "*Ye courtiers, drain the cup,*
>   *Shout, and smile :*
> *Richard is towering up*
>   *From exile.*

> *Before your Lion bow,*
> *England! now.*
> *What though the whole world failed?*
> *For him one friend availed. —*
> *Be he*
> *For ever great and free!"*

" Bravo!" cried Loïc, clapping his hands. " Bravissimo, my worthy fellow-students! Ah, the faithful hearts that you have in them, my lord ! They would never allow you to be led to the block, without thumping the watch well for it ! "

" I believe it readily ; for thumping the watch was ever their favorite pastime. But, by all the saints of Brittany, it would appear that you are in a fair way to lose whatever shreds of wit Heaven allotted you. Why all this flutter on account of a mere ballad ? "

" That ballad, my dear master, is a signal ; this flutter means that in default of rescuing you by main force, the whole University, from to-morrow on, will importune the King to liberate you. They will save you, despite yourself. *Noël* to the students ! " continued the youth, in a transport of enthusiasm. " *Noël* to ballads too ! Long live the fools ! because it is only they who can get the better of the wise."

" Mercy ! I have no page any more, but a regular fanatic," said Guy. " He will soon make me deplore the absence of Master Piteux. You were too adventurous, getting yourself into this cage, my flyaway falcon, and you will break your wings on the bars. No more conspiracies, or I shall denounce you to Artauld the jailer. Let us sleep in peace to-night, and may inner light come with the morning!"

Only one of the two slept in peace, and that was Loïc. Guy de Fougereuse did not close his eyes, and the morrow's dawn found him at prayers. The rays of the rising sun were gilding the limpid surface of the Maine, and peering timidly into the tower cell, when Guy heard the door being pushed ajar slowly, and with unwonted caution.

"Go in quickly." This from Artauld, in a confidential whisper.

A shadow withdrew from the half-open entrance, which was noiselessly closed. Fougereuse rose briskly, and found himself confronted by the hermit of Avrillé wood.

"You here, Father!"

"My dear son, my poor child!" answered the good monk, embracing him. "Were you not expecting me? Did you think I would abandon you? What! gyves? . . . They have spared you no humiliation."

"Father, have you come to prepare me for death?" asked Guy in low, firm tones.

"Happily, Guy, we have not reached that crisis. I bring you a message from the Abbot of Saint-Aubin." The old man drew from his bosom a parchment covered with fine writing, which he held towards Fougereuse.

"Give it me! give it me!" exclaimed the

prisoner eagerly, taking the script. "But speak softly, I implore you. I have a comrade asleep here whom we must not waken: Loïc, my Breton page."

"Very well, my son. Would it not be more prudent to hold our conversation in Latin, as Loïc, if I remember accurately, is no great scholar?"

Guy made an affirmative sign. Bending over it, by the glimmering daylight piercing the wall, he scanned attentively his consoling letter. When he had read it through, he raised his head, breathing like a man from whom a great weight had fallen. "The Right Reverend Abbot is full of kindness," he said, re-folding the parchment; "I shall always be grateful to him for his good counsel."

"But not grateful enough, perhaps, to follow it?" questioned the monk, noticing the anxious face before him.

"Father, tell me what I ought to do. Dom Maurice officially relieves me from my oath of silence, and presses me to disburden him in like manner of the secret of the confessional. He would inform the King of everything, and at once. What do you think of it?"

"I agree with him; only the avowal would come with better grace, it seems to me, from your own lips. Your oath was an ill-advised thing, which would never have been pronounced had you deliberated longer. You have played, as it were, with the flame, and now we must put out the fire. God grant it may not be too late!"

"You know I am not the only one to consider. My guest in the turret knows naught of it; and I would not act without his permission."

"What are you saying, Guy? He knows naught of it? . . . I will hasten to him, and bring him hither, that he may unlock your lips and bid you justify yourself openly."

"A moment, Father! One other expedient is worth trying, before we make all this fuss. It was on the King's account that I was imprisoned: a direct appeal to him may yet right everything. I trust he will never refuse to believe my word, and " —

"'*Put not your trust in princes*,' " the old hermit interrupted, gravely shaking his head. "You cling to a hollow mockery, my lord."

"Have a care, lest you misjudge his Majesty. He cannot soon forget the many good offices I have rendered, the many confidences and testimonies of affection between us. Had I served God half so passionately, I should be a great saint to-day," the baron added, with a deep sigh.

"Oh, that you had done so, dear son! But this is not the time for regrets. Believe me, for I have had long experience of men, the King will be all the more likely to forsake you, because he once loved and seconded you. Give him, therefore, the proofs of your innocence, and not mere declarations."

"Well, Father, the issue will decide it. I wish to put my theory to the test," answered the captive, standing with fire in his eye. "I shall make one final effort: I will learn whether our sovereign's heart holds only forgetfulness and indifference for me; whether I have been to him a friend whom he trusts, or a toy to use and then to break! If the hand of God sever this old tie, nothing can hinder me longer from taking your advice. But until that day, I would be the master of my own secret."

The extraordinary vehemence with which Guy spoke impressed the hermit, who listened thoughtfully.

"Follow your own convictions, son," he said at last, with resolution and gravity, "and may they lead you in the true way! I pray Our Saviour to strengthen your shoulders for the heavy cross you are preparing for yourself, and which I would fain have had spared you; but *per crucem ad lucem:* wisdom springs from sorrow. '*Ought not Christ to have suffered these things, and so to enter into His glory?*' And your heart will have to be overwhelmed with disillusion, before it finds peace. Drain the final drop of your chalice, and satisfy yourself. Have you anything else to say to me?"

The younger man came slowly towards him, and knelt at his feet. Bowing his head, he began, in a voice which revealed something of the emotion within: "Bless me, Father, for I have sinned." And the venerable monk, inclining towards his penitent, lent an attentive ear to the confession of Guy de Fougereuse.

.   .   .   .

Aside from the loyal affection of Villepreux, and the gratitude of the poor folk of Angers, how hate and envy flourished! The most odious reports were those most willingly received. All the crimes of Giles de Retz, increased in number and intensified in degree, were attributed to the unfortunate Fougereuse. Court and city vied with each other in false testimony and in silly credulity. "Fougereuse is a vampire. Fougereuse can make gold with blood. Fougereuse goes to the orgies of the sorcerers, and leads the Devil's dances. Fougereuse changes himself into a wolf, an owl, a snake." Everybody had met him under one or the other of these disguises. "Fougereuse weaves spells, and, being a witch, causes all the misery in Angers. He blights those whom he does not like, and depopulates the town in order to fill the cemeteries." These accusations were exchanged on the threshold of every shop, at the corner of every street. And at court it was added: "Fougereuse is a traitor. He has been bought by King Louis of France, or else by Edward of England. Fougereuse is a regicide, sworn to compass our liege René's death. Fougereuse is a rebel who incites the people, and spawns sedition." It needed less than this to furnish matter for ten indictments, each calling for capital punishment. Villepreux began to think that the only way to save his friend alive, was to have him carried off before he could be brought to trial.

Isabelle, nevertheless, did not lose courage. Her young dignity, her sweet reserve and modesty, her unwavering confidence in her brother's virtue, and her faith that she should see him freed, impressed many minds. She concealed her tears and her aching heart, and prayed without ceasing. She found a way to check Robert's impetuosity, to uphold the good repute of her race, to touch and convince Queen Margaret, who ended by espousing her cause.

"Poor little maid! How proud you were of your brother!" Margaret had murmured on the evening of Guy's arrest.

"It is to-night that I am proudest, Madame," replied Isabelle. "For yesterday I was the sister of a proscribed man; now I am the sister of a martyr." And this brave answer won her the approbation of the royal woman who had known adversity.

Isabelle's hope hinged on the King's recovery. She longed to approach him to plead for Guy, and to reveal the motives of that malevolence with which Walter de Maulny pursued him. The mask of disinterested friendship with which Walter covered his dark dealings was no longer needed, now that the baron was out of the way. No other person in the city was quite so eager to rend his cousin's reputation, and repeat the vilest slanders. He affected extreme grief to think Guy should be guilty of such infamous treason. He assumed so well his affectation of absolute attachment to the King's person, that he succeeded in getting admitted to the sick chamber, although the two Queens and Prince Edward had been hitherto the sole visitors tolerated by the domineering Cornelius.

On the fourth day of the King's illness, Queen Margaret was preparing to go to her father's chamber, intending to speak a word to him in favor of Fougereuse. She was passing through the long galleries leading to the royal apartments in the palace, when a stifled sob caused her to turn around. Against a great piece of tapestry, which, serving as a curtain, divided the gallery into two unequal parts, stood Isabelle de Fougereuse, pale and tremulous, but with anger, not with fear. Her eyes shone with tears; the sobs which shook her breast seemed bred of intolerable pain, and yet were suppressed by a gigantic effort. With her hand clenched against the folds of the tapestry, and her head bent in the attitude of listening, Isabelle motioned to the Queen to approach noiselessly. Margaret advanced, astonished at her odd summons, and wondering for the moment if her troubles had affected the poor child's brain. She spoke very gently. "What are you doing here, Isabelle?"

"Listen, Madame: listen to what they are saying!" the girl replied, in a barely audible, quivering, broken voice.

A confused murmur was borne from the other

side of the gallery. Margaret knew that an eager crowd must be gathering there, in order to obtain from Cornelius the latest tidings of the King. And she understood also how Isabelle, who came thither to await her, found herself brought to a standstill between his Majesty's apartments and this assemblage of persons hostile to her brother. Fougereuse: his was the one name mingled with all their gossip; and the tones of hate, anger, mockery, and scorn in which it was pronounced, pierced his young sister to the heart. For the first time she heard it all. She scanned the abyss of shame into which detraction had cast him; she saw his pure record trailed in the mire; and her whole soul revolted against the dishonoring of her race.

"The cowards, the cowards!" she panted, her face suffused; "what! all, all persecuting the innocent? Not one objecting, not even one? Is there no courage left in the world?"

She trembled so, that Margaret passed her arm around the girl to sustain her. The words "degradation," "torture," "the stake," came clearly to their ears. The Queen spoke hastily, and in disgust. "This is too much!" she said. And she stretched forth her hand to raise the curtain and show herself, in majestic antagonism, to the eyes of the elegant mob, just as a soldierly voice, at the far end of the gallery, threw a defiance to the enemies of Fougereuse. A tumult arose at once.

"Are you not a noble champion of sorcerers and

poisoners!" they cried. "Lion, you are blinded and duped. Roar as you will, and unsheathe all your claws, your friend will nevertheless be burned as a witch. His name will be struck from the roll of knighthood, and sunk in infamy. And that will be simple justice."

"Carry it out, then, my lords," replied Villepreux without excitement, "since it would be a deed so worthy of you. But I do not expect to act as your accomplice. If you drive Fougereuse to the stake, I shall go along with him, flanked by my Penitent Thieves, and protesting against the sentence. It will be a bold executioner who will proceed! If you degrade from his rank the noblest and the bravest among you, I shall stand at his side, and be proud of my post. Each time that the herald-at-arms pronounces a charge of felony and bad faith, I will cry out that he lies, and drown his voice. And when Guy is placed in the ignominious cart, I shall bend my knee before him, and ask his pardon, in the name of all the chivalry of Anjou. Thus I intend doing, my lords and gentlemen. It is for you to say whether you will oppose me."

A storm of comment arose in the wake of this fierce apostrophe. The Queen of England, judging that it was now her opportunity to intervene, raised the heavy draperies, and stood suddenly confronting the startled group. She imposed silence upon them with a gesture. Before the censure in her eyes their own eyes fell.

"It was well spoken, my Crusader!" she said first, addressing Villepreux. "Be the baron de Fougereuse innocent or guilty, he has one strong heart to defend him. My lord Robert, will you do me a service?"

"Name it, Madame, and you shall be obeyed," Villepreux responded, bowing low.

"Then, pray, go seek Prince Edward, my son. I know not where he may be at this moment, and I desire him to join me, without delay, in the King's chamber. Tell him that I await him there, and that he must make haste."

As soon as Robert had left the gallery to carry the message which was the means of withdrawing him from the unfriendly company, the Queen turned again towards them.

"The court of Anjou has changed sadly since my youth, gentlemen! There was a time when any knight would have blushed to hear the absent vilified, and to see the fallen struck anew. You force me to regret the past." And before aught could be uttered in reply, Margaret had vanished behind the tapestry. Once more she found herself alone with Isabelle, whose eloquent blue eyes thanked her and besought her, better than any words.

"Come, Isabelle," continued the Queen, "come with me to my father: you shall speak to him at once. And let us go quickly, my daughter, for we have no time to lose." Margaret had experience and clear-sightedness. Even as birds of prey anticipate a man's death in the desert, and hover around a breathing body which will soon be but a corpse, so these calumniators foretold ruin and disgrace, and gathered together furiously to rend the reputation of one who was given up for lost. It seemed that Fougereuse must already be condemned, that only thus could be explained such a dismemberment of his good name, by his flatterers of yesterday. The exiled sovereign, leading Isabelle, entered the royal apartment, which was strictly guarded by the doctor Cornelius.

René I., Duke of Anjou and Lorraine, King of Sicily and Aragon, whom history has rightly named " good King René," was then an amiable old man, fatherly and sweet. When Margaret advanced, her arm resting on that of the trembling girl, he received her with most tender welcomes. Stretched in a great armchair drawn close to the window, the august invalid wore a long robe of black velvet trimmed with fur, and his cap, of like material, was richly embroidered with the arms of Anjou. His venerable countenance, with its mobile features, bespoke an unimpaired mind, and his vigor and vivacity were astonishing at his age. Illness had left no special traces upon him. His Queen, Joan, seated near, was turning over the leaves of a magnificently illuminated book; and René, who was the author of the designs, was smilingly explaining to her the thread of the allegory. Not far off, a little group of familiar attendants, among whom Maulny and Cornelius were conspicuous, followed, with respectful attention, the remarks of the royal artist.

"Here, at last, is my dearest daughter!" cried René, when Margaret sank down at his side to receive his blessing. "Here is my Pearl of Anjou, the brightest jewel of my crown, whom I should never have intrusted to the rude hands of the English. . . . May Heaven keep you, my child. May your filial heart glean a little gladness from your old father's returning health!"

"Our joy is very great, sire; so great that I would have every soul share it!" Margaret answered. "And therefore I felt confident I should not incur your displeasure by bringing with me a petitioner, whose only hope is in your sovereign bounty."

"Bid her approach, my daughter. God has been too merciful to me that I should refuse mercy to my subjects. . . . But who is this? Isabelle de Fougereuse? You, my poor little one?" And a murmur of surprise ran around the room, when the girl, almost fainting, fell on her knees beside the King's armchair.

"My liege, my liege, listen to me!" Her voice was weak, but her clasped hands, her face uplifted, her cheeks wet with anguished tears, her whole mien and attitude, pleaded loudly for her.

"What would you have, Isabelle?" said the kind René, touched at the spectacle of so much suffering in so gentle a creature. "Come, do not shake so, but tell me your wish. Whatever be your brother's misdeeds, you are not smirched with them ; and your prince desires to be just."

" It is to your sense of justice that I make my appeal," Isabelle began, forgetting her fears in the advocacy of a cause she held so dear. " Pity me, sire : help a lonely and abandoned orphan who has none to befriend her save God in Heaven and her earthly King. I have placed my trust in you; I entreat you to preserve me against the enemies of my brother and my house."

" What is your meaning, child ? Has any one wronged you? If so, do but name him, and we shall learn whether there is justice in Anjou. You will not have called in vain upon my protection."

" You ask whether any one has wronged me, sire ! What, then, in your judgment, is the unforeseen arrest of the baron de Fougereuse without the royal warrant, and his detention in a dark cell, as if he were the lowest malefactor ? What, then, is the abominable accusation of would-be murder, what are these infamous calumnies continually dinned in my ears by all your court? What is this bitter sentence of degradation and death pronounced on him, beforehand, by lips which have no authority? What is the brand upon his honor, and upon the honor of our ancestors, if not a mortal offence to me, and the most cruel injury I can sustain? Why should I complain to my sovereign lord, if not to claim justice against persecution ? Sire, I am the sister of an innocent man ! Guy is the victim of tyranny : he has been condemned without a hearing, and struck down when he was unable to defend himself. They have taken from your side the most loyal of all your servants and subjects. So sure was he of your good will, that he scorned precautions in his danger. The hand of his master had ever been righteous towards him. His foes seized upon an hour of confusion to wrest him from you, and bury him alive between walls silent as the tomb. Sire, will you sanction an act of iniquity committed without your knowledge? Will you incriminate one whom of late you loved, in whom you trusted? I beg you," cried Isabelle, beginning to feel the chill of the silence around her, "I adjure you, my lord and King, by the salvation of your soul, by the fear of the awful judgment of God, set Guy free: give me back my brother!"

This proud and high harangue, very different from the plaint expected from the delicate girl, caused a great commotion. What had been looked for was an appeal for pardon in behalf of an offender; and here was an indignant remonstrant, haughtily invoking the rehabilitation of the oppressed. Walter de Maulny grew pale with uneasiness, and dreaded to see his prey escape him.

"It is a strange discourse that you have addressed to me, my lady Isabelle," René gravely replied. "When Fougereuse's guilt is proven, do you dare maintain him to be blameless, and demand that action be taken against his accusers?

Sorrow has deranged the poor child," he added compassionately, as he beheld her burst into tears. " Your brother was bold indeed to dictate to you such language."

" Guy dictate to me, sire! Are you not aware that no person is admitted where he is? He is in solitary confinement, and for four days now, I know not whether he be living or dead."

" This is too rigorous, seneschal." René spoke to Philip de Beauvau, who had just entered the room. " However bad a prisoner be, one ought not to deny him the means of repentance and salvation. And, henceforth, grant permission to this lady to visit her brother at any time. Isabelle, do you heed my words. If you desire to save Guy, an ingrate who was once dear to me, inspire him with more humble sentiments, and obtain from him an acknowledgment of his fault. He may be less culpable than he seems. No one is more eager that I am, to have him clear himself from the charges brought against him. For the sake of the services rendered me long ago by your father, baron Amaury, and out of consideration for you who lose in Guy your sole natural protector, I am disposed to be very lenient with him. But I exact a full confession of these secret arts, these mysterious and abhorred measures. Bring that proud temper to submission, and I promise you . . . yes, I can promise you, my dear child, to be propitious to Fougereuse. ' *God wills not the death of a sinner, but rather that he be converted, and live.'* Arise, Isabelle. Go and tell your brother that his deliverance is in his own hands, and that his future depends upon his candor!"

"Must I say to him, sire, that his King supposes him to have sought and willed his destruction?" Isabelle queried, as she rose to her feet. "Can you truly deem Guy capable of that unspeakable sin? Is it that which you invite him to avow?"

"No, Isabelle: I do not accuse him of poisoning, for such black ingratitude is incredible. But he must answer for having practised magic, for having woven spells; and it were far better for him to admit as much to his indulgent sovereign, rather than to the implacable judges. Tell him that too, my child. It is not the King who reasons with you, but the old comrade-in-arms of your brave father."

"Alas, your Majesty!" sighed the girl, again joining her hands. "God knows that I am thankful for your liberal kindness; but is this all I can obtain from you? I can read my brother's choice. He would prefer a cruel death, rather than that the least suspicion should enter your mind against him. You send to him, with this word that he must admit such enormities in order to save his life, me, who am his sister! me, who have had from his boyhood the key to that Christian heart, and believe that it has never forfeited the grace of his baptism! me, whose honor is forever one with his own! Can I obey you? I implore you on my knees to alter that message! I assure you, I swear to you, Guy is guiltless. Be not generous by halves, sire. You, who soften towards convicted offenders, suffer yourself to be persuaded in favor of a just man! Can you not put faith in what I say, sire? Is there nothing in your conscience which sides with me, when I proclaim the innocence of Guy de Fougereuse?"

"No more, Isabelle, my poor child. You move my compassion. You are too loyal, too pure, to have an understanding of evil. At my age one is wiser, alas! Long since, I was betrayed by those in whom I trusted, by my most intimate servants; and the conduct of Fougereuse gives me no new pang. I pity you, Isabelle; I am most willing to pardon a repentant culprit. But more than this I cannot do. Go now, and visit your captive. Margaret, take the child in charge. . . . Yet another word with you," the King added, motioning to the girl to approach him again. "You were wrong, my lady, in stating that all your kinsfolk had forsaken you. I know one of them who is devoted to you: your cousin Walter de Maulny."

Isabelle's blood stirred; she raised her golden head apprehensively. Maulny, hearing his name, came forward. "Walter loves you," continued the King; "your misfortunes have not dampened his sincere attachment. He has told me something of his longing to see you installed as the châtelaine of Maulny. What do you say?"

"I beg my beautiful cousin not to reject my suit," added Walter himself, bowing before Isabelle, with that patrician grace and exquisite courtesy for which men and women had admired him in the heyday of his career. "My most sacred wish, for a long while, has been to see our destinies united; but I should not have presumed to aspire to such an honor, had not our gracious sovereign seen fit to encourage my hope." He spoke further in the same strain, for Isabelle's silence misled him: yet he stopped short in the middle of his distasteful compliments and hollow phrases, when the young eyes met his own. That glance of icy scorn, clear and penetrating as a steel blade, was characteristic of Guy in certain moods, but it sat strangely upon sweet Isabelle. Her fraternal love, her pride of temperament and of race, awoke in her every energy of her soul. For the moment, the girl looked so like her brother that Maulny was confounded; and bold as he was, his words failed him.

"Guy will answer you for me, cousin!" She contented herself with this short response, delivered in the best Fougereuse manner. Then, turning towards René of Anjou, she went on: "I beseech your Majesty, speak not to me of marriage, while my brother is in danger. I have no thought for any but for him."

"Very well, very well; Walter will wait," replied the King, in a good-humored concession. "May God help you and uphold you!"

Isabelle de Fougereuse took a respectful leave of the aged monarch. Queen Margaret accompanied her, mournfully shaking her head. She had expected a better result from the interview. Queen Joan withdrew at the same time.

Meanwhile the King was musing. "That child has a true heart, and very fine courage. She is Amaury de Fougereuse's own daughter, and for her sake I must show mercy to her unhappy brother. . . . What are you saying, seneschal?"

"I was saying, sire, that mercy would be a difficult as well as an unnecessary thing. That wicked ally of Fougereuse, Robert de Villepreux, is trying to thwart the law: his arrogant behavior is insufferable. He has converted the baron's residence into a veritable stronghold, guarded by his rascals out of Palestine. He is sowing rebellion amid the people. He defies and insults whomsoever mentions his friend in his presence. Finally, he has just welcomed to town an armed troop, composed of the Fougereuse and Villepreux vassals: I expect at any moment to see him unfurl his standard, and lead his own Thieves to an assault upon the prison!"

"Villepreux a rebel?" the King cried incredulously. "You assert too much, my lord seneschal. I know my Lion: he is proud, impetuous, and fond of fight, but he is docile and gentle to me, his master. Send him to me, and we shall discover the meaning of this muster, and of these seditious intentions."

Cornelius murmured: "I fear the King could hardly bear the fatigue of another audience."

"Send Villepreux to me!" René repeated authoritatively. "I must speak with him. Go seek him, Fleurenville, and do not return without him."

The young page bowed, and was setting forth to fulfil his duty, when the door swung open before Prince Edward of Lancaster, followed by Villepreux himself.

"Welcome, dear grandson!" cried the King. "You bring me the very man whom I most wished to see. Come hither, Robert de Villepreux, and explain yourself to the seneschal! Some persons are disturbed to find you fortifying a house in the city, assembling there your vassals and men-at-arms, and pursuing other measures which are hardly in conformity with your sworn allegiance. They allege, besides, that you defy and insult my servants, in the name of Fougereuse. What does all this signify?"

"If the King question me, I will answer," rejoined Villepreux; "but I will not acknowledge the right of Philip de Beauvau to interrogate me concerning anything I choose to do. Who am I, that I should receive his orders? Under God, I derive but from the King, and him alone will I obey."

"It is the King who commands you to speak," said René. At the bottom of his heart, he was flattered to be so addressed by the untameable Lion, who was meek to no one else.

"Then here is the truth, sire. I gathered my

soldiers together at the palace of Fougereuse, that I might thus prevent them from seeking public quarrels, and causing public disorder. They are exasperated at Guy's detention; they would not have lacked opportunity to fall foul of some of your officers. If I have the doors watched and guarded, it is because I have good reason to beware of spies. One may have nothing to conceal, and yet object to those gentry! As to defying and insulting your servants, sire. they must have taken small offence indeed, since I have had no challenge from any among them. All the world knows that an outraged gentleman may seek redress with his own right arm, instead of lodging a complaint with the grand provost. If there is some one who desires satisfaction, I am quite ready to proffer it to him, at the point of my sword. It is weary of the sheath, and only asks to see the light of day!"

"That is not the real issue, my hot Crusader," interrupted René, secretly satisfied by the other's open and martial reply. "The Saracens have given you too good practice! and I am no whit anxious to have you split and cleave my excellent subjects. What is the meaning of this uprising of the tenantry of Fougereuse?"

"I wished to speak about them to Your Majesty. The poor fellows are deeply attached to their lord: they could not bear to think he was in trouble without endeavoring to relieve him. They are armed at present with nothing worse than cudgels, if Beauvau will permit me to make that statement.

They have marched to Angers in a body, to inquire whether Guy has been shut in the tower by the order of the King, or merely by the whim of the seneschal. Now what shall I tell them?"

"Of all the impudent questions ever asked since the world began!" cried Philip de Beauvau in a transport of rage. "Since when have I to render an account of myself in the discharge of my office? I do my duty; and the King my master will not disclaim me."

"I should never offer you such an affront, Philip," responded René. "Nevertheless, I should have preferred less haste in so serious a matter. Your zeal was too active."

"Active rather than commendable, sire, you will allow me to add," continued Villepreux boldly. "What a spectacle for our nobility, to see its virtue treated as rag and bobtail! Is the chivalry of Anjou fallen so low that its membership must be searched, because somewhere there is a traitor? The King faints, they say, the King is dying, the King must have been poisoned! and it is upon us that suspicion lights! The word is spoken to arrest — whom? Not a valet, not a spy, not a stranger nor a poor Jew, but the very noblest and best among us, the man to whom you gave unique distinction when you allowed him to rank as your friend: the baron Guy de Fougereuse. What had he done to deserve his fate? During the six years when he enjoyed constant favor at his prince's side, did any man ever find a flaw in his honor?

Did he enrich himself with royal gifts, or with bribes from place-hunters? Were there intervals when he laid by his devotion to the King? Who among you can convict him of a meanness? You do not answer, gentlemen! You who praised so once the fidelity, disinterestedness, courage, justice, of the minister, you have not a syllable to utter in defence of the prisoner. It does not seem strange to you that a brave knight should sigh in chains, while an intriguing alien, an upstart of the vilest origin, enjoys his freedom, and holds between his fingers our most precious concern: the health, the life of our sovereign. Were I seneschal of Anjou, sire, it is possible that the tower dungeon would not be empty: but I swear to you that the name of its occupant would not be Fougereuse!"

"*Pasques-Dieu!*" cried Cornelius, who was as ready at an oath as the King of France himself, "are you in a high fever, sir knight? Is it my personality which you mean to designate by those gross epithets? Dare you to hint that you consider me guilty of the infamous act of treason, from which my skill alone has saved my royal patient? Were it so" —

"No threats, minion!" Robert rejoined coldly. "I did not name you: you are proclaiming yourself. Surely, it is permissible to feel astonished, when, so soon as the entire city rings with the cry of poison, doubts accumulate on the head of the soldier, and never so much as graze the charlatan."

"Charlatan! I!" shouted Cornelius, purple with wrath, and losing all self-control. "Dearly shall you atone for this blow, my able beheader of Saracens! Know that you are dealing with the pupil of Master Coictiers, the chief physician of His Majesty Louis XI., with the friend of Oliver le Daim"—

"And a colleague of Tristram l'Heremite," concluded Villepreux. "I should advise you not to boast of your friendships: they smell of the gallows-tree. Behold, sire, the man chosen to replace your faithful Antonio, that noble nature, that true hero of science, who went proudly into voluntary banishment rather than endure such inferiority for rival. It is a sad thing for those who love you, to see your present councillors so different from the men who once surrounded you. Instead of Antonio, this Cornelius; instead of Fougereuse, a Walter de Maulny!"

"Villepreux!" said Maulny, "thank your stars that you are in the royal presence. Save for the respect due to our venerated monarch, I"—

"Enough!" interposed the King, with a gesture of command. "That due respect seems to be forgotten by all here, and I would recall it to you. Master Cornelius, I do not for a moment question your fidelity."

"And why, sire?" asked Robert. "Because he is the friend of Oliver le Daim?"

"You take too great liberties, Villepreux!" said René, frowning. "I have been patient with you:

more patient, perhaps, than befits my dignity. But you must know that I cannot tolerate this constant provocation offered to those of my household, nor your remonstrances against my choice of associates. I excuse your outbursts, because I am aware what you suffer in contemplating the fate of Fougereuse. But I am showing him an undeserved indulgence. I have just promised Isabelle that I will pardon him, whenever he frankly reveals his dark secrets. I permit his cell to be thrown open, from to-day on, to any of his friends who will have the charity to visit him ; and I rely upon them to persuade him to repentance. I am according him all that I can, for the sake of his father, and of his own past services. But you presume too far, my lord of Villepreux, in coming hither to menace my seneschal under my very eyes. And it is only a foolish piece of bravado to maintain, thus obstinately, the entire innocence of that unfortunate man. Proofs are at hand ; and they are overwhelming."

"May I dare ask my liege what these proofs are? Are they worth the pledge which Guy gave me of his innocence? Would you see me thus defending him, if I had not absolute certitude that he is free from blame?"

"Fougereuse has given you some pledge, then!" the King repeated, while Maulny repressed a gesture of surprise and apprehension. "Of what were we dreaming? I might have remembered that the Lion of Villepreux is not the man to stake his soul on hearsay and unknown quantities.

Speak! What do you know? What evidence have you?"

"The word of honor of Guy de Fougereuse!" Robert replied proudly. "Sire, it never errs."

"Is this your pledge, your only pledge?"

"The only one. It suffices me."

"It would suffice no other!" cried Philip de Beauvau. "'The word of honor of Guy de Fougereuse!' Does not every suspect swear that he is above reproach? It is but toying with us, to proffer us such coin."

"What does the King think?" continued Robert, taking a step towards René. "Is the oath of a knight worthless in his eyes? If you would have me go bail for Guy's sincerity, I do so without fear. I am ready to "—

"Heigh-ho, my brave Lion," sighed René: "you belong to Palestine."

A smile danced on every lip. Maulny's expression was malicious, triumphant, and meant to drive Villepreux mad.

"Even so, sire," said the intrepid friend, crossing his arms over his breast, and looking down upon his companions, from his giant height. "I realize that you have foredoomed Fougereuse. Any move against him is legitimate, but to fight for him is to confess one's self a fool. Well: I shall stand steadfast, nevertheless, though I become involved in his own disgrace. I have but one more word to add, before I take my leave. In those two at your side, Cornelius and Maulny, you have two sworn enemies of my unhappy comrade. Their hatred does not date from yesterday; their measures to ruin him are perfectly plain. I also have 'proofs'! I also can denounce traitors! What have you to answer, Walter, when I ask "—

"I appeal to his Majesty!" Maulny exclaimed. "He knows that I could not hesitate to choose between my noble prince and my ignoble relative. It was painful to me to turn light in upon the intrigues of a member of my own family. But perish all my line, before I perjure my vassal's faith!"

"There are witnesses to the fact that Fougereuse bewitched the King," Cornelius announced. "It is certified that in the house of the dead sorcerer, Wolfram, he concocted philters and beverages which "—

"Leech!" Villepreux addressed him with withering scorn. "Leech! as I said once before, you are a viper. And you — O Judas de Maulny!"

"Rebel and conspirator that you are!" cried the angry knight. "All this rhodomontade is but a mask for your own conduct. You will not deny having harangued the people in the Cathedral square, this morning, exhorting them to demand 'Baron Guy's' release. Neither will you deny having declared your intention to oppose, with an armed force, the execution of the royal mandate, in case Fougereuse shall be condemned. Twenty gentlemen who heard you are prepared so to testify!"

"This is going beyond all bounds!" Robert protested. "But I ought to know what to expect from Guy's enemies. You would strike anew at him through me, his last defender. So be it! I will not stoop to cleanse myself of a stain which cannot cling to me. I understand you, hypocrites and felons! You stand here to represent those who clamored of old for the death of the Just One. '*What evil hath he done?*' No matter! '*Crucify Him, crucify Him!*' My liege, once again: will you yield to an envious, heartless faction? Is it worthy of Your Majesty to play, at their beck, the *rôle* of Herod or of Pilate?"

René of Anjou arose, as a ruler before one who braves his authority; as an old man before one who respects not his gray hairs. "Insubordinate! Is it thus you talk in the presence of your sovereign? Dare you so far outrage him, that you compare with him the wicked murderers of Christ? Never has a like insult been offered me, even in my day of bitterest trouble. You have deserved death. I commute it to banishment. Go! Depart hence, and let Anjou behold you no more. Obey, I say!"

"Sire, I obey. My King shall never again see the subject he has charged with rebellion. And before I go, I desire to restore whatever I received. I renounce the tenure of Villepreux, and I am no more now than the captain of my horsemen, my Thieves. Here is the collar of the Order of the Crescent, which I throw at your feet. And finally, here is Hauteclaire, the sword with which you yourself armed me when I was made your knight! I beg you to accept it, for your royal hand alone has the right to take it from me."

Dropping on one knee, Villepreux drew his blade from the scabbard, and presented it respectfully to the offended King, who declined it by a gesture. "Keep it," he said, "I do not recall my gifts. A pretended submission serves but to aggravate your fault. Sheathe your sword!"

"Not so, sire. Hauteclaire has never been drawn save in your service, and has never retired save with glory. If you reject her, let her perish! for death was ever better than shame." And Robert, taking the steel in both hands, bent it across his knee, and with a single effort, broke it off short, next the hilt. "Farewell, Hauteclaire!" he said feelingly, "and farewell, my liege!" He rose up, and adding, "May God preserve you!" walked out of the chamber, his step firm, his chin held high, his look controlled, and proudly sad. René's attendants turned aside. But Prince Edward grasped his hand as he went by, and the old King's eyes followed his disgraced vassal, who withdrew without having turned his head.

When he had disappeared, René of Anjou fell back, exhausted, into his ducal armchair. "All, all!" he murmured. "Antonio, Fougereuse, Villepreux! they all forsake me, one by one. . . . I shall die friendless and alone."

At this juncture a page arrived at the threshold, announcing that the University students in a body solicited the pleasure of presenting to his Majesty their congratulations on his happy recovery. René rose with a brisk effort, and steadied himself upon the arm of the young heir of England, saying, "Come, child! these faithful youths will be our consolation. . . . Page, usher the students into the gallery, for I am fain to see them all, and forget my griefs and vexations in their company."

.   .   .   .

On leaving the palace, Villepreux hurried to the tower cell, which was henceforth open to the friends of Fougereuse. Guy and Isabelle were seated together. Her fair head bowed on his shoulder, she wept bitterly, for he was gently withstanding her every plea. The hermit and Loïc, retired to the crack-like window, were talking in undertones. Villepreux, pale and excited, came into the shadowy room, seeking the beloved prisoner whom he had so bravely and so disastrously tried to vindicate. Guy, perceiving him, uttered a cry of joy, and advanced to greet him; but Robert, with a great sob heaving his breast, took him in both arms.

"What is it? What is the matter, my lord of Villepreux?" cried Isabelle, stricken with mortal terror.

"Why such emotion, dear friend? Does it mean that I am to be executed at once?" asked Guy.

"All is lost," Villepreux answered; "and lost through my fault. Guy, I am an attainted and banished man." •

" You, Robert! " . . . " You, my lord of Ville-preux! " exclaimed the others in the cell.

" Call me not the lord of Villepreux: my lands are no longer mine. I have given up my fief, and renounced my allegiance. At this moment I pos-sess no domain, no castle, no inheritance. They accused me of treason, their King sends me into exile; his orthodox subjects look on me as muti-nous, and my renown is sullied. The lord of Ville-preux is dead: you see in me the knight Robert, commandant of the Penitent Thieves. But I could bear it all, Guy, if my degradation did not involve you. Let me snatch you from this accursed dun-geon! Let us flee our ungrateful Anjou and its blinded monarch, and go to found, in Jerusalem, a barony of the Holy Sepulchre. And I make oath I will never again expose myself to the reproach of having returned from Palestine! "

" Robert, my friend! . . . Robert, calm your-self. What is all this about? . . . Is it credible? Is it possible? Are you in earnest? "

" Am I in earnest! " said Villepreux, after him, pointing to the empty scabbard at his side. " Look, Guy: I have broken Hauteclaire in two! " And Guy, with genuine consternation, learned of the violent scene between his friend and the King, and all that had resulted from it.

" My poor Lion, what have you done! " he ex-claimed, when Robert had finished his tale. " God grant that the good King may be willing to pardon you! "

"I have no need of his pardon, Fougereuse, but only of yours. It was my anger which lost the cause I hoped to win. Oh, I was mad! That demon Maulny, and that serpent of a Cornelius, drove me out of myself; and even René of Anjou refused to believe me, when I pledged my faith for yours. Why will he accredit the guilty, and refuse justice to the innocent? How can he arraign for treason, and for commerce with hell, the most loyal knight and the best Christian in his duchy? Should I lose you, Guy, my life would be nothing worth. If they convict you, I will follow you to death!"

"My lord Robert!" murmured Isabelle.

"If they convict me," Guy answered gently, dragging up the massive chains as he placed his hand in that of his friend, "then that will not be the time for you to follow me to death. I need you for my survivor: while you breathe on, I shall not utterly die. Now hear me out. My will is made, and I have appointed you my heir. No protest, Robert! Should you wish me to prefer my cousin de Maulny? I speak neither of my wealth nor my estate: things sure to be confiscated when I perish. But I bequeathe to you my honor, and the vindication of my memory. I bequeathe to you two devoted spirits whom adversity could not drive from their master's side: Vincent Govier, and Loïc de Kernis. The equerry is a veteran soldier, who can be of splendid service. Loïc (you know him), is a child: but in that roguish breast beats a fine heart, and you, far better than I, will be able to make of him a perfect knight. Loïc, do not cry out! I am not separating you from me, in giving you my second self to love and serve; I count upon you to be true to him. Robert, will you take the legacy?"

"Yes: before God who hears us!" said Robert in an altered voice.

"My friend, I do thank you! There is one precious jewel more, which is dearer than all to me: my sister. My death will leave her alone in the world, without"—

"Oh, no! not while I live!" Villepreux's voice was full of vehemence, and the girl, in a torrent of fresh tears, threw herself into her brother's arms.

"Guy, you break my heart! What could I do without you? Let me enter the convent, and pray for you there to my dying day!"

"Did you hear that, Robert? The child is in such low spirits, since Maulny besought the King for her hand! She thinks she can never put barriers enough between herself and that unwelcome aspirant!"

"Maulny!" Villepreux exclaimed, straightening himself where he stood in the middle of the dim cell: "how hard honor and justice find it to live in the same universe with that man! Maulny! Our only truce with him will be when I have stretched him in his grave. A malison on the traitor! Hell is too good for him!"

"Do not say such a thing, my lord!" Isabelle implored. "And you, brother dear, why do you begrudge to me the peace of the cloister, and the grace of God there?"

"Because it is your sorrow which urges you thus to seek shelter, Isabelle; and not the call of Christ which urges you to choose Him for your portion forever. Not so should one give one's self to God. But have no fear: Our Lady will send you a defender. Would that before I leave this world I might see you betrothed to a lover worthy of you! Tell me, Isabelle, have you never favored any of those young nobles who "—

"Do not mention them to me." She spoke resolutely, raising her head, and looking straight into her brother's eyes. "They have abandoned you, abused you, belied you! Never picture me as the wife of one of those cowardly wretches!"

"Very well, my darling. You demand a hero, and I shall not set myself against that. There was a hero once, to whom I tendered your hand in vain."

The girl flushed, and turned away. "Guy, I entreat you!" whispered Villepreux, evidently in agony. "This is neither the time nor the place "—

"I am the best judge of that," Fougereuse said. "Listen to me, Isabelle. You know how, for generations, the head of our house maintained a feud with a rival race?"

"I know," his sister admitted, very low.

"Until the last descendant of that race," continued Guy, "and the last one of ours came to feel that between the two there had been enough bloodshed. And I went to my foeman, a stripling then like myself; and I was received nobly and frankly, and we swore to forget the past. And we planned an alliance which should forever unite us. You were very young, and I promised to plight you to my new friend and yours. When he visited Fougereuse, you were his princess always, and he your vassal. But the time came when, of his own free will, he gave me back my word."

"Guy, I say! Let me justify myself!" cried Robert.

"'This is neither the time nor the place!' Let me finish. He gave me back my word, because he was not willing, he said, to take advantage of the inexperience of a child of your age, to hold you bound to any such promise. He aspired to win the voluntary love of her whom he should wed. Your dower was a rich one, and you had many suitors, while my odd friend fled to Palestine, as if to escape you and your fortune. But he loved you, and he kept silence with his whole strength, because he believed himself unworthy to occupy your thoughts. . . . You know the rest, Isabelle. You have seen this valiant knight, unaided, defending the honor and the life of his hereditary foe. You have heard him declare himself ready, for my sake, to end his own stainless career in an opprobrious death. He stands before you, cashiered, exiled, for having espoused with too great warmth your brother's cause. And notwithstanding all this, he will not venture to reclaim his little sweet-heart."

" No! " Villepreux broke in : " God forbid, my lady, that I should throw into the balance the. affection I have for Guy! I beg you to ignore it. I should not wish gratitude, nor the sense of any pact made long ago, to influence a maid in my favor. I have no domain, no wealth, no glory, not even my sword. I could not make you mistress of Villepreux, you whom I once dreamed of crowning Queen of Jerusalem! Were you still the great heiress that you were, I should not have allowed Guy to speak for me. But you, like me, are per-secuted and poor, and, like me, menaced with the loss of your dearest and best: therefore will I lay now at your feet the passion and devotion of my whole life. Let me tell you in this dark hour, and once for all, how I have loved you! You have ruled my very soul within me, and Heaven alone knows to what holy ends! As a child. you taught me a lesson of mercy in coming to intercede for some peasants who had transgressed. You opened to feelings of pity and tenderness, my heart which is naturally hard and wild. Every time, far off in Palestine. that I spared a foe, pardoned a rebel, redeemed a captive, or exhorted a renegade to re-pent — O Isabelle! I did it for you. I longed to awake your pride in the exploits of the warrior, and still more, to make you happy by the deeds of the Christian. The memory of your presence followed me like my guardian angel, and warded me from evil: be you blessed for it all! I never nursed the folly of thinking you could care for me. I shall never murmur, if you would keep your liberty in your own hands. But my fate is there too. Decide it for me, and without fear. If Robert de Villepreux cannot hope to be your husband, he will still remain your brother, your friend, your leal knight, to his dying breath."

While Robert was speaking, Isabelle turned, little by little, towards him. She had listened silently to his manly, self-forgetful plea. Sincere, frank, blunt as it was, it was filled with the gentle spirit of sacrifice. The girl's whole attitude changed. Her drooping head straightened itself proudly; her eyes began to shine under their still moist lashes; and the look on her young face was noble and grave.

"My lord of Villepreux," she said, as Robert knelt before her to hear her decision, "my lord of Villepreux, you and I have nothing to do with light and idle talk. My truthfulness shall be equal to yours. If you would owe your bride neither to some debt of thankfulness, nor to some assurance given in her name; if you wish to leave her to the free choice of her heart"—

There Isabelle's voice failed her. She stopped in despite of herself, and reddened, and breathed hard. Villepreux's forehead bent lower, like that of a man who resigns himself to the death-sentence.

"Well, my dear one," Guy prompted her, "what

must become of Villepreux, if he would owe his bride to the free choice of her heart?"

The sister laid her little trembling hand in her brother's. "Then let him receive this hand from you Guy! and tell him that I had vowed it should never be given to any other."

"Robert," Fougereuse continued solemnly, "here is my last legacy, my treasure. I pass it to him who is worthiest."

The young man pressed to his lips, again and again, the hand so sweetly accorded him. He could not answer. What joyful endearments could the two exchange in the air of that sombre room? What hopeful future smiled on them in the divine moment when their brother leagued them together, standing at the brink of the grave? But Isabelle and Robert had found each other in the day of sorrow, and their love was to strengthen in the shadow of the Cross.

"Come, my Father," Guy called to the hermit, "come and consecrate this betrothal by the preliminary rite of the Church. Isabelle must be able to say to the King: 'Sire, I am bound before God.'"

The aged monk came forward, and after a short, simple exordium, he questioned the lovers. The vows were pronounced, two rings were blessed and made to serve, and their lives were joined in a sacred link which no human power could break.

"*Noël!*" cried Loïc. "Honor to the affianced wife of the Lion! And may that fox of a Maulny die now of rage and spite!"

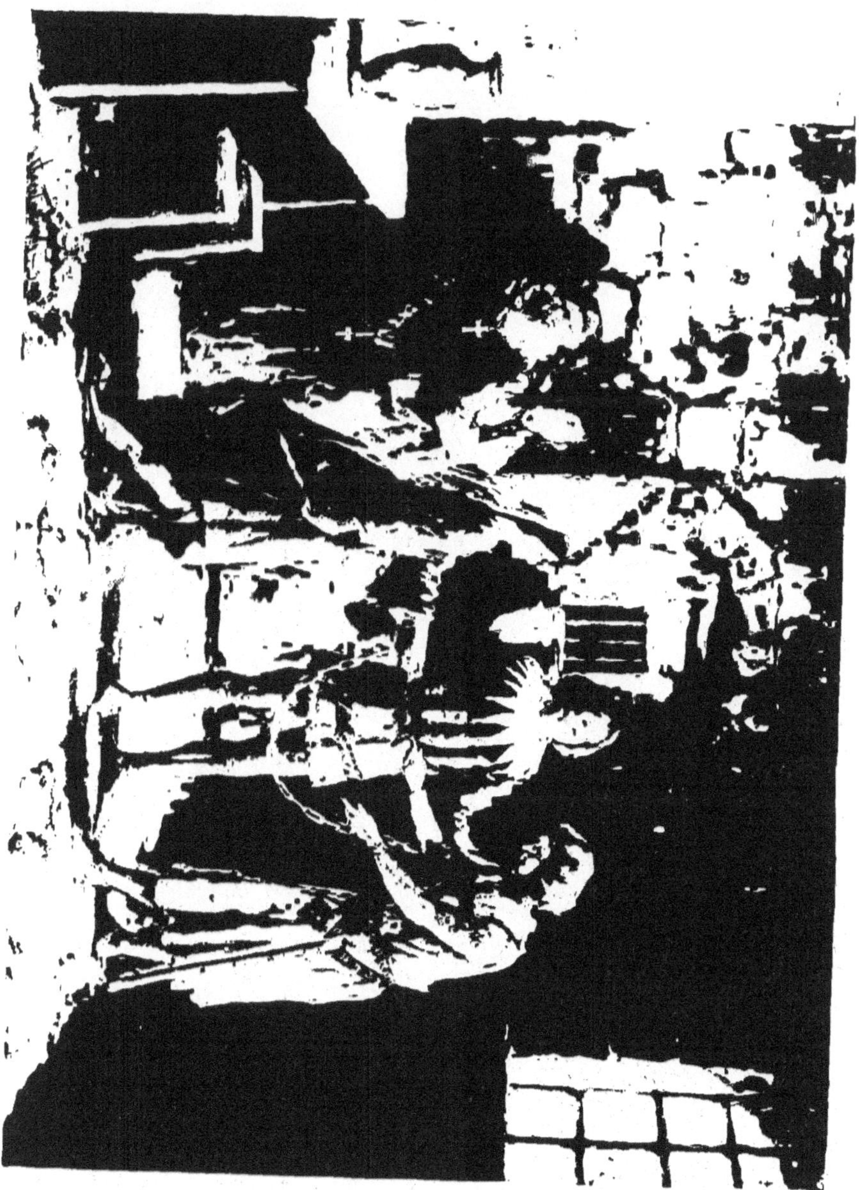

Fougereuse silenced the *enfant terrible* with a gesture. Then he embraced Isabelle, holding her long against his breast, and at last he placed his sister's hand again in that of his friend.

"Take her, Robert, my brother; she is yours. The feud between us is indeed destroyed. May the Lord God Himself be our bond of union, and cement forever the alliance between your line and ours! . . . Good-by, Isabelle. I confide you, without one fear, to your Lionheart. Tell the King that my last thought" —

"Guy, why should you talk thus?" Villepreux remonstrated. "Have you sworn to act like a defenceless sheep, who runs to death? I shall not suffer it. My Thieves are mine yet, and I and they will attempt to save you, be it by attacking the royal troops, contending for your life with the very executioner, or snatching you alive from the burning stake!"

"Isabelle," said her brother, "rather shall you be my ambassadress, since the King appears to have preserved his good will towards you. Here is a ring which he gave me, in a moment of friendly confidence. He engaged never to refuse any request of mine, should this be presented to him in my name. I will intrust it to you. Bring it to His Majesty, and add only this: 'Sire, Fougereuse claims the performance of the royal promise: he demands to be heard before he is condemned.' Go: and God be with you. And you, Father, be pleased to return to the Right Reverend Abbot, and report to him what you have seen; for the hour to act is at hand."

Within a few moments, Robert, the lady Isabelle, and the hermit had quitted the prison. Hours later, Artauld entered.

"Messire, the captain of the guards is outside, to escort you to your audience with the King. Do you wish me to take off your chains? I can obtain permission."

"Be careful, Artauld. They were put upon me in the King's name, and the King alone may strike them off. I follow you as I am."

"You there, Alanik! Come out and get a little air," called the jailer to the page, who cleared the room at a single bound. It was a strange and painful experience for the captive to have to cross the court of the ducal palace, once the scene of his triumphs, surrounded by a guard, and loaded with chains. So short a time before, every one would still have saluted the King's favorite. But now heads turned away, or derisive comment arose. Glory yesterday, and to-day humiliation! The flatterers of yore contemned the object of their flattery: the ancient office-seekers were arrogant and cold. The blight which rested on Fougereuse cleared a great empty space around him; it was due partly to a superstitious terror of the magician, partly to the natural avoidance of a disgraced culprit. The captain, meanwhile, and his men did not hesitate to show themselves kindly disposed towards the prisoner. The rough warriors knew the prowess of the sword of Fougereuse, and had some feeling for the gallant chief who had led them into action. Those hearts whose profession it is to invite death and to bestow it on the field, deal not in mean exactions and useless cruelties. Soldiers, and not executioners, they were open to sentiments of compassion and of respect for misfortune. Guy's own attitude was well calculated to affect them. Though he walked wearily, owing to the weight of his chains, he carried them without embarrassment. Calm, dignified, unboastful, indifferent to what was passing around him, the accused knight went by: never was there a nobler figure.

"Nothing seems to disturb him," some of the guard murmured. "If there is a demon in his body, it is a demon prodigiously brave!"

Just as Fougereuse arrived with his escort, noises began to echo in the court of honor. A ragged throng surged beneath the palace balcony, acclaiming the well-beloved monarch, who had consented to show himself for a few minutes, notwithstanding his still feeble condition.

"Long live King René! Praise unto God who has healed him! Our duke forever! *Noël* to Queen Joan!" cried the poor townspeople, who had come to celebrate the King's recovery. All of a sudden there fell a hush, as of recollection, on the crowd, whose beseeching hands stretched themselves towards the window; they bent the knee and bowed the head in supplication, and a single cry leaped loud from many throats:

"Baron Guy! Give us back Baron Guy!"

"Justice and freedom for Fougereuse!" chorused the students, who at that instant trooped down the great outer steps.

"Sire, sire! Baron Guy!"

René stood up quickly, casting an irritated glance at the gathering below, and withdrew to his rooms, without deigning to answer. But the populace kept to its demand: hundreds of voices repeated ever more warmly and boldly:

"Concede it to us, sire! We must have our Baron Guy!"

Then the students caught sight of Fougereuse, and ran to meet him, waving their caps and shouting:

"*Noël* to the prisoner! Down with the seneschal! Good folk, here is Baron Guy!"

The kneeling crowd started, sprang up with cheers, and rushed upon Fougereuse. The little band of soldiery was overborne, and Fougereuse himself was nearly suffocated. The bystanders kissed his hands and his garments; they examined his manacles, weeping and protesting angrily. They offered to deliver him at once; they offered to carry him in triumph into the royal presence. Fougereuse withstood gently this humane excitement, refused all aid or interference, declared that René was prepared to give him fair play, and succeeded somewhat in quieting the general delirium.

"Men of Angers," he said to those nearest him, "are you truly my friends?"

" Are we ? For life or death ! "

" Very well, then ; what are you doing here ?
You have besought my earthly sovereign in my
behalf ; recommend me now to the King of Heaven !
I once made a vow to Saint Magdalen : hasten to
remind her of it, in her own chapel at Baumette.
Follow them, gentlemen of the University ! "

Docile to their orders, the multitude retreated
through the gates, intoning litanies for the weal of
Baron Guy, not indeed understanding perfectly
what had sent them in that direction, but acting
instinctively together, as mobs will do. The guards
closed in again around their singular captive, who
awaited them with a smile, and the ducal doors
were swung wide before them.

The gallery leading to the King's private apartments was filled with courtiers hostile to Fougereuse. He expected to make an all too leisurely
passage under the fire of their sarcasms, their whispers, their disdainful gaze. A sort of malicious
curiosity shone in every eye. At the entrance to
the gallery Guy had paused for an instant, as if
gauging what warfare lay before him. His head
erect, his face perfectly serene, inexpressive either
of pride or of suffering, he advanced, dragging his
chains over the marble tiles as carelessly as if he
were trailing after him a velvet mantle. But as
he went he brought his slow significant look to
bear upon face after face, and more than one
turned aside with heightened color. His penetrating glance, full now of sadness and pity, sad as a

reproach, pitying as a forgiveness, was that of a judge reading the consciences of men, and condemning the disloyal to the pain of their own remorse. Murmurs died away, a few heads were bowed; not one insult was proffered the prisoner, as he marched through the ranks of his enemies. The King was pacing to and fro in his own room, when young Paul de Fleurenville announced the baron of Fougereuse.

"Let him enter," was the reply.

The curtain was lifted, and Fougereuse appeared on the threshold. His eyes met those of the King, nor did they droop under that severe scrutiny. The aged monarch, standing with his fingers resting on the carved back of a high chair, silently confronted his former minister, who came forward fearlessly, yet with no presumption, sure of his cause. The royal attendants ceased their conversation, and moved aside, interested in a decisive audience whose issue they could not foresee. The subject saluted his sovereign on bended knee, but arose at once, and remained on his feet, in a deferent but resolute attitude. René was painfully impressed at the sight of the iron gyves; they weighed upon him rather than upon their wearer. A melancholy expression crept over his changeful features, and drove all wrath away.

"You wished to speak with me, did you not, Fougereuse?" he began in more sympathetic accents than his present position called for. "In the faithful performance of a promise made to the

friend of long ago, I yield to the claim of the per-
vert of to-day. What would you say to me that
can excuse or mitigate your transgressions?"

"Sire, before I enter upon any defence of myself,
allow me to lay at your feet the expression of my
joy, and also an apology. For my joy is very
great to see your health return. The sharpest
pang I knew in my cell, was when I feared for
the life of my venerated liege. And it is to my
regret, my sincere and profound regret, that I
learn how I was the innocent cause of an offence
to your Majesty. I have seen Robert de Villepreux "—

At the name, the King frowned, and made a
little gesture of vexation. " First Villepreux," he
said, " then the students; and lastly a siege of
beggars. Baron, you have a hot set of partisans!
I would to Heaven they had as much awe of their
ruler as they have ardor for the promotion of
your interests."

" I beseech you, sire, to make allowances for
those who are too true to a disadvantaged man.
If some one must atone for their misdeed, I am at
hand: strike me alone. The quick-tempered youth
of the schools, and the poor honest working-people,
acted without premeditation, and in the heat of
their generous concern for a prisoner. Villepreux
. . . you know the Lion, sire? No vassal of yours
is more deeply devoted to you. But he is used to
the camp rather than to the court; a little spurt of
feeling carried him away. His crime is to have

loved too well a friend cast into disgrace, and to have forgotten that he was addressing his sovereign, and not a comrade-in-arms. Or rather, he never dreamed at all, in his strong veneration for his master, that his soldier-like rudeness of speech could be laid to deliberate discourtesy. Is it an irredeemable fault? Consider, sire, what Robert has had to bear, almost ever since his return from the Holy Land, in hearing his closest companion constantly maligned! Consider what his thoughts must have been during those days when everything conspired to make him expect the death of his prince, the execution of his friend! Remember that he himself was accused before you of felony and of rebellion, and pardon him if the blood of his ancestors mutinied in his veins! The Lion's spoken word may have been lacking in respect, but his heart has never wavered from its allegiance. To-morrow he will be ready, as he was ready yesterday, to die for you! My liege lord, I implore you, estrange not from yourself such servants as he."

"Is it to plead for your associates that you asked for this audience?" said René, ill-pleased. "Have you nothing to urge in your own behalf?"

"Before I think of myself, I must think of my King. It is my duty to repeat to him, for the last time: 'Beware of Louis of France; beware of his creatures!'"

Guy had lowered his voice, but Cornelius heard, trembled, and endeavored to protest. Fougereuse appeared not to have noticed him, and the King hushed him with a movement and a look. Then, turning towards the fallen favorite, he said, in a sorrowful, fretful old voice: "Baron de Fougereuse, you abuse my patience. Answer the accusations brought against you."

"I must know them first! I was thrown into prison on the suspicion of poisoning. I made oath that I was guiltless, before the entire court. Afterwards it was admitted that your Majesty's swoon came from another cause. What more can I say?"

"They charge you with black magic, with witchcraft, with damnable operations" —

"That I might win and keep the affections of my King!" Fougereuse finished the sentence. "Let it be his part to declare whether his friendship for me was due to Satanic influences, or whether it was his own free gift."

"Your proceedings speak against you. Wolfram's house, your secret room at home" —

"Without lock or key: oh, aggravating circumstance! How does that affect me? Has not your Majesty a private closet where the profane cannot enter, and where your master-illuminators do their work?"

"The disappearance of Vincent and of Loïc after your arrest" —

"Vincent and Loïc are not so far but that I can summon them to reappear, not as the accomplices of a sorcerer, but as the witnesses of an innocent man. I am quoting the words of my cousin Walter de Maulny, since your Majesty chooses to rehearse his indictments of me. Am I to suppose that on such grounds my sovereign condemns me without appeal?"

"I demand the truth, Fougereuse!" said René, fixing his bright eyes upon the prisoner. "You cannot deny that there is something to conceal in your career."

"Ah, that is my real crime!" cried the young baron bitterly. "I will state to my King what I have stated to my comrade-in-arms: that I have indeed something to conceal, and that I am under vow not to make it known; but that my conscience and my honor are without a stain. Villepreux was satisfied, sire, with this much; yet you know him to be hard to satisfy in all such matters."

"But I will not be satisfied with it!" cried the King testily. "My toleration is exhausted. On your allegiance, vassal, I order you to reveal to me your life's secret! On that condition I will pardon you."

"Have I not explained to your Majesty that my solemn oath obliges me to be mute?"

"It is a lie!" rejoined René, transported with his vexation. "I do not believe you. You are trying to evade the acknowledgment of your guilt, haughty Fougereuse! But I will be deceived no longer. My eyes are at last open to all your intrigues."

At the word "lie" Guy straightened himself in his chains, and there was a lightning flash in his eyes. He contained himself, however, by a sheer effort of the will, and these words alone fell from his lips: "I pity you, my liege!" For in a silence which was to last several minutes, the aged King had thrown himself into a chair, and sunk his head in his hands, as if exhausted with his emotions.

Fougereuse, still as a statue, wore his most impassive expression, and schooled himself not to give way at all. It was a trying hour for both. The incidents of the long, painful day drawing to its close, had drawn upon the physical strength and the patience of the convalescent old man. He who had been so paternally gentle with Isabelle, so noble and calm with Villepreux, so benignant toward the students, until their insistence had tired him out, had been, nevertheless, deeply hurt by the lively demonstration of his poorer subjects. These friends of the prisoner had bequeathed to him the consequences of the irritation they had awakened. It was on their account, in short, that Fougereuse found the mood of the judge so soon replace that of the indulgent master, in René of Anjou. As for Fougereuse, his own soul was heavy with disgust at the perfidy of the court, and the faithless conduct of Walter; he was full of bitterness, and by no means disposed to comport himself humbly. Attacked on every side, and with his very sovereign prepossessed against him, Guy stood upon the defensive, and refused to take one step towards conciliation.

Cornelius and the seneschal approached the King, but he repelled them with a feverish animation. "Bid every one retire!" he commanded, "and let none be so bold as to approach without an express summons. Come here, Fougereuse! . . . Nearer! . . . Well, listen. I saw what impeded you. You did not wish to talk before those others. Now we are alone, and out of hearing of the indiscreet. Do not harden your heart in this obstinate pride of yours. Speak without fear; whatever you say to your King goes no farther. Can I push my clemency to greater lengths than I do?"

"Alas, sire, I desire only justice. But I thank your Majesty for your graciousness."

The old man continued, with most persuasive goodness. "Remember the deeds of your famous father, Baron Amaury; the hereditary loyalty of your house; the honorable renown of your kindred; remember your orphan sister, that dear child, that noble-spirited woman, who begged your life of me. Would you break her heart?"

"It is because I think of my ancestral past, because I think of Isabelle's future, that I refuse to go back on my word. Would not those knights of old rise from their graves to disown me? And my sister has herself told me that she would rather weep at my tomb than to lament my damnation!"

"The dumb demon has taken possession of you. What strange delusion is upon you? Once you fall into the hands of the law, your ruin is certain.

But I cannot forget that I have loved you, Guy, and that before you shut me out, you had for me in return, an all-trustful affection. Even God does not forgive a sinner, until he shall have confessed his sin. I offer you, even at this late hour, a plenary reprieve for one open avowal! Forget that you are with your King and arbiter, and confide in your old friend. Guy, I long to have you profit by my good will towards you! But if you leave this room without having earned your pardon, your life is forfeited."

"There are other issues more important than life. What is it to live if one must live without honor? If my King refuses to hold me blameless, whom can I convince? But no, sire! I must have misunderstood you, did I not?" continued Fougereuse with great feeling. "You are but trying me; you wish to know how far my courage will lead me, and learn the true stuff of which my soul is made. It is a cruel sport, but yet I will not complain. This persistent effort to wrench my secret from me — what can I think it but a ruse? For you do not believe me capable of the deeds of darkness; you would never accuse me of commerce with the Evil One; you cannot seriously maintain that I have woven spells and practised magic! Look at me: read **my** face, my eyes, my whole being. Hear me once **more**: I tell you that I have no such flaw in me! Can I not arouse some faith in that heart of yours? My royal master, my well-beloved lord, I would awake whatever chord responsive to my touch is still in the depths of your soul.   Sire, sire ! do but trust my honor ! ”

Fougereuse had unconsciously raised his voice. His last words rang in the great room like a supreme, despairing cry.   The King, shaken by the poignant sincerity of things spoken by a conscience at bay, rose up and turned towards his attendants, who were far withdrawn.

“ Hither, my trusty ones !   Come and help to save a foolish knight who refuses life, oblivion of the past, restoration to favor !   I no longer require you, Fougereuse, to unbosom yourself of your secret; only ask for mercy, and you shall receive it.   One word, one sign of regret, and the rest shall be buried forever !   I shall never again recall these days of error and of folly.   Guy, your King is waiting for you.”

“ Yield, Fougereuse, yield, my lord ! ” exclaimed the group of courtiers with one voice, carried away by the compassion and sympathy which the sight of heroic courage will always inspire.

“ Do not play too obstinately the part of Lucifer, baron ! ” said the seneschal.   “ Be our loyal yoke-fellow once more.   I was loath to proceed against you.”

“ Accept the mercy offered ! ” the others pleaded as they came close about the prisoner.

Guy was silent, and tranquil too, amid the general excitement.   But, nevertheless, aware that he must put an end to the scene, he took a step toward René.

" I will obey you, sire. And since you all wish it, my comrades, I earnestly implore the King to accord me " —

" Pardon ! " the old monarch interrupted, with a joyful gesture.

" A trial, sire ! "

" A trial ! " exclaimed at once the King and his lords. " This is madness ! "

" I claim my right. When I was apprehended, I said I should appeal to the royal justice. The royal justice having failed me, I appeal to a jury of my peers. And to them my secret shall be told."

" You shall have your wish, Guy de Fougereuse," answered King René. " To-morrow you shall be tried and judged."

CHAPTER IV.

THE TRIBUNAL.

"Judge me, O God! and distinguish my cause from the nation that is not holy. From the unjust and deceitful man deliver me, O Lord!"
Psalm xlii.

"I HAVE brought you what you wish to wear, my lord. Your servant followed your instructions in choosing these garments, and hopes that you may be satisfied."

"Very well, Artauld: I thank you. Lay the parcel on the floor. Alanik will help me to dress."

"They have ordered me to remove your manacles. The King does not wish you to appear in them before the court, as it gives him pain to see them. Place your foot on this little stone bench, my lord, and I will file the iron links."

"I am grateful to his Majesty," replied Fougereuse, obeying the jailer. The latter seemed impatient to have his captive's fetters fall.

"It is little enough to be grateful for!" muttered Artauld, energetically beginning work on the circlet which had bruised the baron's right ankle. "But it is a good omen, in the main; and I prefer this mandate to some others."

"Did not the servant make some blunder, cousin?" asked Loïc, who was examining the package of clothes. "I spy a great many broideries. Surely, this poor gentleman is not bidden to a feast!"

"What is the little fellow saying?" the jailer inquired of Guy. "I am a bit deaf. . . . Your other foot now, my lord. One must not allow that simpleton to prattle more than is good for him!" And his eyes, raised for a moment, encountered Guy's. Artauld laid a finger on his lip, furtively, and Fougereuse nodded.

"I cannot understand Low Breton speech, my good Artauld; but I perceive that your kinsman does not approve of my costume. That is a misfortune I can hardly bear up under! For I would have Guy de Fougereuse stand before the tribunal with head held high, and in the noblest apparel of his rank. Should my judges acquit me, I would not receive their welcome verdict in a disorderly dress. And should they condemn me, I shall have arrayed the victim! . . . Have you finished? Can I walk freely?"

"Just one stroke more of the file, messire . . . There! It is done. Those villanous chains are more pleasing to me where they lie, than they were on your limbs. It is my wish never to have to rivet them on you again!"

"*Amen!* master Artauld. At what hour ought I to be ready?"

"The captain of the guards will come about two o'clock; he arrives always too early, as you know.

Have you aught else to ask?   If there were any service I could render, which is not contrary to rule ”—

“ There is none, friend.   I am thankful to you for all your good will.   You may go now: Alan will suffice me.”

The man took a step towards the door; then suddenly recalling something, he cried: “ What a threefold beast am I !   I was forgetting this.” He drew from his bosom a small box, which he handed to Fougereuse.   “ Your vassals sent it to you.   It is a medal which they had blessed on the altar of Our Lady of Pity, and they wish it may bring you better fortune.   One finds those poor villains everywhere in the churches, weeping and praying for the preservation of their lord!   It is truly touching . . . I lit a candle of my own for you.   Be of good courage, my lord!”   And the jailer went quickly out, shutting the door with a bang.

Fougereuse opened the leaden box, and took out a medal stamped with the image of Saint Christopher, the great protector against dangers and mortal accidents.   “ *Who sees the saint’s face at waking shall be joyful all the day,*” ran the quaint inscription around the rim.   A small piece of parchment, rolled, and tied with a silken string, slipped out, and fell to the baron’s feet.

“ Bring it to me, Loïc.   Some prayer, I suppose. . . . May God heed them, my poor villains, as Artauld calls them !   Let us see what their devotion has invented. What? . . . What does this mean? . . . Oh, the absurd creatures!" exclaimed the baron suddenly, crushing the little scroll. "Imagine me permitting that!"

Loïc's big eyes were sparkling with curiosity, as he came closer to his master. "Pray tell me what it is, my lord?"

"Have not these simple peasants actually persuaded themselves that they can purchase my liberty by giving hostages!" Guy continued, half in tenderness, half in distress; "and such hostages! They offer no fewer than fifty fathers of families, if that be sufficient! Vincent Govier approves strongly of all this, yet he made them send me written word of it, as he was not willing to have them act without my leave. If I consent, I have only to wear the medal over my doublet, where it may be plainly seen. What think you of the brilliant idea?"

"It is just like that old dunderhead of an equerry!" said Loïc, with a most contemptuous shrug of the shoulders. "As if one ought to go asking permission for a move like that! The thing to do is to take it, and let come what may!"

"How now, sir page? Are these the lessons you learned of me? In truth, I do not know what folly possesses every one of you. It is only a question which shall sacrifice his blood and his life for me (things I have no use for!), and dispense himself from all obedience. My old Vincent, at least, has some regard for my wishes. It is fortunate that I have time to hinder this fine hecatomb! . . . What have you to say, Loïc? If you wish to be useful to me, untie that parcel, and give me my court costume. Make haste. The captain may come at any moment; and it would be graceless of me to keep him waiting."

"Ah, if you had only been willing, my lord!" sighed the page, laying on the straw the separate portions of a rich suit. "If you had only been willing!"

"Do not let my scarf trail so on the floor . . . Well, if I had been willing. What follows?"

"You might have been a free man on the soil of Brittany! Our duke Francis would have received you with open arms, and he would have told you "—

"By all that is idiotic! Will you tease me unto everlasting, with your regrets for a conspiracy which was never perfected? You dreamed of it all last night; you wasted incredible talk upon it. Can you not console yourself for having lost the prospect of being hanged or beheaded, in the company of your dear students? . . . I believe this boy is possessed!"

"It would matter very little whom they hanged or beheaded! No price would be too high to pay for the joy of saving you, and of thwarting Maulny."

"Ah! that is what stirs your soul, is it? Do you know, my poor Loïc, I begin to fear that I have brought you up very, very badly. . . . Help me with this doublet. I cannot help asking my-self what Villepreux can do with you when he becomes your master."

"Villepreux will never be that," answered the youth, with emphasis.

Guy turned, looked him in the face, frowned, and asked gravely: "Louis de Kernis, is this a revolt?"

"It is not. God forbid, my lord. It is only a vow which I made. I have sworn never to serve any knight but you. While you live, I will follow you anywhere: yea, into exile or imprisonment. When you die, I shall enter a monastery to pray for your soul. I have made a vow, as I said before. That is all there is to it!"

"The saints assist me!" murmured Guy, vis-ibly troubled and anxious. "Come here and listen to reason." The page approached. Fougereuse placed his two hands on Loïc's shoulders, and gazed into those clear honest eyes which were lifted fearlessly to his. "My dear child, I am going to give you pain; but it is not in my power to avoid it. Know that, alive or dead, acquitted or condemned, I must part from you. I *must*. Do you comprehend?"

"My lord!" . . .

"After this, it will be impossible for me to keep with me my best servants, my dearest friends. You belong now to Villepreux, who has inherited all my duties and my rights. Your vow is null and void; you can readily be dispensed from it."

" I will never cancel it."

" Loïc, I exact as much, in the name of your allegiance! Obey me for the last time. Do not try to unriddle to-day what will be made plain by to-morrow."

" I understand that you drive me from you!"

" You are mistaken. Have confidence in me, Loïc."

" You have the right to drive me away, but not to give me to another. I will not serve my lord of Villepreux!"

" But what have you against him? He is my choice for you among a thousand. Have I not confided my own sister to him? I am not aware that Isabelle took offence at it!"

" It is different with me." argued Loïc, in a voice trembling with annoyance. " I am not your brother. I am not your vassal, nor your serf. I am not your grayhound Fergus! When you took me away from Brittany, I followed you of my own free will. I served you because I loved you : in all this world I never loved any one but you. But if my life is yours, my fidelity is my own, to do what I please with. You may kill me, but you shall not give me to somebody else ! "

He threw back his head, with the air of a young lion at bay, shook off his master's touch, and withdrew a step or two. Guy said nothing. His sad, compassionate glance was itself a call to peace, to submission : but Loïc's wild nature was too deeply wounded. " If you had but told me sooner that you were tired of me, I would have rid you of my presence. Be satisfied now, messire; for you will see me no more. God forgive you!" He ended with a sob, which he did not succeed in repressing.

Guy answered gently: "*Amen*, Loïc."

There was an instant's silence. The child turned towards his master a look of sorrow and reproach; then, covering his face with both hands, he threw himself on the stone bench, and burst into a torrent of scalding tears. Fougereuse attempted to quiet him, but the other sank deeper and deeper into his passion of despair.

"Command me to die, but let me die yours!" he wailed, in the most forlorn accents. "Remember that you reared me in your house, and will be responsible for me at the Judgment Day. You have been more than a friend to me, kinder than any father; I loved you alone; I existed only to serve you. Would you make a present of me, as if I were a horse or a falcon?"

"Silly boy!" said the baron, shaking him by the shoulder; "do you know what you are saying? Mercy on us! Did any one ever hear a page talk so to his lord? Where is your respect, sirrah?"

Loïc threw himself at Guy's feet, contrite and heart-broken.

"Please pardon me. I did not mean to offend you! Every fault I ever committed against you weighs on me like a mountain. Your last impression of me will be one of disobedience and obstinacy; and now I have been disrespectful too! I would give every drop of my blood to wash away the memory of those days of my rebellion, but you will not let me, any more. If I am too great a care for you, if you dismiss me from your side, could you not at least, out of charity, give me shelter at Fougereuse? I could sleep on the threshold of your door; I could groom your horses, or keep your armor. And if I might sometimes see you passing by, I could be happy yet. Then by and by, on the battlefield, I should know how to find my place again, how to pay my debt! You would never have to blush for the orphan of the Kernis line!"

Guy de Fougereuse was touched. He raised Loïc up, and clasped him in his arms. Hitherto, the blows aimed at the captive had not disturbed his empire over himself. But before this affection, so frank, so warm, and these entreaties, so humbly poured forth, his heart beat very fast, and his eyes moistened.

"Take not away my courage and control, Loïc," he said, "for we shall both have need of them. I obey a will stronger than my own, in separating you from me. Yet how can you think ill of your best friend? Do not mention your faults again, for they are forgotten; all I can recall now is your dauntless confidence in my honor. You believed me stainless, when my King himself accused me, and when even Villepreux needed my oath to banish his doubt. And for that, beloved child, I pray God to bless you, as I do bless you, in the name of your father, who was dear to mine. But as for following me " — Guy hesitated. Loïc's pale, imploring face affected him, and turned the balance. "Well, I leave you free: and may Heaven not impute it to me as a weakness! Do not exult too soon! Trial and sentence are yet to come," he continued, crowding his sentences, and trying to quell the fiery lad's outburst of joy; "and then, perhaps, you will ask for time to reconsider. Meanwhile, count de Kernis, I will promote you a grade towards knighthood. Be my page no longer; for I make you an equerry."

Noël!" shouted Loïc. "Brittany-Malo! Here am I, a champion. Let the Devil himself come on, and I will not budge an inch!"

"I would not jest so, Loïc. Sometimes I ask myself whether indeed we have not dealings with the Evil One and his imps, in human guise: the events of these last few days seem to me so strange. Maulny might pass for a demon in disguise."

"Maulny would be a pretty disguise for a demon!" the boy replied scornfully. "If I were Satan, I would get a better mask. This one shows his face through it! . . . Who comes? I hear Artauld's keys jingle. Could it be the guard already?"

The door opened; a slender, graceful figure glided into the cold room, and a sweet voice announced: "Guy! it is I, your sister."

"Isabelle!" exclaimed Fougereuse, embracing her fondly: "I feared they would not let you come this morning. You are too pale for a betrothed bride, darling! And why do you shiver? Are there bad tidings?"

"Speak low, brother. I am here against the King's command, against even Artauld's wish, to tell you important news, and bring you a message from Robert. Every moment of my visit is counted. The seneschal has given the command to search your palace."

"That is a prudent measure, and one that, were I in his place, I should have taken long ago. What else?"

"You know the house is guarded by the Penitent Thieves and their captain," murmured Isabelle, raising her blue eyes to her brother's.

"Which is as much as to say that the grand provost and his bowmen will have a hard time getting in. What is Robert doing?"

"He awaits orders from you. For nothing in the world would he allow any man to cross your threshold, unless by your own consent."

"How proud you are of your Lion, Isabelle! To offer resistance would be absurd. Let our Villepreux know that I have no objection to have them search the house. I dread no discoveries which they may make."

"Alas, Guy! I would I were as confident as you are; but you cannot guess what things are devised against you: lies that I hear every hour of the day. They say now that the haunted house at Pouillé hides a guest: some call him a sorcerer, some a poisoner; some will have it that it is Satan himself. The King means to send down a company of armed men, to seize the supposed magician."

"That is a wise precaution, too. There is naught in it to make you anxious, dear. . . . Well, well! Here you are in tears."

"Oh, have I not good reason for tears, brother?" said the girl, between her sobs. "My strength is gone! All these mysteries, these unknown dangers, this trial you have demanded, this death that you are braving . . . Guy, Guy, tell me they will not condemn you!"

"How can I tell, my poor child? Do you think I am a sorcerer, you also?"

"God forbid, Guy! But remember how we are following you through dark places, and do not blame me if sometimes I long for the light. I have suffered so much!" she ended, leaning her forehead against the prisoner's shoulder.

Fougereuse spoke very gravely. "Had I known how bitter this trial was to be to you, I would have done all in my power to spare you! The hand of God has brought events to a crisis, and now I must drink my chalice without looking behind. Forgive me for all you have suffered through my fault, Isabelle, dear little sister, my last sweet joy and comfort! If it cost me anything to preserve my sworn silence, it was chiefly that I felt for you, hurt by every arrow aimed at me. Forgive me that I made your young heart acquainted with grief and unrest; perhaps even with doubt."

"No!" cried Isabelle. "No, not doubt! Could I suspect you, Guy?" She raised her head, and looked at her brother with proud and trustful affection. "I have trembled, and wept, and despaired of your life; but suspected you, never! Do not reproach yourself: you have done right."

"Every one has accused me."

"Because they do not know you! They have never known you, they who dared to bear false witness against you! They were not worthy to know you!"

"Well said, my lady!" murmured Loïc under his breath.

"It has been a cruel ordeal for you, Isabelle. They tried to make you blush that you were my sister; they tried to make my name an unbearable burden to you."

"It is all the dearer to me, and so is my brother. If I have any cause of thankfulness to Heaven, it is that I am sister to-day to the prisoner, not to the judge."

"The disfavor into which I am fallen reacts on my few friends. The noblest of them all, your lover, is banished merely for upholding me."

"As for him," said the young girl, with reddened cheeks, "I prefer him, in his ruin and disgrace, to the heir of a throne. I shall go with him into exile, without a regret. Nor will I begrudge the tribulation which was the means of revealing to me our Lion's noble heart. I should not have learned how it beat only for me, Guy, save for the anguish of these days; and I should not have found out that a fund of delicate tenderness could lie under armor. I am in hopes to make him forget his Hauteclaire," she added with a little smile, "and to give him happiness in exchange for glory, and for whatever he has sacrificed for your sake."

"You are aspiring, Isabelle! Hauteclaire and glory were your only rivals. But since neither you nor Robert complain of fate, I can only thank Heaven for it all. Here I stand, delivered from every bond, seeing clearly through every illusion, every lie; alienated from my false friends, and cut off from those who paid court to me for selfish ends; retaining, in my misfortunes, the devotion of heroic hearts, and my own peace of conscience. You have one more hard day to live through, sister dear! Will you be at the hearing?"

"Yes, Guy. I shall be near Queen Margaret. I pray God to make your innocence clear, to assist your witnesses, to direct your judges."

"That is well for me. Your presence will encourage me like that of my guardian angel, and your prayers will help me through my last fight. I am staking more than life, more than honor, even: for I must fix my eternal destiny. This is an enigma to you yet; but patience, Isabelle! A few hours from now, and you will hold the key. You trust your brother, do you not?"

"I trust you blindly!" she fervently answered.

"Believe me, then, that this is the last confession of faith I shall ever ask of you. Whatever danger I seem to run during the trial, whatever be the testimony of my enemies, or my own bearing under it, do not fear at all. My farewell word is: Hope! Here comes Artauld. Go, dearest. God bless you: Our Lady hear you!"

The jailer showed himself in the crack of the door, whispering uneasily: "Make haste, my lady: the guards are just leaving the palace."

Isabelle laid her smooth forehead once more against her brother's lips, and danced away, light as a fairy. Very soon afterward, the captain of the guards entered the cell.

"The court awaits the baron de Fougereuse." Guy made the sign of the Cross, and followed the officer.

The festival hall had been selected as the scene of the solemn hearing demanded by Guy de Fougereuse. At the request of the accused man, the palace gates had been thrown open to the citizens, and the entire aristocracy were ranged about the enclosed space. The clergy, who, as a party, were favorable to the prisoner, sat upon a platform next to that of the judges. The latter, chosen from among those equal to Fougereuse by birth and rank, were presided over by the King in person. René of Anjou appeared in public for the first time since his illness. He had wished to display the royal regalia, but a great cloak edged with ermine covered him from head to foot, to

protect him against the winter cold, and the ducal
crown, which was too heavy for his feeble brows,
was replaced by a richly embroidered cap. The
wan, sensitive face of the old King was outlined
against the reddish hangings embossed with the
fleur-de-lys. Behind his armchair leaned Cornelius, flask in hand, watching him closely, and
holding himself officiously ready for emergencies.
All about was crowded the group of nobles, dressed
in black velvet, sworded, bareheaded, thoughtful.
Many of them were yesterday the foes, or at least,
the detractors of Fougereuse; yet now every sentiment of envy, hate, and resentment, as well as
of friendship, fell into abeyance; for justice must
speak. The summons of Fougereuse had roused
in their knightly bosoms a sense of honor, a conscious love of right. It was a board of soldiers,
and it might be severe; but it would scorn to
employ quibbles and trickery, in order to extort
a confession from the prisoner. Guy had made a
wise choice, in summoning his comrades-in-arms
to try him.

No one knew how it came to pass that Walter
de Maulny, bound by ties of blood to Fougereuse,
contrived to obtain a place among them. Walter,
in his brazen policy, thought this move necessary
to save his credit. Should Fougereuse triumph,
his rival was undone. It would never do for
Maulny to be examined as a witness or a plaintiff.
Only a seat with the judges could exempt him
from making any statement, or taking part in any

debate; and therefore he had most eagerly sued
for it. The King yielded to him, at a time when
he was embittered against his former minister.
René's compassionate mood had passed away,
never to return. Nothing could have so wounded
his heart, nothing could have struck so direct a
blow at his royal pride, as the refusal of Fougereuse to accept pardon, and this haughty appeal to
a jury of his peers. All was indeed over, between
the vassal and his sovereign: friendship was
broken, bounty cancelled, long service rendered
void. The gentleness which was withstood, had
changed into cold sternness which no power could
disarm. Acknowledgments, repentance, entreaty,
became thenceforth of no avail, nor could ever
pacify the offended King. Guy had exhausted
the wells of mercy; and all the more inflexible
was the wrath deserved by such ingratitude.

In a dark corner of the staging, walled by the
tapestries, were the two Queens, and young Prince
Edward. He stood aside from the company, and
appeared to ignore the proceedings; Joan of Laval,
then as always, showed herself sweet and benign;
but Margaret, in her high-spirited indignation,
seemed ready to enter the lists to overthrow the
wrong. At her feet, in shadow, was Isabelle de Fougereuse, fearing, hoping, praying with all her heart.

The throng were uneasy and excited. Curiosity
and dread and wonder were stamped on many
faces, and there were impatient murmurs and
whispering while they awaited revelations. One

or two phrases, in particular, ran from lip to lip, and were more than once repeated:

"Do you know, Fougereuse refused the King's grace!" "Did they tell you that Fougereuse asked for a trial?" "We shall know at last, what mystery there is about him!"

The students, by determined elbowing of the peaceful burgesses and the common people, had managed to range themselves in the front rank of the auditorium. No one sought to eject them, as quarrels of that sort led to many complications. They, meanwhile, wore their most professional air: bold, aggressive, ready for defence, and eager for attack. Save for the actual presence of the King, various civilities would certainly have been exchanged between these fiery champions of Fougereuse and his adversaries: lively arguments, harangues, affronts, and probably blows.

In plain view of the populace, the titled classes and the court held their own animated discussion. Not one felt himself indifferent to this question of Fougereuse's secret, which for more than a month had agitated all minds. It was no longer a matter of piquing a rival, but to behold acquitted or else condemned, a knight of ancient lineage, with whose career, honorable or dishonorable, every man had intimate concern. Some were heard to blame him for "making a scene," for having brought about all this formal pomp and show. Why not have hushed the whole thing up, so long as the King was prepared to condone it? Others charged the prisoner with foolhardiness, and expressed themselves as dumfounded at his insolent action. Suppose he were innocent, such conduct would lead only to his ultimate ruin! Was he not already too deeply compromised, unhappy being that he was, to dare attempt a public justification?

Among the minstrel-poets and the artists, there was many head-shakings, and comments of "What a pity!" for an adverse verdict seemed to them inevitable. They were sorry for Guy, for they could not defend him, nor, above all, save him. If but half of the counts brought against him were true, there would still be enough to set fire to ten stakes, instead of to one! But the chief sentiment which dominated the vast assembly was that of eagerness to see the drama end; the desire to possess the clue; the hunger for the show, which is the passion of crowds.

The soldiery, drawn up in line before the platforms, and clear around the enclosure, formed, with their impassive figures, an odd contrast with the restless multitude which filled the hall. In their helmets. and with lances at rest, the rough, sunburned men stood perfectly still. Such was their wont, under orders; and if need there were, they would have remained until the morrow, in the selfsame attitude, without the revolt against duty of a single muscle. But a sharp observer might have read dejection in their eyes. They fretted to have been called out to see the brave baron Guy arraigned as a criminal.

The cathedral chime struck two. A confused stir in the outer galleries, into which the press of people had overflowed, indicated that the waiting was soon to be over. The doors of the audience-chamber opened before the captain of the guards. After him, marched four armed men, and in their middle, Guy de Fougereuse. As he advanced, silence fell. All eyes were turned towards the once fastidious gentleman, brought as a captive from the dungeon straw. In a general thrill of astonishment, the citizens and the court beheld the Fougereuse of the old time, in whom nothing betrayed the caprices of fortune. or the change in his own destinies. Carefully dressed in a splendid costume of the royal colors, in a stuff shot with gray and silver threads, and worked with arabesques of black, and adorned with an emerald necklace, the richest heirloom of his family, the young baron stepped as if going to a festival. His clear, keen eyes had a sparkle of energy and will. His carriage had the "grand air of Fougereuse;" his whole person was stamped with proud and quiet dignity. In vain would any one have searched his face for a trace either of presumption or of fear. Master of himself, he would not seek to brave his judges, nor to cow them. His easy gait belonged rather to a prince condescending to his subjects, than to a vassal summoned before his liege lord; yet it was far from effrontery or affectation. This intrepid serenity, which used to characterize him in battle, conferred, on this occasion, a very especial charm. It was as though Guy de Fougereuse had outsoared all human authority, and had given his allegiance only to a Power not of earth.

The singular spectacle of an arraigned man in gala attire, amid judges in mourning, and a sombrely clothed assemblage, struck some present with superstitious horror. More than one person crossed himself with a trembling hand, while he gazed at Guy, as if he came from the unknown world of spirits.

"Apollo!" was the comment of a Provençal troubadour, as the prisoner went by.

"No; Oberon rather, King of Fairyland!" replied another from Lorraine, whose imagination was seized by the poesy of the North.

When Fougereuse reached the students, they began to wave their caps. "Courage, my lord!" they cried. "We are all for you!" René frowned. Guy gave them a look and a sign, and suppressed the too enthusiastic manifestation.

The accused knight arrived at the foot of the platform where the tribunal was, respectfully uncovered his head, and bowed low to the sovereign; then he slowly scanned the faces before him. His glance crossed that of René of Anjou. It was but instantaneous, yet long enough to let Guy de Fougereuse know that he had lost his King. The others were not pleased at this mute inspection. At a sign from René, the seneschal rose, to begin the examination. In answer to Philip de Beau-

vau, Guy briefly declared his name and his titles.
When he was asked to swear upon the Gospels
that he would answer truly such questions as were
addressed to him, he reflected for an instant, before
laying his hand on the holy book.

"I myself convened this gathering," he said, in
a ringing voice, "and thus do I take oath in its
presence. I swear that I am innocent of treason
towards my lord and King, and innocent of all
practices forbidden by the Church. I promise on
these Gospels to reply truly; but I reserve my
right to make the whole truth known at such a
time, and in such a manner as my conscience thinks
proper. So help me God, and the ever-glorious
Virgin Mary."

The judges looked at one another, with surprise
and disapproval. They had expected some sort of
exoneration from the defendant; but here he was,
on the offensive. and deigning to expound his
intentions! What was behind this superb assurance? Did it spring from a pure record, or from
supernatural strength, strength from hell? Fougereuse's attitude had never been more enigmat-
ical.

"My lords and gentlemen, my compeers, my fellow soldiers!" he continued. "I have demanded
your decision of these things, so that I might clear
before all men a name which all men have slan-
dered. I confide my cause, without anxiety, to
your hands, and rely upon your impartiality. But
I also require that you shall acquaint me with the

motive underlying my imprisonment and condemnation. I seek satisfaction from you, for having been arrested and judged without a hearing!"

"You have not been judged, baron," said René, straightening himself in his chair. "What is this inopportune plaint to us? You strangely forget both decorum and the favor which was extended to you."

"Sire, I forget nothing; but I owe the truth to the tribunal. . . . The King offered me my pardon yesterday, in exchange for an avowal. My lords, whom does one wish to reprieve, if not a man already condemned? I knew, therefore, that my sentence had been passed. I knew that more than one mouth, in this company, had pronounced it." Guy turned himself slightly towards the courtiers, who began to murmur. There was a moment of general uneasiness. Seeing the King's features contract and his eyes kindle, Beauvau hastened to intervene.

"There has been neither judgment nor sentence, my lord of Fougereuse. To assert it is to proffer a gratuitous insult to the royal justice. In your situation, it would be more fitting to suppress these audacities, which do not serve to deceive us."

"I have nothing to suppress, sir seneschal. I have lost all I had, save honor; and that I must defend at the cost of the rest. Meanwhile, I accept your assurance. I will content myself with asking whether it was by regular orders that a spy was imposed upon me in my prison."

"A spy!" cried René, whose good heart abhorred the thought of cruelty or craftiness. "What does it mean, Beauvau? Are you not aware how repugnant these measures are to me? What bold interloper has committed so formal a disobedience?"

"I know not, sire," the seneschal quickly responded. "I never uttered a word which could authorize such a thing. Let the captain of the guards be brought hither, and the jailer Artauld."

Maulny dared not breathe, but he called all the powers of evil to his aid. He cursed Jacob, of whose fate he was ignorant. He cursed Fougereuse, whose untoward boldness upset his calculations. To what would it all lead? The captain and Artauld were already on their feet, and prepared to testify. Walter leaned over towards Cornelius, and said something in a low voice. The physician left the King's chair, and advanced to the front of the staging.

"The order originated with me, sire," he announced, with his usual pompous air. "Fearing for your precious life, suspecting the accused of promoting the disease which was wasting you, dreading, in short, his abominable and sorcerous spells, I decided that it was necessary to have Fougereuse watched. I take upon myself the whole responsibility for an act of zeal dictated by disinterested devotion, and which was approved by several officers of your household."

The captain of the guards protested. "I believed it was the King's own order, for as such it was given to me! Otherwise "—

Artauld declared that there could be no great harm done, taking into consideration his choice of a spy: a Breton idiot, who could not speak two words of French. The brave jailer added that he should never have had the heart to admit a shrewder fellow, who might have brought his prisoner to an evil end.

"You, at least, acted like a Christian!" exclaimed René, whose eyes shot fire. "Our laws may be severe, but I wish them to be fair and open, even to the worst of criminals. I see what was in your minds. You considered me as practically a corpse; you looked forward to an interregnum! *Pasques-Dieu!* as swears my nephew of France, the hope of some who wished me dead shall be crossed. I shall not so soon require you to wear mourning for me : I mean to live long enough to see my wishes respected."

A silence ensued after these words of the aged monarch. Cornelius took his place, with an air of ruffled dignity, and Walter thanked—Satan. Owing to the docility of the leech, who was only too glad to push himself forward, Maulny succeeded in warding off the danger; he could not now find himself compromised, though he had been the sole author of the obnoxious deed. Cornelius, who was obtuse and slow, served willingly as his shield. There remained but Jacob to consider. What had become of Jacob, if he never had entered the cell at all?   Where did that indispensable witness hide himself, he whose deposition, dictated in advance, was going to be Walter's revenge, and Guy's certain fall?   Could Fougereuse have won him over? . . . Had Villepreux done away with him? . . . Was he lurking there in the crowd? . . . If he should be missing when he was wanted! . . . At this thought, Maulny bit his lip, in a fury of anxiety.   Surely, an evil star pursued him.   Could he never escape it? . . .   And yonder was Guy, calm and smiling.   What demon possessed him, that he should be so sure of himself, in the very hour of his ruin?   What was it, — the secret of Fougereuse?

A debate arose between the seneschal and the prisoner.   The question of the poisoning had been waived, but the baron insisted that it should be brought into view, and claimed the right to have it sifted.

"What, gentlemen!   Was I not imprisoned on the strength of that calumny, and do you now refuse to give me the reason for your suspicious? You allege that I am no longer considered guilty. So far, so good; but I wish to know how I ever came to be considered guilty of the odious crime. You cannot deny me that privilege!"

Somewhat embarrassed, the seneschal threw the blame on circumstantial evidences, and on malicious reports.

"Strange rumors touching you were in circulation, Fougereuse, and your behavior bore them out. You affected to devote yourself to occult researches, and it was you who poured into the King's cup the beverage which instantly caused him to faint away. The physician declared it to be a case of poison; I gave the order for your arrest. Since then, it has been established that no poison was administered. Let this suffice you. Why do you take pains to recall so horrible a charge, when many another one is heavy on your head?"

"Because I wish to clear myself completely. I find it unbearable to have been accused of assassination and high treason by my King, my friends, and the whole city. I invoke his Majesty as witness. When the hunt was over, sire, you commissioned me to get you a flask of Naples wine. I respectfully urged upon you that it might be detrimental to your health, that Antonio Blandini had positively forbidden it to you, especially in the season when fever is prevalent. But you answered that my duty was to obey. I bowed, and sent young Fleurenville ahead to the appointed meeting-place, telling him to find out whether any of the huntsmen had some Italian wine with him. At the very moment when we rode up, the little page handed me a flagon with a chased silver stopper, and a cup of the same metal . . . Do you not remember, sire?"

"It was quite so," René replied. "But what is the use? I do not reproach you with that crime."

"Some others did and do reproach me, your

Majesty. I took that cup and flagon from the boy, without inquiring how he obtained them, and under your own eyes I poured the Naples wine. A few moments later came that swoon which threw us all into consternation, and I was despatched to the tower, by mandate of Philip de Beauvau. I have not learned yet to whom the cup and flagon belonged. Fleurenville alone can tell us."

"Let Paul de Fleurenville be called," said the King.

"There is no need of it, my lord and father," a voice began, close to the aged sovereign's ear, "for I know the owner of the silver vessels, and I would ask the court to accept my testimony." And Edward of Lancaster, Prince of Wales, stepped forward on the platform, and stood before his grandfather.

"Speak then, my son," said René.

"I declare," continued the heir of England, "that both cup and flask belonged to me, and that Fleurenville received them from me when he brought them to Fougereuse. The Naples wine was my refreshment after exercise. I had already used a portion of it, before lending it to the King. Unluckily for the prisoner, my horse was carrying me homeward, when I met the page. Had I been present at the time, I should have opposed the arrest of the baron de Fougereuse. This is the truth, on the faith of a prince and of a Christian."

René turned toward Cornelius, who grew pale

with spite and fear, and, in his heart, wished young Edward a thousand miles beyond sea. " I disapprove your hasty action, doctor. How could you have spoken so lightly that fatal word 'poison,' which has engendered all the distresses we suffer under to-day?"

"My zeal for your Majesty's welfare. . . . Sire, the alarm being apparently justified . . . deceptive symptoms. . . . Science is not infallible! . . . I knew I was wrong from that same evening."

"And yet I was kept in confinement," Guy added slowly, "although. almost from the first, my enemies themselves exonerated me. Do you call that justice?"

"There are other counts against you, baron," resumed the seneschal, "and I doubt if you can so readily dismiss them."

"Before turning to these, sire, I beseech you that I may force the court to declare whether I am relieved from this odious accusation of poisoning!"

The judges conferred for some minutes in a low tone, then they spontaneously rose. "We attest that Guy de Fougereuse is entirely innocent of having attempted the murder of his sovereign lord by poison, and we demand to hear the remaining indictments brought against him."

A sympathetic thrill ran through the auditors. The students openly applauded. Maulny, disappointed, clenched his fists. Yet he took heart, reflecting that, according to his own canons, his cousin Fougereuse had committed the worst of blunders: he had proved to his superiors that they were in the wrong. Walter felt that henceforward the jury and the defendant would be at swords' points.

Then the regular legal process commenced. The accusations ranged themselves under two principal headings. One was, that Fougereuse had bewitched the King, and harmed his health by evil influences, in order to secure that empire over the royal mind which Cornelius disputed with him; and that these spells and sorceries employed, originated in the closet which shut without lock or key, in his palace in town. The second was, that Fougereuse gave asylum to a magician in Wolfram's house, and resorted to him by night, that he might study damnable arts, and conjure up infernal spirits.

"I deny it absolutely," replied the baron, when the seneschal had read the allegations. "It is an absurd tissue of inventions and popular fables, with no basis but maudlin gossip. During six years, I held the perfect confidence of the King, and it was only six weeks ago that men began to impugn my motives and my actions. I protest strongly against these calumnies."

"So you deny it all?" asked Beauvau.

"All, without exception."

"Fougereuse, that is not tenable!" cried the old count d'Etriché, who sat in the front row of officials. The whole jury repeated after him: "No! It is not tenable."

"Will you be so good as to tell me why not?" the prisoner exclaimed.

"Because we have evidence," answered Felix d'Etriché. "Your commerce with hell is a matter of public notoriety."

"'Everybody says so:' is it not that?" said Guy, with his light sarcastic smile. "I am familiar with the argument, for I have heard it many a time on frivolous or ignorant lips. But I hardly expected to meet it in a hall of justice!"

"You have never refuted the general opinion, before to-day. What was your object in strengthening it by your silence?"

"Since I have lived the life of courts, gentlemen, experience has taught me this: foolish is he who would undertake to chain up a mountain torrent, and yet more foolish he who would stop the flood of detraction and malice which flows from idle tongues! I scorned to notice the chatter, or to contradict it, so long as the King honored me with his favor. Nothing else mattered much! But to-day, my illustrious master doubts me; and therefore have I invited a solemn judgment, that to all these falsehoods I might give the lie."

"The tribunal has the right to exact proofs of your bold statements."

"'What you freely deny, I may as freely affirm,'" Fougereuse rejoined, quoting an old philosophic axiom. "I await your proofs before producing mine."

"You passed the night of November fifteenth

in the haunted house in Pouillé wood. Do you
admit it?"

"I will say neither 'Yea' nor 'Nay.' Have you
witnesses to the fact?"

"Call Jacob Piteux," ordered the seneschal,
raising his voice. The bailiffs called. Silence
answered. Maulny felt the cold sweat stand on
his brow.

"What has become of Piteux aforesaid?" inquired Philip de Beauvau, irritably.

"Disappeared!" cried some one in the crowd.

At the seneschal's request, the man who had
spoken came forward, making an awkward salute.

"Who are you?"

"Martin Bodin, messire, proprietor of the Red
Rose, the best inn in Anjou."

"Are you acquainted with this Jacob Piteux?"

"He is my cousin."

"How do you know he has disappeared? What
was the manner of his disappearance?"

"How do I know it? Because the day before
yesterday he came to me in the evening, and
asked for supper and lodging. And the manner
of it? It was in the manner of robbers, to wit:
Jacob decamped by night with a good fur cloak
that I had from my uncle Jasper, and with a fat
purse belonging to a travelling gentleman. And
you need never expect master Piteux to return to
you!"

The seneschal made a negative gesture; Maulny
bit his lip for anger. Jacob had tricked him, and

had escaped at the critical moment, with his gold and his secrets! The flight of his spy threw Walter into a great perplexity, for in Piteux he lost his certain aid to success. Nevertheless, he resolved to strive desperately to win this last fight with Fougereuse, and he put on a bold face.

Philip de Beauvau detained the innkeeper, and questioned him thoroughly, concerning the night of the fifteenth of November at the Red Rose. Bodin related in detail all that had taken place, speaking slowly, recollecting himself now and then, and endeavoring to reassure the court as to the trend of the adventure. According to him, it was a mere spurt of fun, following a drinking-bout. Vincent Govier made a jovial fellow's brag; Loïc was playing a fantastic joke, as boys are wont to do. The very next day, were not both of them present at the tourney, full of health and spirits? What could be brought against the proprietor of the tavern, in regard to their going to the Devil's House? He had done everything in his power to hold the equerry back, and he had carefully nursed the page. Since that time, he had had no dealings with them: he had no desire to compromise himself by getting entangled with current gossip. The Red Rose was a well-kept, well-patronized, decent, Christian place; and Bodin was a good son of holy Church, and a faithful subject of King René. All the harm came from Jacob, who would never stop telling stories of the supernatural, to amuse the guests and bring the inn into disrepute.

No one had ever noticed anything strange or suspicious about the east side of the turret, up to the last November.   "And notwithstanding the fact that you see *that* from the windows!" Martin concluded, with a sigh.

"Is this all you know?" asked the seneschal.

"All, my lord."

"The equerry and little Kernis could tell us more," remarked Felix d'Etriché.   "Neither of them fled away from the lodge without some good reason."

"You see, gentlemen," said Walter de Maulny, "that the absence of the witnesses is an intentional part of the defence!   It is easy for Fougereuse to defy us to establish the crime, when our means of doing so are withdrawn."

Guy smiled, not without disdain.   Turning towards the great assemblage, he cried:

"Vincent Govier!"

"Present, my lord!" replied a burly voice.

"Come.   You are needed."

Govier obeyed.   No one had encountered him since the imprisonment of his master, and the sight produced something of a sensation among the people.   A hundred grotesque rumors had been circulated about him.   They had had him carried off by demons, drowned in the Maine, shut up in the magic closet, changed into a werewolf: yet here was master Vincent in his own flesh and blood, perfectly stolid, and in the correct military attitude.

"Whence are you?" King René asked.

The veteran saluted, and answered: "From the palace of the baron de Fougereuse."

"Why have you lain hidden recently?"

"I was under orders."

"Whose orders?"

"My lord of Villepreux's."

"Robert wished to save my servants from the rack," Fougereuse interpolated. "I know that his Majesty held no threat over them, but they were in some danger, so long as we feared the death of the King."

"What zeal!" commented René of Anjou, casting a cold glance at Cornelius and at Walter. "Reply without fear, Vincent. What was your motive in going to Wolfram's house?"

"To cut short the talk of my lord Walter de Maulny, in regard to my master."

"I should like to remind the court," interrupted Walter, "that it is the policy of the supporters of Fougereuse to mix my name with all their fictions and imaginings."

"Fictions!" echoed Vincent hotly. "Is it any fiction, messire Walter, to maintain that you never loved the Fougereuse family, and that you cherished always a particular grudge towards my young lord? Will you deny having told me that your cousin had given his estates in fief to the Devil, and that his tenant would yet lure him to the scaffold? And imaginings!" growled the old soldier, with rising wrath: "who ever knew Vincent Govier to imagine anything?"

"Well! that is by no fault of yours, my trusty one!" Guy said gently, while the nobles on the judicial bench exchanged an involuntary smile.

"What did you find at the haunted house?" continued the seneschal.

The equerry turned towards his master.

"Answer, friend: for this is the proper time," the prisoner assented.

"I will do as you wish, my lord. . . . The first thing that I found, sir seneschal, was Val."

"Val?" repeated the seneschal.

"The baron's horse," Govier explained. "The poor dear beast was standing in a hut of branches, and whinnied joyfully when he saw me. I feared some misadventure had befallen my master; and I threw myself against the turret door, beating it with my fist, and shouting with all my might."

"No one replied, no one opened to you?"

"Yes, indeed yes! A voice came through the window: 'Vincent Govier! what are you doing here at this hour?' I said: 'I am looking for my master, the baron de Fougereuse, and I mean to have him, alive or dead!' After a few minutes the door was unlocked, and I nearly fell backwards, I was so amazed!"

"What did you see?" Several of the judges had spoken together.

"My young lord himself, with a lantern in his hand."

A shiver ran through the audience, at this unexpected revelation. The judges looked at one another. Guy remained calm, and gave no sigh. "Go on," he commanded his equerry.

"Then," resumed the witness, "the baron accosted me. 'Govier,' said he, 'you are not at your post. Return at once to Angers, and get my household ready for a tourney which the King intends shall take place to-morrow. And keep silence until you receive fresh orders!' Well, I obeyed, item by item. I took the road to Angers, and arrived home after two o'clock. That is why they did not see me again at the Red Rose. At dawn, my young lord appeared there among his retainers; he examined my preparations, and he ended with: 'Vincent, you have done well!'"

"And then?" prompted Beauvau, as Vincent came to a pause.

"That is all, sir seneschal."

"What explanation of the affair did the baron offer?"

"Why, none!" exclaimed Vincent, surprised. "He never spoke of it at all."

"And you never sought to find an explanation?"

"My master had warned me: 'Keep silence, until you receive fresh orders.' I waited for those orders."

"Did you report aught of this to any one?"

"Not even to my confessor. I repeat, I had instructions to hold my tongue."

"Yet it is impossible that you did not think about it!" cried René.

"I had no instructions to think about it."

" You are playing the machine, soldier," the seneschal resumed, " but you cannot deceive us. What do you know about the little closed room in Fougereuse's house here in town?"

" That it was built by the first Lord Amaury, God rest his soul! after he became gouty and deaf; for he needed a place like that, where he could safely confess to his chaplain."

" Does it serve the same purpose with Baron Guy?"

" I do not know. My lord does not tell us anything about his private devotions."

" Have you sometimes seen your master go into it?"

"No, messire."

" Did you ever enter it yourself?"

" Never."

" What does the baron conceal in it?"

"Sir seneschal," broke forth the equerry, who could hardly keep his patience, " for two hundred years the Goviers have lived and died in the service of the family of Fougereuse, not in the quality of spies, but in that of followers-at-arms!"

The students cheered this answer on the part of the old soldier. The court deemed it useless to interrogate him further. Vincent had said all that he could say; they could have cut him into inch pieces, sooner than extract a word more from him.

"Baron Guy de Fougereuse," called Philip de Beauvau, " to what do you object in the deposition of Vincent Govier?"

" I object to nothing."

" Do you agree that it is true?"

" It is very accurate. Vincent can neither lie nor invent."

" Do you now acknowledge your presence at the haunted house, on the night of November fifteenth?"

" I acknowledge it."

" You remember having commanded your equerry to keep your secret?"

" I do."

" What was your reason for being there at that hour, and why did you constrain Vincent Govier to silence?"

" I will answer in due time. Summon the other witnesses."

The court deliberated. The imperiousness of the prisoner displeased them, and his refusal to explain was thought to be incriminating. The seneschal beckoned to the bailiffs, and whispered a name.

" The young count de Kernis!" cried four nasal voices in chorus.

There was a commotion in the crowd, as a Breton peasant, with loose curls and tanned cheeks, turning the brim of a huge hat round and round in his hands, emerged, bowed to the tribunal, and stood waiting to be questioned.

" What is this?" asked the seneschal, scrutinizing the strange creature, whose bright eyes and roguish smile belied his rustic appearance. " I summoned Kernis."

"And this," murmured Walter, "is some familiar demon, which the Evil One has placed at Fougereuse's disposal."

The witness poised proudly his supple figure, and tossing his long locks, announced:

" I am the last descendant of Noménoë, King of Brittany. My name is Louis Artus III., Count de Kernis."

" Loïc!" exclaimed several of the lords. "Impossible! Such a transformation is beyond human power! "

" There is no sorcery at work, messires. I beg his Majesty's pardon for presenting myself before him with my hair and my complexion dyed, and in shepherd's clothes. I put on this disguise that I might obtain entrance into my master's dungeon."

" What!" exclaimed René. " The newly arrived cousin who spoke no French, the idiot Alanik!"

" That is it," said Loïc modestly. "I fooled Artauld."

" And you do not hesitate to avow it? " Beauvau went on, in a severe tone. " Wretched boy! do you see to what you expose yourself by this complicity in the intrigues of Fougereuse? "

" To a share in his fate, I suppose! Far from dreading that, I desire it. Sir seneschal, treat me no more as a child whom one can frighten. I am no longer a page. I have been appointed equerry."

At this declaration, made with intense pride, the judges had to smile again. Walter de Maulny made the new equerry an ironic salute, and whispered teasingly: " A thousand congratulations on your brilliant good fortune!"

" And what do you call the intrigues of Fougereuse?" Loïc boldly resumed. " If I altered my own appearance, so that I might join him in his cell, are you going to blame him for it? I did it of my own accord, without any person's advice. My master had nothing to do with it, and I am the only one responsible."

" With what design, messire de Kernis, did you so disobey the royal orders? Wherefore this trick, unworthy of a gentleman? Why such haste to communicate with a prisoner who was then suspected of an attempt to poison? "

" Why? Because I wished to .serve, in his adversity, my betrayed and forsaken lord. Because I rather thought it was my duty!"

" Can you swear that your service embraced no secret message, no plan of escape, nor conspiracy of any sort? "

" I besought the baron to fly, and to leave me as hostage in his stead. An escape was possible. It all depended upon him, and he refused."

All eyes were turned on Guy. King Rene asked: " Fougereuse, is this true?"

" Yes, sire: it is true. But there is nothing to wonder at, and no reason why merit should be imputed to me. I had no plot against the State to defeat. The whole matter was but an enthusiastic dream on the part of a child who is blindly devoted to me, who has sworn to die for me or with me, and who was determined to sacrifice his life. If this be a fault, it is one rare enough to deserve indulgence. I do not believe that your Majesty will permit it to be construed as high treason."

"The King is moved, you see!" Maulny breathed into the ear of the viscount William de la Bohalle, who sat next him. "Guy knows how to touch a responsive chord. On my soul, what consummate skill he has! If we do not control things better, this Devil's piper will play upon us all. Say a word to change the present theme, will you?"

"Answer, then, my good novice equerry!" exclaimed the viscount. "Did you not deem your master guilty, since you endeavored to arrange his escape?"

"I was convinced that my master was above reproach, but I could not forget the low, fierce hates and jealousies of which he was the object. Common talk would have it that the King was dying. Messire de Maulny was already crying victory."

"Impudent little liar!" cried Walter harshly, wincing under the dart. Loïc had aimed at him. "Dare you utter my name? What reliance will this tribunal place upon the word of a vagabond stranger, brought by Fougereuse from Lord-knows-where, associated with his own detestable deeds, caught in the act of murdering a faithful attendant of the King, and heard to utter outrageous criticisms on our venerated King himself? A hundred times have I refrained from punishing your arrogance, but now you force my hand, and I demand "—

"Demand whatsoever you please, Walter de Maulny!" Loïc sang out, eying his adversary with scornful bravado. "Your threats cannot make me alter a word of my testimony. What is this you remark concerning vagabonds, in your contempt for me? A scion of the old royal house of Brittany, I can never ask of you, 'Where are titles so ancient as mine?' but, 'Where are my equals by birth?' I see before me but one: René, our sovereign lord!"

The chivalry of Anjou was visibly disturbed: those nobles on the platform as well as those in the hall. Protests and murmurs arose against Loïc's boldness. He, standing motionless, his head thrown back, his face white with emotion, his nostrils trembling like those of the war-horse who hears the bugles, was elated with his first battle for the honor of Fougereuse. The indomitable energy of his country, its iron determination, had full swing now in the descendant of Noménoë. He was resolved to dare everything, and push on to the end, overturning all obstacles, never pausing, never flinching, never looking back, not even for love of his master. And God would do the rest!

"Now then, gentlemen, silence!" The command, in the shrill voice of the King, surmounted the din, and hushed it. "Why such astonishment, and such a clamor? The blazons of my fair

province need not blush, though they must own
that they are not derived from the kings Hoël,
Gradlon, and Noménoë. For my own part, I consider that this child flatters me, in calling me his
equal. Come hither, my dispossessed prince, and
confer with me. ' *Good blood cannot lie.*' Your
ancestors bequeathed you, instead of a throne, a
wonderful courage, if not much policy. I wish to
question you in person ; for it would be a pity that
my seneschal should set traps for one like you!"

Loïc approached the dais, and faced the King,
looking at him alone, and seeming to ignore or
disdain the others.

"Plague take the monkey!" was Walter's
thought. "With his blunders and silly speeches,
he has managed to gain the good graces of our
estimable liege, who is smitten with heroism of
the moral sort. What hallucination leads him
wantonly to ruin his career, by so clinging to a
disgraced peer? My one spy, hired on liberal
terms, has to play me false, while Guy has a free
gift of hostages, rescuers, champions, frantic at-
tachments, and reckless companionships in misfortune. And they do not impute it to sorcery! . . .
What else, first and last, is the luck of Fougereuse ?"

Having secured a witness to his liking, René of
Anjou took his time in examining Loïc de Kernis,
not indeed on the subjects of political plots, which,
to him, were of small concern, but in regard to
Guy's own habits, the mystery thrown around

them, the occupations which he concealed from all men, even from René himself, and the mainspring of the exclusions and the distrust which had wounded his old heart to the quick. The King would gladly have exculpated Fougereuse from every other offence, but he could not forgive his favorite for having secrets which he was not invited to share.

The boy's responses were clear and prompt, and without a shade of hesitation. He contradicted fearlessly whatever he thought was wrong; made sport, with his fiery, student-like humor, of the legendary tittle-tattle dear to credulous spirits; called upon a member of the jury, at need, to corroborate him; and, in general, conceded nothing to public opinion, but let fall one positive statement after another, without qualification or change. The truth was given with utter candor, and Walter de Maulny followed it with keen attention. Loïc had just been reproducing, with appallingly accurate mimicry, the language, accent, gesture, the whole little dramatic prologue, of that evening of November fifteenth. The hearers hung upon his lips, entranced by so picturesque and striking a narration. As their interest grew, their curiosity and sarcasm came into play; nor were these exercised now at the expense of the prisoner. Walter felt that he was becoming a target for sinister smiles and stolen glances, and for the biting comment which buzzed on all sides. To this volley of little steel arrows he presented his cold natural pride as his best shield. but his apprehensions were gaining upon him: for he could not prevent Loïc from making him ridiculous. There was no possible point which could be raised in opposition to a scrupulously exact, indeed, a far too exact, deposition. The page never failed to show forth Maulny's real sentiments with telling emphasis, though Maulny flattered himself that these had been impossible to divine. The young scrapegrace must have been well tutored by his master: it was not his wont to be so circumspect! One must lie in wait for the first misstep of this merciless good memory.

"Did you succeed in looking into the turret chamber from the tree?" René inquired.

"I did. sire."

. "Was Fougereuse there?"

"He was."

"Alone?"

"With one companion." Excitement stirred again among the crowd.

"Are you perfectly sure of this?"

"Yes."

"Can you tell us who the man was?"

"I do not know who he may be; I did not see his face."

"Describe him."

"He was very tall. He wore a scarlet robe, like that of the officers of the ducal palace. He had a skull-cap of the same color."

"What were they doing, he and the baron?"

"The unknown was bending towards the hearth, stirring the fire. My master was studying some manuscripts by the light of the lamp."

"Had Fougereuse the custom of visiting this house?"

"It was the first time I had ever seen him there."

"Was the unknown a transient guest, or an habitual resident of the turret chamber?"

"I do not know. I never heard any one speak of him."

"What explanation did your master offer, when you told him of your discovery?"

"I only told him of it in his dungeon. He said that my eyes had not deceived me. He said also that I was not to suppress any part of the truth, when I came to the witness-stand."

"Baron Guy," cried the King, "do you hear this child?"

"Yes, sire. Every word is correct."

"What companion had you that night? I wish to know."

"Your Majesty has given orders to have Wolfram's house searched. In a few minutes, the person desired will stand before the court."

"Do you refuse to name him?"

"I do refuse: absolutely."

"Wretch! You are risking your life."

"I am bound by a promise, and I mean to keep my word."

"This is but a pretext!" the judges objected. "Name your accomplice."

"What do you call an accomplice? Am I so notorious for sorcery that any man seen in my company must pass for an infernal agent? Since when have I forfeited my right to converse with Christian folk?"

"You cannot thus impose upon us. Acknowledge that you were entertaining Satan!" . . . "You conceal a magician there!" . . . "You are conjuring up spirits!" . . . "You conspire with traitors against our King!"

"Enough, gentlemen!" said the prisoner, in steady tones. "You were summoned hither to judge me, not to abuse me."

The haughty reminder raised a storm of indignation. But in the face of the obstinate silence of Fougereuse, there was nothing to do but resume the examination of Loïc.

"What did you think, my pretty page, when you surprised your master in a colloquy with Satan?" ironically continued Felix d'Etriche.

"I did not think, certainly, that there was likelihood of Satan's being mixed up in my master's affairs! I said to myself: 'My lord is housing somebody in trouble.' And you smile at that? Why, it is not the first time he has done such a thing! He had a leper once at Fougereuse; he used to dress his wounds in secret."

"Come, come!" was the cry all along the platform; "will you try to make us believe that you hold the baron to be a saint?"

"Yes! That is just what he is!" answered the

boy, quite beside himself at the sight of this contemptuous scepticism. "I never held him to be anything else! You will not find one of his own household who does not agree with me! Listen: I will tell you the real secrets of Fougereuse!"

And to the multitude before him, by this time worked up into a passion of interest and curiosity, Loïc de Kernis spoke. Simply as a child, fearlessly as a gallant gentleman, he began to outline broadly the inner life of Guy de Fougereuse: that life shut away from men, which could not go undetected by one in daily contact with it. Piety and charity, most fervent, most generous, had filled up the leisure hours of the King's elegant favorite. A holy soul dwelt beneath the smooth and sparkling carriage of the courtier. How often had Loïc surprised him at prayer, during the hours set apart for sleep! How often had he been the prudent go-between, when good offices and almsgiving were in question! He set forth the great love the baron had for the poor: how he sacrificed to them his time, his physical strength, his fortune; how he dedicated to them, at the hospice of Saint John, his early morning hours, day after day; how he shrank from no service he could render them, nor from any hardship involved. Kneeling before these unfortunates, he would wash their feet with as much reverence as if they were the Lord Christ Himself! . . . And what could be said of his conduct towards his own vassals? During the last epidemic of typhoid, did not Fougereuse travel into the country to his own estates, where the fever raged, and stay there till it was allayed? Was he not the only physician, the only comforter his people had, in that terrible hour? Did he not heal the sick, and bury the dead, until he was himself stricken down? And if he did not die of it all, that was Our Lady's miracle! "Believe me, my lords and gentlemen!" cried Loïc, in ardent conclusion, "believe an orphan who has slept under Baron Guy's roof, eaten his bread, tried his patience! These are the only secret circumstances, the mysteries, of his life: and this is he whom you treat as a reprobate. Saints of Brittany! who, then, are God's elect?"

The acclamations of the crowd greeted this apostrophe. Over all rang the shouts of the vassals of Fougereuse:

"Give us back our master! We offer hostages. Takes our lives, but deliver Baron Guy!"

"Liberty, liberty!" chorused the students, waving their hands.

"This is very much like sedition," said the seneschal, rising to his feet. "Guards, remove the ringleaders."

"No, Philip," the King interposed, with animation. "It is your severity which alienates my subjects from me. Their affection may express itself in questionable ways, but it is warm and true; I am unwilling to have it taken from me. . . . Answer, baron de Fougereuse. Is it a work of mercy which you have been so carefully concealing at the haunted house?"

"No, sire."

Again the group of lords exchanged a significant look. They had remained impassive and incredulous while Loïc presented his frank plea. With these worldly men, far more inclined to accredit evil than to spend their enthusiasm upon virtue, the venomous hints of Maulny outvalued the fond revelations of the young page. For a long time, Fougereuse had been a suspected character. It cost too much to acquiesce at once in his innocence, and even good King René sadly shook his head.

"I affirm," Loïc continued, "nay, I swear to you, that my master has been cruelly belied. I have .proofs of it."

"Eh? Let us have them!" the King replied impatiently. "We are not here to hearken to panegyrics."

"Then let me draw up an arraignment, sire. . . . There lives one who holds Baron Guy in immortal hatred. He glides along in the dark, like a thief, to keep track of his operations; he sends spies to dog his footsteps; he does not blush to defame, by means of the most brazen inventions, the honor of a family which nurtured him. I, even I, have seen this traitor waiting, at the corner of a disreputable street, for the miserable informer whom he hires, and I have heard them planning their infamous revenges. To pierce an adversary to the heart with a poniard, — that is a vulgar business. But to wound him in his reputation, by a calumny, without running any risks, without compromising one's self ; to see him fall into disgrace, droop under condemnation, and die a shameful death on the scaffold or at the stake ; — that is a stroke of genius ! And that is what the two accomplices engaged to do. They made a division of labor : one was to destroy the standing of the favorite, at court, by innuendoes cleverly strewn about ; the other was to excite the popular imagination with gross rumors. On that particular evening their chief industry had been to represent the baron as a vampire who fed by night on the bodies of the dead. The spy undertook to get him accused, in time, of all the crimes of Giles de Retz. before a single voice should be raised in protest, so infinitely befooled can people be ! Both of them laughed aloud at the docility of their dupes, as at so many long-eared asses. But they began to quarrel as soon as ever the underling claimed his salary. The gentleman drew his dagger, and said in a fury : ' Villain ! I will pay you with this.' Then the poor devil shook with fear, and started off, shouting ' Help ! ' I ran up, and received the slender blade full in my arm, for it had been thrown like a javelin, in the Italian fashion. Of course it was not meant for me, but I kept it, without scruple, as my share of the booty. I have it with me, sire. Behold it ! "

" You lie ! " roared Walter de Maulny. " You stole it from me."

" Take your own property, my lord," added Kernis, with a withering smile. " I did not mention your name, but your conscience has a voice louder than mine."

" I proclaim, sire," cried Maulny, " that a bolder imposture never saw the light of day. This page is Fougereuse's imp of wickedness, and would sell his chance of salvation to benefit his master. Falsehood is his element. How can we endure the presence of such an impudent trickster? Away with you, son of a sorceress! "

" You forget yourself, Maulny," said the King dryly. " I alone have the right to order any one hence. If you be accused unfairly, vindicate yourself. You will be heard, according to the law of equity, which it is our duty to maintain."

" I shall not stoop to a vindication," Walter replied wrathfully; " and I am astounded that any should be expected of me. My honor is above suspicion! "

" Ah! since when? " cried several sarcastic voices from the group of University youths. The smiles and whispers which this sally evoked so exasperated their victim that he lost control of himself. He began to abuse Loïc, to brave his equals beside him, to threaten the students; he even offered to put out any pair of eyes which ventured to look insolently at him. Cornelius, who endeavored to quiet him, was brutally repulsed, and dubbed a poisoner.

" He is crazy, sire; crazy clear through! " exclaimed the doctor in consternation.

“Walter, Walter!” arose to right and left of Maulny. . . . “It is a delirium, gentlemen.” . . . “It is an attack of insanity!” . . . “It is more like a possession.” . . . “He has been bewitched!”

“Sire,” the seneschal broke in, “whether Maulny be guilty or only demented, we desire that he shall no longer sit as one of us.”

“Maulny, leave the platform,” René commanded sharply. “You are no longer a judge, but are yourself upon trial.”

“Who dares accuse me, who dares?” Walter gathered himself together, and faced the King, as Lucifer, in his defeat, might turn under the heel of Michael the Archangel. “I defy every one of you!”

“It is I who accuse you, Walter de Maulny,” Loïc said: “I accuse you, in the presence of God and of your earthly sovereign, of having, through your calumnies, attempted to destroy the life and the good name of the baron Guy de Fougereuse. Do not deny it; you have betrayed yourself.”

“Varlet! Ape of a Breton! You lie.”

“You know I do not lie, my lord of Maulny!”

“The honor of Fougereuse was as dear to me as my own. How then, could I have contrived the infamous campaign which this infernal young scoundrel assigns me?”

“You had always a jealous grudge against your cousin Guy; you have hated him beyond redemption, since he prevented you from paying suit to the lady Isabelle. You have never ceased pursuing him with your rancorous perfidy. Have we neither ears nor eyes, we of the household of Fougereuse, here in Angers? Is not there one among us whom you have not tried to corrupt, or tempted to talk! They will witness to it. And what baseness did you not employ in my own case, when you knew I had fallen under my master's displeasure? What did you not say to me, to estrange me from him, and extort some confession from me, to his disadvantage?"

"You and your master have sworn to ruin me, because you feared my knowledge of your seditious intrigues, and diabolic customs, and heathenish crimes. You have both been seen performing your wicked incantations; you have been heard"—

"Oh, go on! I know the whole rigmarole. Your worthy associate composed it for you, piece by piece, at the corner of Chaperonnière Street, on the evening when I had the honor and happiness of overhearing your conversation."

"Whelp! Jacob Piteux never used such language. It looks well for you to blame him, when your master has treacherously caused him to disappear, in order to escape being condemned by his testimony! I require"—

"You are compromising yourself, my noble lord. It is not Piteux whom I denounce."

"A truce to your fits of temper, Maulny!" exclaimed René, as he saw the enraged knight take a step forward, with bloodshot eyes. "You admit, then, that you are acquainted with this Piteux?"

"Yes, sire," Walter answered, desperately holding out against hostile circumstance; "yes, sire: I am acquainted with him, and I would give my right arm to have him here, as his mere presence would drive this barefaced liar underground. But Jacob has vanished. His silence was necessary to Fougereuse. Dead men tell no tales."

For some moments preceding, the attention of the public had been drawn from the hearing, and had concentrated itself on a certain part of the hall, where some disturbance had arisen. Just as Walter, in his hardihood and fancied security, deplored the absence of the important witness, a sonorous voice rang from the crowd: "You have your wish, messire de Maulny: here is Jacob Piteux!"

Every head turned immediately towards a side door, which swung to. There Villepreux's manly countenance towered over the crowd; and a little less tall than he, were two bronzed, dark-eyed figures, with glittering white teeth: a couple of Penitent Thieves in silhouette against the light.

"Jacob!" was the cry. "But where is Jacob?"

"Make way!" commanded Robert, stretching his hand over the heads nearest to him. And as if by magic, a path opened through the surging multitude. One could see in quick advance, emerging from the confused mass below, the three casques of Saracen steel, flashing as they came. Once they had reached the enclosure, there appeared, between the soldiers, a little, shrunken, shaking, pitiable being, who had been indistinguishable until now. At a sign from their chief, the Thieves released their unhappy captive; and Villepreux, picking him up by the sleeve, shoved him to the edge of the tribunal, saying: "Jacob Piteux, my lords!"

The judges bent forward curiously, to examine the witness so eagerly reclaimed. Looking rather like a trapped fox than like a human creature called in to further the ends of justice, Jacob bemeaned himself more and more, wriggling his spine, and casting sullen, furtive glances from side to side. Maulny stood speechless before his inopportunely recovered spy, whose arrival cut the ground from beneath his closing statement.

"Your Majesty, and you, my lords," Villepreux began, "accept my testimony in regard to this man. Three days ago, my soldiers caught him in the very act of espionage, outside a lower door of the palace of Fougereuse. For that matter, he did not deny his honorable calling, but maintained that he followed it for the benefit of another, a fine gentleman, whom he accused of paying him very irregularly. As he said he had just been hurt by the hoofs of one of my horses, I had him charitably cared for, and kept out of sight until further orders. He was willing enough, until I let him know that he would be wanted at this trial in the quality of witness. Then terror seized him, and he implored me to let him go. I refused; but he dispensed with a per-

mission, and succeeded in escaping from the house.
My Thieves, however, are not dismayed at a little
thing like that. They scented the runaway, over-
took him in the open country, some miles out,
and brought him home. Here he is."

"Very good, Villepreux," René said with some
stiffness; for the sight of the captain of the Penitent Thieves brought back to him the memory
of a painful scene. "Very good: the tribunal
thanks you. . . . Approach, my man, and speak
without any misgiving. Under the shield of
your King, you have nothing to fear. If you are
not exempt from blame in this affair, confess your
wrong-doing frankly, and receive your certain pardon. But remember that we must have the truth,
and the whole truth. Do you understand?"

"I understand, my dread sovereign lord, and
I swear to reply as honestly as at the Last Judgment," responded Jacob, bowing down to the
ground. "I throw myself entirely upon the clemency and the gracious protection of your Majesty,
which were never invoked in vain."

"I require no flattery from you. What is your
name?"

"Jacob Piteux. My family is connected with
the middle class, and my relative Bodin, who was
formerly under arms for the King, will go bail for
me."

"Will I, monster?" shouted the innkeeper,
leaning forward over the railing of the enclosure.
"You wait until I go bail for you!" The inter-

ruption hardly reached the tribunal, but Jacob heard it, and winced.

"I am but a poor wretch, sire, slighted by every one, and trodden under foot, like a worm, by my own kith and kin. Those bound to me in friendship have cast me off, because they are ashamed of my misery. Great and small scoff at me and maltreat me; the rich drive me away, and the poor are jealous of me. What would become of me, saving your lordships' presence, if I did not live by the wits which Heaven bestowed on me? It is no discredit to have tact and cleverness!"

"You are too conversational. Let us come to the point. What has been your office between my lord of Maulny and Guy de Fougereuse?"

"This, in truth, most noble prince. I was at the Red Rose one evening, when Vincent Govier and the gentle count de Kernis took the notion to visit the Devil's House. It did not suit messire de Maulny to follow them, but he sent me on the trail. In fact, I found the young baron of Fougereuse coming out of Wolf's turret."

"We know he passed the night there. What then?"

"Then I informed messire Walter. He seemed much pleased at the news, and desired to learn more. So, to oblige him, I agreed to watch the baron's proceedings."

"Did Maulny pay you for these services?"

"Sire, my fortune has never been so considerable that it could secure me the luxury of working for nothing. Messire Walter promised me a good deal; but as for having paid me, that is another story!"

"Knave, equivocator!" cried Maulny. "Vile serpent! Do you attempt to assert" —

"Silence is enjoined upon you, Walter," declared René, in a tone which he rarely employed, but which no man was inclined to disobey. "Continue, Jacob. Omit nothing."

"Your Majesty can see that it is not always well to resist the will of the lords of the land. They have two irresistible arguments: menaces and money. I was faithful to my commission; and every evening I waited for the baron as he came forth from his town-house, and followed him like his shadow."

"Whither did he go?"

"Oh! to a hundred different places. He never took me twice to the same spot. Sometimes to church, sometimes to a den of cutthroats, sometimes" —

"I advise you to boast of your acuteness!" interrupted Loïc. "Here you have been spying the page, for the last month, instead of the master. It is I who made you lose your breath, racing after me, wherever I cared to lead you!"

"Oh!" said Jacob, in a mournful surprise. "Surely you are joking, my sweet sir?"

"I am not your sweet sir, and I want no familiarities. Nor am I joking. You followed my

lord of Fougereuse just once; and that was on the
first day of your professional engagement. He
went to the Cathedral. Afterward, I cut short
your opportunities of that sort, by occupying your
nightly leisure, myself. Great George, comrade!
but you and I have had some famous walks together. Do you remember a certain attack that
sent you scampering like a hare down to the bank
of the river, and almost into the bed of it, you
were so scared? Do you remember certain confidential interviews at the cross-roads, with some
individuals who must have been unhooked from
the gallows-tree, if one might judge by their appearance? And lastly, you do remember, do you
not? certain plans and programmes laid out by
you and your worthy employer, whereby you aimed
at nothing less than the burning at the stake of
Guy de Fougereuse? Ah, ha! my prudent Jacob!
I have profited by your teaching. You may en-
title yourself The Spy Espied. This court knows
everything that passed. If you would save yourself, you have only to avow the facts."

"I am betrayed!" exclaimed Jacob, springing
up, with malicious hatred in his eyes. "But if
you have given me over to destruction, Walter
de Maulny, I will destroy you, in my turn. Sire,
the baron de Fougereuse is innocent of all crimes
with which he is charged. I can confirm it better
than any one, for I invented every one [illegible]."

"False witness!" yelled Maulny. "Villepreux
has bribed you."

“Have you so utterly lost the fear of God, messire?” asked Jacob, clasping his hands, in hypocritical alarm. “I am sorry for you, but I am resolved to save my soul. It is bad enough to risk hell for one’s own sins, without shouldering the sins of others! You have made me lie abominably. I am tired of that; and for once in my life, I am going to be honest.” Desiring to avenge himself on Walter for his parsimony and his scorn, pursued by the dread of the law, and impelled, above all, to escape the gibbet, Jacob now studied only how to win the royal pardon, by a thorough declaration, and by an earnest of repentance. For Loïc had reminded him that “this court knows everything.”

Therefore Piteux confessed, heaping up details and proofs, anticipating questions, throwing responsibility upon his accomplice in order to free himself, revealing all the particulars of the falsehoods manufactured between them, shivering lest he should omit one bit of evidence already familiar to the judges, and ending by begging for mercy, in a lamentable whine. The entire scaffolding of calumnies, built up with such intelligent care, crumbled piece by piece, under the eye of its designer, until not a board of it remained standing. Light began to break in on every man’s mind. The crowd listened, in a profound hush. Walter de Me[illegible], dark and tongue-tied, quaked with r[illegible] and humiliation. Loïc and Villepreux struck hands, and looked meaningly at each other. Isabelle's delicate and winsome face peered forth eagerly from the draperies, and her eyes were shining with hope, through their tears. Guy, apparently calmer than ever, followed the processes, without taking part, with the curious attention belonging to a mere spectator, rather than with the emotion of one personally concerned in them. His expression was, for the moment, something inscrutable. The lords who were to decide the verdict drew closer together: some were shocked and indecisive, some shook their heads obstinately, and only a few accepted frankly the data which upset all their prepossessions, and humbled their judicial pride. They had been played with, and treated as credulous children, or easy dupes. They would yield to incontrovertible evidence alone, and would admit their mistake only when driven to the final extremity.

Jacob had at last done with his cowardly revelations. The voice of René of Anjou arose, steady and solemn: " Walter de Maulny! have you nothing to say?"

Maulny darted to the forefront of the platform, steeled to attempt a desperate effort. Standing in all his pride, braving the court, reckless of consequences, cowing, by every look and gesture. his miserable satellite who trembled before him, he said:

" I request that yon clown be put to the torture: he would then talk after a different fashion. By the eternal right! what outrage is this, gentlemen? Since when has a peasant's drivel been considered as good as the oath of a knight? Have you all determined to debase yourselves with me, that you suffer the mob to pelt with mud the escutcheon of the Maulnys? Are you content to be the docile minions of Fougereuse, and let him throw dust in your eyes? Guy is jeering at you now and here. He congratulates himself at having gathered you together, that he might bid you rend limb from limb a kinsman whom he hates, and buy his immunity at that kinsman's expense. Will you be blinded by this coarse artifice? Will you acquit the prisoner, and let him go free, without having produced an explanation or a proof; maintaining his arrogant reserve; delivering my honor over to you, and carrying his own counsel with him? That would be to make yourselves the laughing-stock of the populace, and not without cause!"

"Halt there, fair cousin!" Guy began, striding forward a little. "You lend me, gratuitously, intentions which I never harbored. Nor do I know what intimate relationship with you, on my part, has authorized you to speak in my name. I have no desire either to wrest your honor from you, nor to jeer at my judges. I have promised to unfold to them. in due season, my secrets, and that promise I shall keep. Sire! and you, my lords! do you not hear the clash of arms, and the shouting, in the great courtyard outside? It is my destiny, on its way: in another instant it will be knocking at the

door. Remember that you brought it about! Let
it be accomplished without opposition!"

Before Fougereuse had done speaking, a tumult
of voices, loud, quick footsteps, stern orders and
demands, arose in the adjoining apartment. A
halberdier sergeant came to the threshold of the
audience hall, and uncovered his head. "My
dread lord and King," he said, "the constables
sent to search the haunted house and the palace
of Fougereuse, have returned with their trophies,
and await your Majesty's pleasure."

"Let them appear at once," was René's answer;
"and bring what they have found."

The sergeant turned to repeat the royal command, when he was energetically pushed aside by
a tall old man in a scarlet robe, whom the guards
had some difficulty in holding back. At the same
time a vibrant voice queried imperiously: "Is Guy
de Fougereuse safe and sound?"

At this spectacle, at this word, a distinct agitation swept over the crowd, and communicated
itself to the tribunal. The constables advanced,
escorting two prisoners, one of whom was the hermit of Avrillé wood. But upon his companion
every eye was riveted. That face and figure were
thrown into noblest relief against the background
of dull-hued tapestries. A cry of amazement
leaped from every throat; then an impassioned
cheer was launched by a group of students, and
carried away the whole assembly on a wave of
frenzied enthusiasm.

" Is Guy de Fougereuse safe and sound ?"

"Antonio! Antonio Blandini!" . . . "Hail, master!" . . . "Long life to the King of doctors!" . . . "*Evviva messer Antonio! . . . Evviva il maestro!*"

Quite indifferent to his triumphant reception, the new-comer hastened rapidly forward, preceding the bailiff and the guards, and never vouchsafing a look either at the lords in council or the people. When he came to Fougereuse, he seized his hand, and then turned towards the tribunal with a magnificent movement, full of defiance and indignation.

"Condemn me with him. ye blind judges! The executioner has not his due number," Blandini cried, imposing silence with his extended arm. " You have but the pupil, and now I deliver over to you the instructor!"

"Antonio!" a dozen on the raised floor exclaimed at once. . . . " Is it indeed you, or your ghost?" . . . "Has some demon taken your shape?" . . . "Where have you been living?" . . . "What miracle brings you hither?"

"You are welcome, dear and learned friend!" added King René, whose old eyes kindled with a ray of heartfelt joy. "We have longed greatly to see you again. But how is it that my watchmen restore you to me? Does it rest with you,— the key to this strange enigma?"

"I pledge you my oath to clear Guy de Fougereuse, sire! He is innocent of all treason, of all necromancy, of all underhand dealings. The baron's guest at the Devil's House, his mysterious comrade, stands before you: it is Antonio Blandini."

The King made a gesture of incredulous surprise. A long murmur of astonishment echoed among the crowd.

"You! by all the saints, Antonio," numerous voices protested; "what should you be doing in that den?"

The physician seared with a lightning glance the officers of the court. "Den! The dwelling of the great Wolfram! You blaspheme, my lords. Let me tell you that the duchy of Anjou and the kingdom of Sicily are not worth the tenth part of the treasures which that unjustly decried turret chamber has yielded up. One small manuscript of that misunderstood man of genius contains a wealth of knowledge and a depth of wisdom, undiscovered by the divine Aristotle himself! . . . But what is it to you? I forget that I speak to the deaf. Fougereuse alone is able to understand; and you have reputed it a crime in him!"

"Explain yourself clearly, master. Have you spent there, in Wolfram's house, all the time which has elapsed since your departure? Why so strange a retirement? It is an odd fancy: what is its meaning? What end, what interest, did it serve?"

"Hear the truth, sire, and let God be the judge! When I left your court, resolved to shake the dust of Anjou from my sandals, you did everything in your power to detain me; by promises, by prayers: perhaps you remember?"

"I do remember, Antonio. But you were inflexible!" said René with a sigh.

"You had opposed a rival to me; you wished to keep him beside you. My profession does not admit of these dualities," continued Antonio, with an Olympian frown. "I would have buried myself in the earth, sooner than pretend to authorize the presence, and the methods, of Cornelius. On the very morning when I was ready to sail away on a ship lying in the river, my favorite pupil, Guy de Fougereuse, came to beg me to delay the voyage for a few days. He had lately bought the hunting-lodge where the famous doctor Wolfram lived and died, which was full of precious manuscripts, and he begged me to consent to examine them with him. I let myself be persuaded, but under the condition that it should be kept an inviolable secret: Guy swore to me to reveal to no living soul, under any pretext, whatever might befall, that I was still in Anjou. The following night, I accompanied him to Wolfram's turret, and I determined to stay there, where I might be able to live in peace and privacy, while our researches lasted. I do not even yet realize how the hours and the days went by. . . Fougereuse had asked me for a week, but the week has unfolded into six long months, and we have not yet finished half of our labors. Guy has seconded me with ardent zeal, visiting me by day and by night, devoting to me all his leisure, and with his quick intelligence and his young eyes, helping out my old memory and my enfeebled sight. I never knew that he was in training for a death at the stake! Could I have known that my pupil was risking his life and his reputation on my account, never would I have suffered " —

"What! Did Fougereuse tell you nothing? Did you suspect nothing?"

"Nothing, sire. Guy was silent as the grave, on that subject; he did not allow me to dream that there was the least shadow of danger. This holy hermit, who was our only confidant, brought me, this very morning, the first news I had had of my young friend's misfortune. While I learned, with a shudder, that Fougereuse had been arrested as a poisoner, and thrown into a dungeon; and that he was to be arraigned for sorcery, and, in all like- lihood, condemned to capital punishment, your officers, sire, broke into my dwelling, crying: 'Death to the magician!' As soon as they recog- nized me, they drew back, astounded; yet they had to obey orders. They searched the turret, overhauling my manuscripts; they seized upon us two as circumstantial proof, and brought us hither . . . The rest you know. I bless Heaven for it, that I have arrived in time to save you from com- mitting a murderous injustice!"

Antonio's noble character for disinterestedness and sincerity, forbade all doubt as to the truth of his testimony. He was too religious to have the black art even indirectly laid to his charge; and for that matter the presence of the good monk of

Avrillé would, of itself, be enough to drive away suspicion. The judges were taken aback and startled; but they were not satisfied. Such a simple ending to so complex a matter overturned their preconceived ideas, and left them in a strange perplexity. Was it possible that this was all there was to the secret of Fougereuse, and that Antonio had offered them the clue to the formidable comedy?

Guy could not repress a smile, observing the embarrassment of the court. The men about him sat in bitter vexation before their mute defendant, their breathing Sphinx, who would neither confess nor explain, but left to events themselves the task of pleading his cause. "If you have laid a wager, baron de Fougereuse," William de la Bohalle exclaimed abruptly, "say so, and have done with your smiling! Truly, this passes comprehension: that you should weave such a web of mystery, get yourself apprehended and tried, and formally convoke a jury of your peers, all in order to inform us that you are taking lessons of the learned Antonio! This to make a mock of the whole Angevin aristocracy, and you owe us satisfaction for it."

"You shall shortly have it, messire," Fougereuse answered gravely. "Hitherto I have held my peace, that my friends and foes might speak their fill. But I feel, as you do, that it is time to sum up. Antonio has told you his half of the truth; but the secret of my life I alone can utter. Now listen: for what you shall hear is known to but one man living besides myself."

Appeased by these words, the tribunal ceased all conversation, and the old King leaned forward expectantly. Guy recollected himself for an instant. His heart beat furiously; his voice shook as he began.

" First of all, my sovereign lord, I ought to implore your pardon. You have believed me your servant, attached to you alone : a leal vassal, belonging to you in body and soul, with no ambition but to live and die in your employ."

" Well ? " René ejaculated, growing pale.

"For three years, sire, I have served a master other than René of Anjou."

" Traitor ! Felon ! " cried some of the judges. And the King, uplifting his eyes to the Crucifix in the hall, cast on it a resigned look, and murmured only : " Ah, Guy ! you also."

" I beseech your Majesty to hear me out ! My fault, if it be a fault, cannot now be atoned for : it is forever. For a long while I resisted the call of my new King ; I strove with his ambassadors ; I intrenched myself strongly upon the faith which I had sworn to you, and on my duties as your subject and your minister ; and my spirit rose against the thought of forsaking you. . . . But to-day the battle is over. I am persuaded, defeated, conquered. An attempt to retain me would be useless. I would choose torments and exile, sooner than delay my response to my true liege ; nor even in death could I be separated from him. My lord René of Anjou, I am yours no more ! I implore you to release me from my allegiance."

This singular apostrophe gave the hearers a sense of uneasiness. ·Each man among them felt that it clothed some hidden meaning, with which Guy alone was conversant. The King made a little gesture of weary disgust and sorrow. " Go, then, Fougereuse," he said, " go rejoin the master whom you prefer to me. I grudge him not the homage of a perjured courtier, and I absolve you from an allegiance so grossly violated. You are no longer my knight, and I am no longer your sovereign. . . . Unto treachery I am only too well accustomed ! " René ended with a sigh of poignant sincerity, as if he found himself sadly at home there.

"Dear and venerated sire," replied the baron, laboring under more emotion than he cared to show, "when I shall have told you who he is that summons me, you will not reproach me. You will think, rather, that I, who withstood him for three whole years, must have loved you with a great and loyal love. For you, I would have given my life ; for him, I would sacrifice forever, and without a regret, all that may be more dear than life itself : family affections, wealth, glory, honor, freedom ! I value these only inasmuch as I may throw them at his feet. I covet labor and suffering for his sake ; and my one desire is to see every knee bow when his name is spoken."

"The name of Louis of France ! " René added, with a bitter smile.

"The name, sire, of the King of Heaven : the

name of Our Saviour Jesus, who died upon the Cross, and rose again the third day: my Master and your Master, my God and your God. I have vowed to Him my life, and my regained liberty. . . . And there you have the secret of Guy de Fougereuse."

Of all possible conclusions, this was the most unexpected. A thunderbolt, fallen in the middle of the assembly, could not have caused greater consternation. The Abbot of Saint-Aubin was seen to leave the balcony reserved for the clergy, cross the enclosure, and hasten to place himself at Guy's side. With an authoritative motion, he laid his hand on the young baron's shoulder, then addressed the King and the court. "I, Brother Maurice, of the Order of Saint Benedict, declare that this man, by his solemn promises, belongs to Christ and to His Church. I claim him as a postulant of our community, whom no earthly power can longer withhold from God. . . . Finish your task, my son, and may Our Lady help you!"

There was a thrill of emotion felt wherever the monk's words were audible. The students saluted reverently; the people crossed themselves, invoking the saints; the backbiters were hushed; and Walter de Maulney bowed his head in defeat and shame. The monarch beckoned to his old favorite, who came to the foot of the throne, but did not mount the steps. "Why is it, Guy, that you chose to act with such secrecy, such a lack of confidence in me? Why?"

"Sire, now you ask of me a real confession! but I mean to obey you. A vow of my own held me silent, until God Himself should set me free. Many ties of duty bound me to the secular world, and they were well-nigh inextricable. My orphan sister had need of her brother; my King said that he had need of his minister. Though I lived detached from ambition and from the pursuit of pleasure, I had my dream of being useful; still more, of being loved. But God called me incessantly, and that Voice, now imperative, now plaintive, followed me equally into the festival hall, or upon an errand of mercy. I spent my fortune and my strength, I multiplied my vows and vigils, hoping thereby to ransom my future; and all in vain. My Creator would have from me no gift less, or other, than myself. There came the day when I said to Him: 'Here am I. If Thou hast chosen me, break, with Thine own hand, my chains. I promise to seek no aid but Thine, nor to make known Thy dealings with me to any man, until the last barrier is down!' That promise, sire, I have kept, as you know. I will not remind you how it was borne out. The Divine Will scattered to the four winds of heaven my friendships, my good fame, my high station; it suffered my career to be overclouded, my Christian faith questioned, my liberty taken from me, my life put in jeopardy. Isabelle's lover returned from the Holy Land; I was able to reclaim for him his long-promised bride. What held me back?

One last link, stronger than all: your affection, and my fidelity. God and you strove with each other in my breast. While I besought you so passionately to believe in my innocence, I was still undecided. My destiny was in your hands; with one little word you might have secured your vassal. But Our Lady had compassion on my weakness: that was not to be. When I could not convince you, I leaped the gulf. For when I was driven to ask for a trial, then the spell was broken, and Our Lord Christ had no rival in my heart."

"Guy!" René exclaimed pathetically.

"I do not mean to reproach you, sire, or to reproach any one. I am at peace with those who abandoned me, and I forgive my detractors. Nor do I complain of the ordeal: since it taught me what men are worth. Let me, however, do reverence, in passing, to two among those noble hearts whose loyalty to me never wavered. Robert de Villepreux, Loïc de Kernis, you mistrusted not your friend, when the world overwhelmed him; you sacrificed yourselves to him in his adversity. May God bless you!"

The baron's voice broke. His features, hitherto under perfect control, contracted, in a spasm of tender feeling. Forgetful of King, jury, spectators, he held out either hand to Robert and to Loïc, with a look more eloquent than words. That warm, silent grasp, held the three together for a moment, under the eyes of the troubled assembly. "I beg pardon of your Majesty," Guy continued, "but these two have risked much for my sake, and lost. . . . What is there yet, that you would ask of me, my lords? Antonio has unravelled for you the mystery of the haunted house. You see now why I was in love with science! My celebrated little room at home awaits explanation: the room without lock or key. It was sacked. What did you find, sergeant?"

" I should have thought I was in a monk's cell, my lord! I found a fresco of the Crucifixion on the wall; a hard, narrow bed, a mere straw pallet; a missal; and this chest. We were not able to open it."

Guy put his finger on one of the ironwork ornaments of the carven coffer which the soldiers brought him. The four sides, opening all at once, dropped back with a din, and several dark, indistinct objects fell out upon the floor.

" You made no error then, my good fellow," said Fougereuse to the sergeant, motioning to him to gather the contents together. ".It was indeed a monk's cell; and here are the monk's habit, his cowl, his book of hours, his rosary, and his instruments of penance. For a year past, the Right Reverend Abbot has allowed me to follow the Rule, by myself, and to wear the dress of the Benedictine novices, during the hours dedicated to study and to prayer. Now, I had only my nights to give to study and prayer. This parchment is the plan of a hospice which I had hoped to build in my own domain, and of which the hermit of

Avrillé was to be Superior. And, finally, this picture is a copy of Our Lady of Pity, destined for the monastery of Saint-Aubin. These are the items of my treasury. Are you satisfied, gentlemen? For Guy de Fougereuse has no more secrets to conceal!" He paused an instant; then folded his arms, raised his head, and added: "Pronounce my sentence."

The nobles, brought spontaneously to their feet, declared in unison that Fougereuse was innocent, and that the charges against him were withdrawn. The people broke forth in a transport of joy and triumph, and the students' cheers made the rafters ring. It was no mere acquittal, but such an ovation as few monarchs have received. One cry, however, was heard jarring upon the general enthusiasm; and it turned many a shout of gladness into a threat and a curse. Maulny had tried to escape from the enclosure, but Loïc blocked his way.

"Arrest the traitor!" he cried. "Seneschal, seneschal!" White and exhausted, but still sustained by his indomitable spirit, Walter kept his haughty aspect. Though he was fain to speak, his voice was drowned in the mutterings of the angered crowd. "Let us have justice! Let us revenge Fougereuse!" was clamored on every side.

"You must have some quarry to tear to pieces, dogs of Angers!" was Maulny's answer. "Your motto is: ' *Woe to the vanquished!* ' I would have you know that I can have no judges here, for these are my accomplices."

Indignant protests greeted the insulting phrase. The aged King started, and drew himself up with severe dignity.

" Be your own judge, then, and declare your own sentence, Walter de Maulny! You are convicted of imposture, of calumny, of false witness, of indirect attack upon the life of a kinsman. I give you your choice between a degradation from knighthood, imprisonment, or banishment. Decide: and consider that you are fortunate to have escaped death."

" Your Majesty is most generous. I choose banishment. I have lost the game, and I quit, like an honest player. This very evening, I take the road to Tours. Your star is up again, Fougereuse; but we shall meet hereafter. . . . Bah! what would you do? . . . I forbid you to seek pardon for me. Exile is welcome. I expatriate myself without a regret."

" Have him removed ! " commanded René.

The constables escorted Maulny to the doorway of the hall. An instant later, he was without. The schemer had parted forever with his ambitious dreams. Philip de Beauvau alone, among the nobles on the platform, noticed that Cornelius also had disappeared. He said to himself: " The hand of Louis XI. is in all this ! "

" Baron Guy de Fougereuse ! " exclaimed the King, " you are declared victor in the struggle.

Your slanderer is punished, your honor is vindicated; your sovereign and your equals in rank heartily admit their error, and deplore it. A traitor has shaken our good faith; yet God forbid that we should have wrought injustice wilfully! We are eager to atone for our moods of blind folly. Favor, estates, position, all are yours once more; my esteem for your character is greater than ever; and my affection, estranged for an hour, is frankly offered you for the second time. You have leisure and opportunity to forget the past!" The good René was moved; he continued kindly. "Reflect. before you bury your youth alive in the cloister, and throw away your splendid future. Remember, Guy, that your career has barely begun: life spreads before you, full of promise and of hope."

"It is so indeed. sire: promises which are sure, hopes which fail not," Fougereuse replied: "the only perfect things. My future is eternity, Heaven is my heritage, and Christ my King. You have absolved me from my vassalage; nor will I renew it, save to God alone. . . . My Father, put an end, I beseech you, to these importunities," Guy added, seeing several members of his family conspiring, with the King, to raise objections. "Give me, without delay, the livery of the servants of Jesus Christ. I seem to have won the right to it, as it were at the point of the sword!"

"To-morrow, my son, at the Abbey, after a night of meditation and of rest."

"Nay, to-day, Father, now, here! after a ay of agony and battle. God calls me; bid Him not to wait." Throwing himself at the feet of the Abbot of Saint-Aubin, he ended imploringly: "Would you delay, you must answer for my soul!"

The prudent deliberation of Dom Maurice had to yield to the prayers and the strong will of his postulant. The priceless jewels which Guy wore, and his decorations, were cast heedlessly on the floor; his brilliant court costume was replaced by the black Benedictine habit; his wavy blond hair was shorn away, while that forehead, lately held so high before King René and his tribunal, was bowed humbly before the poor obscure man of God.

The baron Guy de Fougereuse had knelt him down, melancholy, and sore in spirit from his recent warfare; but Brother John rose up in great peace, and radiant with happiness, amid the weeping assembly. At a sign from the King, he ran up the steps of the platform, and bent his knee before the aged prince, with tenderest respect. René clasped him in his arms, and yearned over him like a father embracing his son for the last time. The judges, standing, pressed about the comrade they were now to lose. Isabelle came too, close to her brother, weeping with pride and love and sorrow. Guy was saved: but the separation was at hand, to weigh upon her tender, girlish heart.

"No, sire, no. I beseech you, dear and royal

master!" Fougereuse was saying, in the endeavor to arrest upon René's lips some expressions of remorse and contrition. " Be not depressed, and do not accuse yourself; for God has wrought in all. I go from you, bearing you a most grateful affection, and blessed in being cleared so fully, in your eyes, from every shadow of blame. Yesterday you offered me your pardon; let me ask for it to-day, on my knees. You have suffered through me; and on my account others have offended you. Sire, may I demand mercy? The culprit is dear to me: he is my true friend, and the affianced lover of my sister. Robert has his moments of revolt; but I know not how he can live, under the resentment of his beloved liege. I entreat you to overlook his fault!"

"Let him come to me," René replied. "I recall nothing now, save his heroic devotion to your cause. . . . Nearer, Villepreux! I forgive your rudeness. Be as loyal, ever, as you are." And as Robert threw himself at the King's feet, kissing the hand graciously held out to him, the latter turned to Isabelle.

"My lady and dear child, you are the last of the race of Fougereuse, and as such, you owe the crown a vassal's fealty. Your father and your brother conquered new territory in my name : will you not win and keep for me the intrepid heart of the Lion? I see that he is yours, and I trust you for it! You have mourned long enough, Isabelle. Let me hear you laugh and sing again, and let me reclaim my right to lead you to the altar on your marriage morning. . . . Guy, my best Angevin, whom I so wronged! go; for I give you up to Him who needs you. Obey His voice, with my leave, and my benediction. And remember to pray for me at the feet of Jesus Christ Our Lord."

The peers bade Fougereuse farewell, as if they had never known a hostile thought against him. As the brilliant favorite withdrew from the arena, rivals and foemen acknowledged his virtues, and vied with one another in his praise. With perfect serenity, he listened to protestations and regrets, or cut short an exhibition of sentiment real or feigned. Brother John had already forgotten the grievances of the baron de Fougereuse. He was less eager to hear eulogy and lament, than to have them hushed and ended. Yet it was otherwise with him, when he passed through the crowd of men and women in tears, among whom were his own sorrow-stricken vassals, beseeching him not to leave them. He disengaged himself from their hold, and resisted their pleadings; but it was with wet eyelashes and a throbbing heart, that to their cry of "Pray for us, servant of the Lord!" he answered: "Pray for me, dear poor: we shall not live apart."

At last the palace threshold was reached, the strife was done, the victory gained, when a hand touched that of Brother John, and a voice whispered: "I may go with you, may I not? You said I might."

"Loïc!   What do you ask?"

"Only to follow you, to the end.   I was a page, where you were a knight; and where you are to be a monk, let me be a novice!"

Dom Maurice said to him: "Come, my child."

EPILOGUE.

OUR LADY OF PITY.

"If thy brother who hath offended thee ask not thy pardon, beg thine of him: for so shalt thou lead him back to God."

SAINT FRANCIS OF ASSISI.

IT was near the end of April; Anjou was re-clothed in its liveries of laughing green. The new leaves shot forth under the dark twigs of box and holly; buds spread along the branches which winter had laid bare; the ditches were carpeted with wild strawberry vines, the fields with daisies, and the woods with blue violets. Dawn whitened the horizon, and the earth seemed happy at her awaking. The morning lark had begun his sweet concert for the laborer; the huntsman held out his fist for the falcon to light upon, and rode gayly through the thickets. But ahead of the watchful song-bird, ahead of the impatient horn of the chase, the chime of the Priory of Our Lady of Pity had already greeted the unrisen sun. The monks were in choir for the office of Prime, prais-ing and blessing that God who has cast over the natural universe the ray of His love, and the re-flection of His divine beauty. In the footpaths of the valley, many pilgrims were hastening onward, that they might not miss the first Mass. For it was the Feast of Saint Dismas, the Penitent Thief, patron of the hospice with which Robert' de Villepreux had endowed the monastery, and where the sick, and strangers, were received as if sent of God. It was the day of bounties to the poor, and of happy opportunity to the rich: a day of joy for both. The little military troop, preceded by its own banner of three crosses sable on a gold ground, marched through an admiring crowd, and took its customary place in the chapel. Robert de Villepreux, in a gleaming coat of mail, his helmet on his head, his sword strapped at his side, stood before the altar. The standard, carried by the faithful Vincent Govier, was unfurled in the choir; and four of the Thieves, lance in hand, stood around it, sentinel-like. Between the little pillars of her pew in the gallery, might be seen the sweet face of Isabelle de Villepreux in all its touching loveliness, and with the added grace which happy wives and mothers wear. At either side of her, a baby head bobbed inquisitively up and down, one dark and eager, one blond and shy: Amaury and Yvette, nicknamed, by the Thieves, the Lion-cub and the Gazelle; Isabelle's tender care, and their father's joy and pride.

The candles were lit, one by one, around the reredos of the altar: the Cross of Christ, rising triumphantly between the crosses of the Good and Bad Thief, standing out from the rich hangings of dark red velvet behind. Then a side door opened quietly, and the friars came up into the sanctuary, filing two by two, in silence and recollection, wrapped in their black habits, and the ample Benedictine cowl. They reached their stalls, and prostrated themselves, in the attitude of profound adoration. The Father Prior came last, in his priestly vestments, accompanied by a young novice with an open countenance and very bright eyes. This was Brother Louis de Kernis, whose turn it was to serve the Mass of Dom John, once Guy de Fougereuse. His six years spent in the cloister had not altered Guy's aspect of health, nor overshadowed it; a new youth seemed to have been given him for the service of his Lord. In vain, now, might one search at the corners of his mouth for that little sarcastic curl of the lip which was so frequent with the favorite of René of Anjou. The habit of prayer had given a slight forward inclination to the haughty forehead, and long vigils before the tabernacle, and penitential austerities, had made it pale. The yoke of obedience and of humility had left on the proud gentleman the monastic stamp. A steadfast serenity, an inexhaustible meekness, replaced, in the Prior of Our Lady of Pity, the mocking indifference of the courtier of long ago. Every man who saw or heard him, knew that he was in possession of that deep and blessed peace which this world knows not, and with which God fills to overflowing the hearts of His own. As for Loïc, his exterior change was much more marked than that of the knight his master, and many a one failed to guess that this was the same adventurous page, in the garb of a novice of Saint Benedict; yet, in reality, the spiritual transformation was far less thorough. The expression of his face was stilled and softened, the roguish bearing overlaid with seriousness and submission; yet now and then a smile, a tone, a look, a jest, would reveal the fiery nature beneath, which Divine Grace had seized like a glowing coal, and given to the Lord, undivided and forever. Mass began to the chant of the favorite stanza of the Penitent Thieves, which was repeated by the crowded congregation:

> *Tu latronem exaudisti,*
> *Tu Mariam absolvisti:*
> *Mihi quoque spem dedisti.*

> ("Thou the sinful Mary savest;
> Thou the dying Thief forgavest.
> And to me a hope vouchsafest.")

The monks answered in Our Lord's words:

> *Hodie mecum eris in Paradiso,*

> (This day shalt thou be with Me in Paradise!)

sung very low, in harmonies of merciful tenderness and sublime consolation. When the solemn moment of the Elevation came, the little bell sounded, and every brow bent to the ground, under its burden of suffering or of repented sin. Which of us has not been bowed beneath the one or the other?

But the Comforter, the Pardoner, is present at the
Holy Sacrifice, in the hands of His priest; and
through them will He give Himself to these failing hearts, and fill them with light, strength, and
quiet.

Robert, first of all, received the Sacred Host,
with such faith, simple and deep, as the centurion
had of old. Then came his men-at-arms, in respectful piety, and last, the multitude of pilgrims; all
ages, ranks, and occupations sharing in the Christian union. Isabelle de Villepreux, the noble lady,
knelt near a poor old beggar in rags; homespun
touched velvet; the soldier elbowed the peasant;
gentlefolk were mingled with apprentices, children
with graybeards. Youth, beauty, fortune, glory,
fame,—all vanished away, all effaced themselves
before the hidden God, whose infinite love comes
hither to claim the poor, weak love of His own
creatures.

"May the Body of Our Lord Jesus Christ preserve thy soul unto life everlasting!" The Prior
had breathed this prayer over the last of the com-
municants at the Holy Table, and the latter had
but just answered "*Amen!*" when suddenly a commotion arose at the lower end of the nave. The
cry: "Sanctuary! sanctuary!" a hoarse, desperate
shout, rang like the appeal of some being in his
agony. The sea of people fell apart at once, and
left a passage clear for a man, covered with blood,
who had flung himself into the church. "Sanctuary! sanctuary!" he repeated, rushing towards

the chancel like a wild boar at bay. " Sanctuary !
in the name of the Holy Mother of God ! "

A confused murmur began among the crowd.
Dom John stretched forth his hand as a pledge
of protection towards him who asked asylum of
Our Lady of Pity. " The Holy Mother of God
will shelter you, my son," he said.

At the sound of his voice, the stranger trembled
violently, and drew back, turning full on the Prior
his haggard face and demonic eyes. " Guy de
Fougereuse ! " he cried; " it is always Fougereuse ! "   He brought his hand to his head in a sort
of frenzy, tottered, and fell, with a stifled moan,
on the paving.

Dom John was paler than the wounded man.
Kneeling beside him, he raised his head, and tried
to staunch the blood which gushed from a gaping
wound in the unhappy fugitive's breast. " Walter !
. . .   O Lord! accord me his life."

. . . .

The right of sanctuary, one of the most admirable things devised by the Church in times of
bloodshed and persecution, was still respected in
the fifteenth century. Nevertheless, many who
dared not brave the law, nor expose themselves
to the excommunication which devolved upon the
violators of a sanctuary precinct, scrupled not to
employ base means, in order to lure their enemies
beyond the recognized place of refuge. Whither
the dagger or the headsman's axe could not pene-

trate, poison could pass; it did pass, indeed, the gratings of the cloister. Louis XI., according to the chroniclers of the time, was never so much of a devotee, as when he had some treasonable end in view. He multiplied his pious offices toward the Abbeys, and feigned to venerate ecclesiastical rule; yet those there whom it was his policy to condemn, in no wise escaped their doom. The miserable death of his own brother, Duke Charles of Guyenne, poisoned in the Abbey of Saint John at Angély, was a sinister instance.

There were reasons why the Prior of Our Lady of Pity was unlikely to stand in the good graces of the crafty monarch. The merciless hate of Walter de Maulny had not busied itself in vain. Banished by René of Anjou, and defeated by Guy de Fougereuse, Walter had sworn to be revenged on both; and he had kept his oath only too well. René's aforetime minister was received favorably by the King of France, and for six years he was his secret agent: the director of all the underhand dealings, the wicked spites, the course of hateful annoyances which ended by leaving Anjou in the hands of Louis XI. René, harassed on every side, abandoned and betrayed, a childless father, a powerless monarch, loaded with anxieties and mortifications in his old age, let himself be overborne, for very weariness. The loss of his son, the gallant Duke John, and the tragic end of his grandson, Edward of Lancaster, stabbed after the battle of Tewkesbury by the Yorkist princes who had defeated his cause, left the venerable King without direct heirs. Margaret of Anjou, heartstricken by the death of her husband, the unfortunate Henry VI. of England, and, above all, by the horrible murder of her only son, had withdrawn to the solitude of a manor-house at Reculée, to deplore those dear ones, who here below had been her life and hope. Her sister Yolande, the Duchess of Lorraine, had already passed away, and her son, René of Vaudemont, was heir equally to the house of Anjou, and to that of Vaudemont in Lorraine. Two nephews remained to the King: Charles of Maine, the son of his brother, and Louis of France, the son of his sister. Provence was to fall to Charles; Louis XI. was to inherit Anjou. But the greedy monarch determined to possess his own portion even during the lifetime of his uncle. His craft and pertinacity, aided by the strategic intelligence of Maulny, achieved the desired end. A factional riot, and the complicity of William de la Cerizaie, captain of the town forces, delivered Angers into the hands of the King of France, in the year 1473. René had to yield; and he sailed away, with tears, to his beloved Provence, the last resting-place for his white head and his weary heart. But he has still in Anjou some devoted partisans, and in the foremost rank of them stood Guy de Fougereuse, who, generously abetted by Villepreux, had built the monastery of Our Lady of Pity, and had just been appointed its first Prior. The suspicions of King Louis, directed by Maulny, lit upon both

Prior and convent, and they became the objects of constant persecution.

Every day brought its fresh conflict and trial. The unchanging loyalty of Dom John to the dispossessed René, his firm, uncompromising attitude towards the emissaries of Louis, his refusal to put at his Majesty's service his own great influence with the people; — these things were considered equivalent to the crime of high treason. The humble retreat of fervent religious was denounced as a nest of conspirators, and subjected to sharp espionage, such as even the vigilance of Villepreux and his fearless Thieves could not always foil. Were it not that Louis XI. cherished a secret hope that he should win the Prior over to his cause, either by threats or promises, there is no doubt that Maulny's hatred would have succeeded in obtaining his enemy's death-warrant. Such were, at any rate, Walter's Satanic plans; and lo! at the very apex of his career of triumph, the hand of God touched him, and threw him, disarmed and dying, at the feet of his victim; without hope, save in the chivalry of an outraged kinsman, without defence, save the bulwark of protection afforded by the holy walls he had done his best to destroy.

.   .   .   .

The chamber into which the sick refugee was carried, was a crypt cut in the living rock, below the chapel. It communicated, by several passages, with the interior of the monastery, and, in turn, gave it access to the underground ways which led to the Loire. It was, indeed, a little house of refuge; more than one proscribed man had owed his salvation to it. A bedpost hung with antique, faded curtains, a stone table. a few stools, diversely shaped, comprised the furniture of the half-darkened room, which sunlight reached only through the narrow fissures of the rock.

Walter slept an unrestful, feverish sleep. The monks who watched over him walked so softly and spoke so low, that hardly a sound was audible. The hermit of Avrillé, now known as Father Andrew of the Cross, was carefully preparing, by the light of a lamp, a beverage which he had brought from the infirmary. Brother Louis, seated near the foot of the bed, was passing the beads of his rosary through his fingers. His lips murmured *Ave* after *Ave:* but his eyes. roving anxiously from the patient to the Father Prior, bespoke a rush of emotion and of memory which had not their source in prayer. Dom John was standing, with joined hands, his face showing with what deep feeling he gazed upon the sufferer beside him, whose features were. white and livid against the dark draperies. With infinite compassion the Prior looked down on the old comrade of his boyhood, the man of his own blood and lineage, who was fostered and educated under the same roof. Maulny's treachery had already been pardoned by the heart of the cousin and the friend; but who can say what was passing, at that moment, through the heart of the religious? Before that soul, ransomed by the blood of Jesus Christ; hanging, as if by a miracle, over the very jaws of Hell, and divided, it might be, by a few moments' time, from God's searching judgment; before that soul, which a touch, a sigh, could save, and yet which a word could lose forever, what was the agony of the priest! Bitter remembrances lived no longer, nor wounds gone by. A spirit was in danger of eternal death: this alone appealed to the Prior of Our Lady of Pity, moved him to the depths, wrung from him a prayer strong enough to overreach Divine Justice itself. For having sinned against him, Walter became, now, to him, the more dear; since he felt it his sacred right to fold the guilty one in the mantle of forgiveness, and to force, in his behalf, the mercies of God.

Across the silence of the chamber where mortal pain hovered, a brisk step resounded from the stair, and the door leading to the chapel was thrust open by an incautious hand. Dom John frowned, and advanced quickly to the newcomer, hushing him with a decisive gesture.

"But I must speak with you!" said the voice of Villepreux.

"Then speak with me here," answered the Prior, passing out into a narrow corridor, and gently closing the door. "Walter would be in the gravest danger, were we to wake him."

The knight and the monk found themselves in a sort of natural grotto of curious conformation, arched irregularly, and lit only by a hanging lamp, which resembled those kept burning in burial vaults. Robert's coat-of-mail gleamed in the dark, and threw off little fantastic reflections, under the flickering light poured upon it. Dom John's black habit and cowl were indistinguishable against the sombre walls, but his features, pale, thoughtful, and pure, seemed to draw to themselves every ray of light, and shine as if within an aureole.

"I have important news, dear friend," Robert began eagerly. "We have got ourselves into a terrible hole. Maulny is not the victim of an assassination, but of an execution!"

Fougereuse's clear eyes expressed no surprise. "I feared as much," he replied.

"He is a condemned man, who has no legal right to exist, but who has broken away from his fate," continued Villepreux. "He was struck down, under orders of Louis XI., by the hirelings of Tristram l'Hermite. Word had been given to sew up the body in a sack, and cast it into the river."

"Ah, the royal code! He has escaped it."

"But Maulny was on the alert. It seems that he defended himself desperately, killing or wounding two of his assailants, and forcing the others to desist. You know nobody is so skilful as he at an ambuscade. Well, he profited by the momentary confusion of his murderers to throw himself into the church crying 'Sanctuary!' and Tristram's bravos did not dare to pursue him, in the sight of the people. Now, the difficulty has only changed its color. Louis of France is set upon having this man's life; and he may command you to deliver him over to-morrow! I learned this from one of those who attacked Walter.; he is grievously wounded himself. In fact, my Thieves found him in a dying condition on the Three Crosses road, and bore him away."

"I thank you, Robert," the Prior said, looking down. "All this is a very serious matter." And in the pause that followed, Dom John fell into meditation, praying God to assist him, while Robert awaited his instructions, without further speech.

Before abdicating his natal rights over Anjou, René had transferred to Our Lady of Pity the sovereignty of the domains of Villepreux and Fougereuse. Thenceforth, the Lion figured as the first subject of the monastery, and paid his feudal homage to its Prior. Never did ruler exact so little, and see himself so perfectly obeyed, nor ask so seldom, and receive so often, and so much. The faithfulness of the friend, and the vassal's loyalty, were welded together with the Christian's respect, and it was easy for the great heart of Villepreux to submit to the gentleness of Fougereuse.

"This hireling, this wounded man." Dom John went on presently, "did he tell you for what reason King Louis had suddenly condemned Walter. his best and most able counsellor. to such a death? It is a prompt revulsion, Robert: too prompt not to call for comment."

"I have had that thought, too," Villepreux responded, lowering his voice; "and I questioned the man closely. He swore that he was not aware of the King's motives: that the King is not in the habit of confiding his motives to the butchers whom he employs. Who, in all the world knows, for certain, the mind of Louis of France? He has never scrupled to break a tool after he has used it. I suspect that Maulny was playing two parts, and carrying on intrigues with Brittany, where the French yoke meets with small favor. And what master has Maulny not betrayed? However it be, King Louis has avenged King René, and royal justice, for once, is the justice of God."

The Prior's countenance became sorrowful and severe. "Justice!" he repeated. "Is it justice to come secretly upon a human creature, and execute him before he understands that any sentence stands against him? Is it the justice of the most Christian King, to speed a soul to the Judgment-seat on high, without allowing him a moment for repentance? What, then, would be considered cruelty, did infidels ordain it? And you, a Crusader, Robert, talk thus to me: you, my brother!"

"Would you plead in Maulny's behalf?" cried Villepreux excitedly. "Have you a good word to say for that man whose life is made up of deceit, who is a stain upon the whole order of knighthood? Surely, he merits another sort of requital! A prince who is set upon punishing ought to punish openly. And yet there are criminals too vile for the block. It is not that which Walter deserves, but degradation and the stake. His presence here soils the sanctuary!"

" Enough, Robert. The miserable being is crushed now under his own disgrace and misery. Have you no pity?"

" Had Maulny any pity on you?" cried the Lion, carried away by his growing indignation and disgust.

The Prior looked at him, and sighed. "Ah, you children of the century! How one loses one's labor, preaching to you the Gospel of Christ! . . . Take your Thieves with you, Robert, and return to your own castle. I and the community will guard the altar, and defend our guest as we are bound to do, by prudence and prayer, and, if so it must be, by our blood, shed in maintaining the rights of Holy Church. Our Lady will give us help."

" Be not unjust to me, Guy. You know well that nothing will ever separate us from you! But before entering upon a struggle with the King, before imperilling your own head and the freedom of your friars, in order to save a wretch, let us see if you cannot obtain your end by less difficult means. My business is to protect you and watch over you; and I discharge it by exempting this monastery from the wrath of King Louis. Listen: give Walter to me. I will have him taken privately to Villepreux; and I swear to deliver him to you safe and sound, as soon as the danger shall have passed away. Why do you hesitate? What is there to fear? Under my roof, my own little son Amaury would not be more secure."

"I believe it, my dear brother; and with all my heart I do homage to your generous intention. But it would be only Walter's ruin, and your ruin as well. There is but one obstacle which can deter Louis of France: respect for holy precincts. If he dares brush that aside, nothing will hold him back thereafter. For me, whatever befalls, I must act as a religious should act. Walter de Maulny is a Christian in distress, who has claimed sanctuary in Our Lady of Pity's chapel. He is under her patronage, and there he shall remain. No human power should constrain me to violate his privilege. A monk, after all, should not be troubled by the wrath of princes, when he has innocently drawn it upon himself: for he is Christ's vassal, and his allegiance is to God alone."

"Well, mine is to you; and it will not be found wanting," answered Villepreux. "No one can harm a hair of your head without stepping over my dead body, and the bodies of my men. No matter whither you would go, we have but one word to speak, and that is out of the Gospel: '*Let us also go that we may die with him!*' But it is hard for us to see you throw away your life, consciously, in order to " —

"Ah! if but my life could do it!" murmured Dom John, bringing his hands together, with flushing cheeks, and with radiant eyes uplifted.

The heartfelt, almost involuntary exclamation cut short Villepreux's monologue. "'How one loses one's labor,'" he quoted murmuringly, "arguing with these saints! Guy, I surrender." And sinking on one knee on the damp rock, he added gravely: "Since it pleases you to die for your enemies, at least bless your friends!"

Their interviews often ended in this manner. The Prior stretched his hand over the proud head which inclined gladly before him.

At this moment, Loïc entered the grotto, whispering: "Come, Father, I pray you. The sick man has awakened, and Father Andrew needs you."

Walter's slumber was ended. He had begun to question his nurses, with an air of harsh distrust which soon exhausted the patience, none too ample at any time, of Brother Louis. Even Dom Andrew replied to him with that deliberate quiet which shows that its self-control is a matter of effort.

"Once more, my dear son, I assure you that you are in a place of safety, and not in a dungeon, and that we are not your jailers, but your physicians. Do you wish me to taste this drink for you? It is no poison, but a very salutary remedy. Take it, I implore you, if you would be cured."

An angry gesture from Maulny overturned the goblet, the contents of which spurted over the friar's robe. "I wish nothing of you or yours, traitor monk! You have sold yourself to Fougereuse!"

Father Andrew sighed, as Dom John came in, followed by Loïc and Villepreux. At sight of the three, the wounded refugee shrank back instinctively, and the spark of rancor flamed up in his eyes. The Prior softly approached the bed. "Are you suffering less, my brother?" he inquired, with gentlest solicitude.

"What matter whether I do, or do not?" answered Walter harshly. "Let me die in peace."

"We hope to heal you, and save you, God willing!"

"It would be better to finish me at once. The King is bound to have me killed, nor will Tristram miss me the second time."

"You are here in inviolable sanctuary. Our Lady of Pity is a rampart which Tristram will not scale. Confide in our hospitality, and in the protection of the Mother of God."

"I confide in you?" exclaimed Maulny, with difficulty raising himself a little. "I confide in you, Guy de Fougereuse? You are too ready to think me your dupe, for I should rather confide in Satan. Drop this mask of holiness! You know that you hate me, in the bottom of your heart."

"I never hated you, Walter. Never: I repeat the word. Let us bury the past. All I desire of you is the salvation of your soul. Will you refuse me that?"

"Ha!" said Walter, with a cold, bitter laugh, "I expected this! You would have me make my confession to you; you would see me at your feet, striking my breast, and crying for mercy. Why do you not require me to don the habit and swear obedience? Would it not be a pretty revenge? But you may as well seek other penitents, my man of God. You will never make over a Maulny into a trophy of your prowess!"

"Miscreant and ingrate!" Villepreux shouted, unable to contain himself longer. "Do you forget to whom you speak? To one mortally injured in his good name because of you: to the betrayed knight, the persecuted religious. He stands here beside you, willing to forget his wrongs, that he may succor you; and you, the guilty person, you, the oppressor, you, rescued by his heroic charity, you repay him but with suspicion and insult! Is there yet in you the soul of a gentleman, Maulny, or have you traded it into the Devil's hands?"

"He has his attacks of eloquence, the gallant Lion!" said Walter. Then, turning toward the Prior: "Tell me, forsooth, my beloved cousin, what spell you cast upon these simple folk, to make them believe so in your virtue!" he sneered.

"Job himself could never have endured this creature!" mumbled Brother Louis, in his indignation.

Guy gazed sadly upon his reviler. To so much sharp and insolent speech, he opposed but a word or two, in a low voice:

"Walter, what did I ever do to you?"

The countenance of the ambitious, fallen courtier changed, and a frightful expression of frenzy swept over it. "What did you do to me? Do you ask me what you have done? You have made me what I am! May you be cursed for it!"

He seized with his fingers, which were burning hot with fever, the wristband of Dom John, thus forcing the monk to bend down towards him. "What did you do to me? You stole my share of life! You profited by my ill-luck, to secure fortune and happiness. You refused me the hand of your sister, only to bestow it on the enemy of your house. You wrought my disgrace and banishment. Royal favor, inheritance, reputation: you took them all from me, you robbed me of them all! And what am I now? A man under the sentence of death, tracked like a wild deer. And you! You are living in peace; you are the contented and honored leader of friars who serve you, as it were, on their knees, and of imbecile vassals who worship the ground under your feet! And you ask me what you did to me? Hangman! Give me back what you wrested from me!"

"Walter!" cried the Prior, grasping both hands of the fugitive, "Walter, listen to me. I implore you" —

"You come, talking to me of salvation!" the other continued, in ever-increasing fury. "You come, burdening me with your generosities! These spectators compliment me as ingrate and miscreant, and will bury me under your 'heroic charity.'

Drop the mask, I say, hypocrite comedian! and let your own face be seen."

" You see it now," answered Dom John, inclining his head, with resigned sweetness : " it is the face of a friend."

" Of the friend Judas!" Maulny interrupted, scornful, implacable. He tore his hands from the Prior's hold, and with savage suddenness struck at him so violently that the latter staggered, from the blow, half across the room. " Away, impostor! I will not be seduced."

At this brutal attack, plainly the act of a madman, both Villepreux and Loïc started forward : one terrible in his passionate wrath, the other trembling with indignation and grief. Dom Andrew impeded Robert, while the novice threw himself on the floor at his superior's knees, kissing his hands and his garments, and looking up at him with that intense affection which had been proven again and again.

Dom John appeared to be conscious of nothing. He took a slow step backward, with his eyes fixed on the Crucifix which hung above the bed, and on those merciful, outstretched arms. Then he joined his hands, and finally murmured : " Our Lady of Pity, blessed Mother! Suffer not thine unhappy child to perish thus."

" Father," said Dom Andrew, "I entreat you not to remain here with us. You see that the man is delirious. Spare your sons further heartaches; and go, instead, to pray to Our Lord. You will be heard by Him, if not by this poor hardened soul."

"Can you assure me that he will not die to-night?" The Prior spoke as he reluctantly turned away.

"I think I can do so. He may live several days. Be pleased, Father, to withdraw at once; and you shall be called, if he should give any sign or token of repentance."

Dom John acquiesced. Villepreux followed him from the crypt, clenching his fists, and mastering his feelings as he could. The Society of the Penitent Thief, drawn up in array, awaited its chief in the quadrangle. Robert signalled for his horse; and when he was in the saddle, he growled, casting his fiery glance all around him:

"Good Lord! what a shame it is to risk the lives of such brave soldiers and such godly monks, all for love of that devil-possessed creature!" Then, in a loud, stern voice, he gave the order of departure. The troops clattered away, and the captain reserved to himself alone the duty of marking the outposts, and of placing sentinels along the borders of the valley.

Meanwhile, Dom John implored the mercy of Our Saviour for Walter de Maulny. Striking his breast, he repeated the words of David: "'*From my secret sins cleanse me, O Lord, and from those of others spare thy servant.*' And forgive me those which my brethren have committed through me." There he remained all night, at the feet of

Our Lady, and there Loïc found him before the morrow's dawn. When he arose, his face had regained its habitual serenity. He led the chanting of the Office with perfect attentiveness, but ever and anon he would cast upon the floor a gaze so intent that it seemed to pierce the marble tiles. As soon as Father Andrew, after having completed his long vigil at the crypt bedside, was seen ascending the choir steps, Dom John started, and turned inquiringly towards the venerable figure. Despite the sacredness of the place, and the antiphonal Psalms already begun, Dom Andrew drew near, and whispered in the Prior's ear. And when Matins were over, the latter raised his voice: " A certain soul in danger is fighting against its own salvation. Let us do violence to the Kingdom of Heaven, O my brothers and my sons!" He was the first to kneel and intone the *Miserere*, to which the community answered from their stalls; then, standing up, and beckoning to Father Andrew to follow him, he glided rapidly from the church.

"Is there no hope for him?" he asked the hermit earnestly, as they crossed the inner court of the cloister.

"I did not say quite that, Father; but the situation is more grave, and death is hanging over him by a hair. He has gone through a terrible crisis: while it lasted, I thought, a dozen times, that he was passing away in my arms. He is calmer now, but his strength is going. The sword is wearing through the sheath. It is dreadful, dreadful, to see a Christian soul choosing damnation."

"What! Could you do nothing with him? Your long spiritual experience, the authority of age "—

"Nothing, Father, nothing. I urged, exhorted, supplicated, all in vain. I tried to touch his heart, or to wake his conscience. He refused stubbornly to repent or to confess, and he broke silence only to indulge in a fit of passion. The poor lost soul rejects Divine Grace; he will sue neither for the mercy of his Redeemer, nor the forgiveness of his fellow-man. Death may come at any moment, and send him unprepared into eternity. God help us! It is an agonizing thought, Father."

"I will go to Walter," said Dom John, in a low voice. He stepped forward, but his aged companion detained him.

"Nay, nay, not you!" he exclaimed, in accents of such meaning that the Prior stood still. "Not you, I beg."

"What can you fear? Has anything happened? Why do you seem so anxious? . . . Hide naught from me, my Brother, on your vow of obedience. I need to know whatever there is to know."

"The sick man cannot endure your presence, Father," Dom Andrew said gently. "The time for that has not arrived."

"Does he hate me, then, so much?" the younger man sighed. "Has it come to this?"

"It is a hard trial for you, my son of former days!" answered the old friar, pressing the Prior's hands between his own. "It is hard, too, for me to own the truth, but I must be frank with you. Maulny, indeed. is losing his very soul through the hatred he bears you: it burns him alive like an infernal flame. Your name is to him a sting, a torment, a lasting nightmare. Your kindness only serves to embitter him; your generosity hurts and maddens. He blames you for all his crimes; he curses the tortures you force him to undergo, when that charity which he, alas, cannot understand, heaps coals of fire upon his head. In fine, if the pardon of God be refused and contemned, it is simply because Maulny feels that in accepting it, he must also accept yours (I do not say even *ask* yours!) and must thus humble himself before you. It is a craze of pride, a sort of triumph in him of the demon of envy. . . I have told you enough, so pray do not question me further," continued Dom Andrew imploringly. "Be not saddened or self-reproachful, dear Father; for you did everything possible to move the unhappy man, and your zeal ran aground on a nature harder than the rocks. But God is strong enough to melt it yet, and has no need of us to help Him in His work! The thoughts of the Lord are not our thoughts, and His ways are beyond our ways as the heavens are exalted above the earth. Let us pray unceasingly, and never despair."

The melancholy, weary voice of the monk belied

his encouraging words. The fact was, that never in his long career had the ancient champion of the Faith met with such obstinate impenitence, at the solemn hour when the breath of the grave is wont to chill earthly passions. Dom John lifted his head, sunk upon his breast, as if under the weight of a burden heavier than he could bear. His eyes were cast upward, with a look in them of invincible confidence.

"Our Lady of Pity will intercede for her guilty son, at the throne of his Elder Brother, who is our God," he said. "And because of that, I hope against hope. . . . What is it, Brother Louis?"

Loïc had neared them with quick steps. along that side of the cloister where they stood, and had come to a standstill a few feet away, waiting, with evident impatience, until the Superior should have ended his talk with Dom Andrew. At the former's invitation, he eagerly approached.

"Reverend Father, a stranger has arrived who wishes to speak with you at once. He will not give his name, but he questions everybody, and he looks at everything. He reminds me of Jacob the Weasel! Were it not for his more rampant air, I should have said it might be King Louis in person. I would not swear"—

"I will receive him," Dom John replied shortly. "When will you learn a little reserve of speech, my son?"

"For which I ask your pardon, Father," the novice humbly replied. Then, encouraged by the indulgent smile which greeted him, he added: "Will you please permit me to watch over Walter to-night?"

"Yes: provided Dom Andrew thinks it well to take you for his assistant. You are not yet perfected in patience, my poor child!"

"Well, I am not!" Brother Louis murmured to himself, as he followed with loving eyes the Prior's retreating figure; "but I know a saint who is. That imp of a Maulny must make his confession to-morrow, or else give some uncommonly good reason for not doing so!"

In the reception-hall of the monastery, Dom John found himself confronted by a small man, of sinister appearance, but of smooth, courteous manners. He was dressed in a plain, brown surcoat, and a well-worn cap. Fougereuse, despite this rural simplicity, at once recognized Master Oliver le Daim, otherwise known as Oliver the Bad, or Oliver the Devil, the barber and the minister of King Louis XI., and his most intimate associate. After having gravely saluted him, his host motioned him to a high-backed seat, and placed himself in his Prior's chair, which was raised one grade above the floor. Crossing his hands under his ample sleeves, he waited for Oliver to speak.

The latter had already taken his companion's measure. For all Dom John's inflexible serenity, Master le Daim felt that a struggle was at hand, and that he should have to play a close game. He began in the ordinary way, and presently

sounded the praises of the monastery, of its regu-
larity of life, of its holy Prior and fervent community; he announced that his Majesty held that
Prior in great esteem, in such very great esteem,
indeed, that now there was a vacant bishopric, he
had thought of him in connection with it. And
why not even a higher honor? The cardinal's
hat, in the opinion of Louis of France, might as
easily be bestowed upon another of his true coun-
sellors as it was upon His Eminence la Ballue!

From time to time, the wary diplomat made an
artfully calculated pause, inviting some response to
his insinuations, and glancing adroitly upward, in
order to detect Dom John's real sentiments. But
he, with downcast eyes, sat silent and immovable,
statue-like.

"The King is your well-wisher, Father Prior,"
was Oliver's concluding word. "He thinks that
he is able to rely upon your fealty."

The monk made a correct and formal bow. " I
am not aware that I have ever given him occasion
to doubt me."

"There was a time when his Majesty was preju-
diced against you." Oliver dropped into a confidential tone. "But your accuser, by his own
felonious conduct, established the untruth of his
statements." And he repeated the sum and sub-
stance of Maulny's slander of the Priory; deepening
the tints. already sufficiently black, of his infamous
charges ; expressing wonder that one relative could
nourish such spite against another, and unfolding,

one by one, the new instances of Maulny's mean
manœuvres

Dom John listened without stirring an eyelash,
in a marble calm. "I knew all this," he said
quietly, as soon as Oliver had done speaking.

"Whew! Your Reverence must have a good
detective service," he had to exclaim, feeling somewhat disconcerted.

For the first time, Fougereuse wore a light smile.
His eyes were on those of the envoy, reading his
thoughts; the astute guest, conscious of it, bit
his lip.

"You are wasting time, friend Oliver. What
would your master with me?"

Put into a position to explain himself, le Daim
hesitated. His way was not a straight way, and
his tortuous policy found itself crossed by this
direct attack.

"His Majesty knows, beyond any doubt," he
replied slowly, lowering his voice, "that Walter
de Maulny, pursued by men who had the royal
commission, sought refuge here, and that you
granted it to him."

"Well, my son?" the monk said, with the tranquillity which comes from a quiet conscience.

The barber decided to burn his ships behind
him, and take the aggressive attitude. thus: "Well,
my lord Prior, the King reclaims Walter de
Maulny! I summon you to deliver him at once
into my hands. I have orders to carry him to
Loches."

It was now Dom John's turn to look at Oliver with astonishment. "I do not understand you, Master le Daim."

"The King will have Walter, dead or alive," repeated the comrade of Louis XI., "dead or alive, if you understand that! I fear you are trying to fool me, Dom John de Fougereuse."

"Not at all, Master Oliver the Bad; but you took me by surprise. For I gave asylum to a victim caught in ambush, and escaping from his assassins, and I cannot conceive your purport. Walter is not my prisoner, nor is he the hostage of the King. He came freely to sanctuary, and when he leaves it, it shall be as freely."

"Are you ignorant that he has committed the crime of high treason, that he was in the pay of Francis of Brittany? His very presence is a mortal menace to your convent and to yourself. You never had a worse enemy than this man. I wish to be hanged, if I can guess why you should befriend him! What can you expect from him? He is lost, he is ruined, beyond redemption."

"He is here, relying on a sacred traditional right," said the Prior, rising to his feet. "I have no need to know more. What to me are your intrigues, or his disgrace and ruin? I am the guardian of the honor of this church: I will maintain it against the whole world. The sanctuary of Our Lady of Pity shall not be profaned by blood-thirsty villains, so long as one friar remains here to defend its threshold."

"Is this your answer, Father Prior? Are you forgetting the allegiance you owe your sovereign?"

The Benedictine stretched his hand out towards a statue of Our Lady with her Divine Babe, which dominated the vast room. "There is my sovereign, and King Louis' sovereign also. I am ready to die in her service."

Oliver crossed himself devoutly, while inwardly he consigned the obstinate monk to the powers of evil. "Pray reconsider, your Reverence. I would not have you subject to severe measures. Yet the King might employ armed force! What else could you do then, save surrender?"

"What could I do? I could resist: not indeed by a rebellion, but by the spiritual authority intrusted to me. I could pronounce publicly the *ipso facto* excommunication incurred by any who profane the holy place. It is for the King to choose whether he will expose himself to it."

"Excommunicate his Majesty!" cried le Daim, bewildered by the threat. "Do you mean it, Father Prior? The scandal of it would overturn the kingdom of France!"

"In any case, the blame will not be mine. My conscience will be at rest."

"You have not spoken your final word," Oliver continued, visibly agitated. "Do not try to impose upon me. See now: what price do you ask for giving Maulny into our hands? I repeat that a bishopric, nay, a cardinalate, has entered his

Majesty's mind as a suitable reward for you. And unless you aspire to the Papal tiara "—

" You alarm me, my son. I must write to King Louis at once, and relieve you of all responsibility in the matter."

Dom John seated himself at a table covered with parchments, and seizing a pen, wrote rapidly, during several minutes. " Read ! " he said, offering the letter to Oliver le Daim.

The latter cast his eyes over it, and shrank back in dismay. " I shall never deliver such a message, Fougereuse."

" As you please. Give it to me : I will seal and send it. Where is his Majesty at present? "

" At Angers castle."

" I thank you."

The barber-minister silently watched the Prior fold the manuscript, and stamp it with the great seal of the monastery, then summon a lay Brother, and hand it to him, with directions spoken in an undertone. A few moments later, the clatter of hoofs resounded on the gravel.

" You may go now, Oliver. My missive will be at Angers before you."

" What a man you are ! " exclaimed le Daim, gazing at Dom John with a sort of admiration. " Are you aware that all this may end very, very badly ? Only a year ago, the Prior of Saint Mark's was thrown into the Loire, by Tristram's orders, for an act less bold than yours."

" It matters little, my son. One must die sometime! Either by land or water, Paradise is accessible. Perhaps I am even more ambitious than you deem me, Master Oliver! You offer me the red hat: but I seek the martyr's crown."

.   .   .   .

Night had come again: one of those lovely, calm, starlit nights which belong to the sweet sky of Anjou. The friars had sung Compline, and were filing through the cloisters, with bowed heads and folded hands, in that absolute silence which monastic rule imposes upon the recollected evening hours. Those who lay ill at the hospice saw the Brother in charge arrive at his post of duty, and light the lamp which burned before the statue of Our Lady. That gracious figure, in the ray of the steadfast, mystical flame, was a consolation to sleepless eyes. The sufferers felt themselves supported and strengthened by Mary's maternal hand, by her whom the Church calls health of the sick, refuge of sinners, comforter of the afflicted; and if they suffered on, it was not without hope and peace and resignation.

Villepreux's Thieves, leaning on their spears, kept watch along the walls; and across the whole width of the valley, the picket posts of the gallant little army stood ready to utter the cry of alarm, at the first scent of danger. Their captain remained at the Priory, and his sharp eyes sentinelled the sentinels as effectively as they would detect the approach of the enemy. Villepreux had employed every precaution which human prudence and devoted fidelity could suggest, and left the rest to Heaven. There could be no such thing now as taking the Priory at a disadvantage, were Louis XI. to come with his Scotch soldiers, or Satan with all his swarm! One leader would find before him a troop ready for battle; and the other would surely encounter the legions of angels which Heaven places at the disposal of its Queen, and who have her name as their war-cry, to strike terror through the hosts of Hell.

In the shadowy crypt, Walter de Maulny tossed on his bed of pain. Near him was Father Andrew, attentive to his lightest wish, humoring him in his worst caprices; though nothing seemed to satisfy or quiet him. Isabelle de Villepreux had made a great effort to lead him into more Christian moods. She had visited him during the day, holding her little daughter by the hand; she had leaned over the wounded wretch with sisterly solicitude; she spoke to him of their childish years passed together, and then, believing him touched by her sweet words, she importuned him to return to God. Walter turned away harshly from the gentle young dame and her angel-like compassion; he shut his eyes that he might not be affected by the innocent beauty of Yvette, who was the very picture of her mother at the same age; he shut his heart, too, to all memories of the old time, as if by so doing he revenged himself for his unrequited suit. She, therefore, departed in tears, without having won any response save this bitter reproach: "You could have saved me once, Isabelle, but you would not. And now it is too late."

Afterwards, however, the vision of those wet blue eyes came back to haunt him in his solitude, and to add to his anguish. Nor could he escape from it. Through his troubled brain rushed a thousand remembrances of his earliest youth, of the days when as yet the passion of envy had not dried up the lifesprings of his heart. He saw again his mother's kinsman, the baron Amaury de Fougereuse, who reared him as his son, and taught him to be truthful and brave; he saw the comely baroness, his second mother, who devoted to him the same care and the same endearments which she bestowed upon her own children; he saw Isabelle, no older than the wee Yvette, laughing, and with golden ringlets, her little hand in that of the boy who was then her champion and slave. He saw also (and this hurt him most), a Guy whom he had not learned to hate, who walked arm-in-arm with him, shared his sports, knelt beside him at morning and evening prayer: a Guy who ever turned upon Walter the eyes of brotherly love. The unhappy culprit would fain flee away from these phantoms which enraged him so; or again, he would cry out upon his own bodily weakness, which forced him to look upon them without anger. He talked much and impiously; he loaded with abuse and profanity the kindly friars at his bedside. Dom Andrew vexed himself but little on that account. He knew, by experience, that such mad outbursts indicated the remorse stirring within, and he prayed God to perfect His work, and send the grace of repentance.

Midnight rang from the belfry. The door opened, and Brother Louis came softly into the room. Bending over the aged monk, he asked a question or two; the latter rose, observed his patient, who had apparently just fallen asleep, gave some brief instructions to the novice, and noiselessly withdrew. Loïc sank into the seat vacated by the hermit, and fervently raised his mind to God in prayer. The war over Maulny's soul was to rage that night between Brother Louis and the Prince of Darkness, and the youth had sworn, by the help of Heaven, to make him relinquish his prey. Maulny remained in the same state of drowsiness real or feigned, his hard features laying by nothing of their fierceness and cynicism. Ever and anon Loïc rose, and brooded over the rebel against God and man. Instinctively his lips, obeying his thought rather than his will, began to murmur that beautiful prayer of the great Saint Thomas Aquinas: "*Supreme Goodness, O Lord Jesus! create in me a heart captivated by Thee, which no sight or sound of this world may distract from Thee: a proud and faithful heart, which never wavers, never descends.*"

Maulny's eyelids fluttered nervously, though they remained closed. Brother Louis went on:

"*A free heart, never seduced, never enslaved: an*

*upright heart, never found in devious ways: a
dauntless heart, that will renew itself after every
storm.*"

" Hold there ! " cried the patient, throwing himself forward in the bed. " Are your prayers canon-
ical, my reverend friend ? In any event, they are
ambitious. You tempt the Lord." He repeated
ironically : " A proud heart, a heart faithful and
upright, and free, and dauntless, and what else ?
Plague upon it ! but that is enough. Do you
think you are everything that is good ? "

" A truce to your sneers, messire Walter ! " Loïc
answered. " They do but harm you, and delight
the evil spirits. It is time to dress your wounds.
Let me examine them."

" Ah ! the old patriarch has given me up. By
Saint George ! I am not sorry for it, for that long,
face of his gave me the nightmare. And you:
who are you ? Something in your voice sets me
against you. I have heard it in my dreams, like
a carillon that mocked me. Come hither, hobgoblin, that I may see you plain."

He seized the novice by the hand, and drew him
to his side, curious to discover whether, in that
tranquillized face, he could detect any souvenir
of the past. Loïc endured the scrutiny without
winking. But at last Maulny shoved him away,
and turned over on his pillow. " Those are Kernis's eyes ! I believe I am going mad." Then,
with sudden fury, he added : " That were all that
is lacking to my death-agony ! Every one of them

come to me here! Why not King René? As for Louis of France, we are two at the same game: against a deceiver, pit a deceiver and a half!" And he broke out into wicked laughter.

Loïc prepared the bandages in silence. Walter looked at him, and continued disdainfully: "Come, pretty page! stop masquerading. I tell you I know who you are. Do you hear me, Louis-Artus III., count of Kernis?"

"I cannot imagine, messire, to whom you think you are speaking. There is no count of Kernis. My name is Brother Louis."

"Make some one else believe that! You played successfully the part of a Breton shepherd, but — a friar? You have fine impudence, on my soul! Confess your mischievous prank. I will laugh with you, and it will soothe me."

"Maulny, I am no friar, but a poor novice, whom his superiors are not yet willing to admit to vows, much as he importunes them. I ought not to answer to the name which was mine when I was a layman. Novices or professed religious, we monks are dead to the world: and that is something which worldlings are determined never to understand! Now then: be quiet, and let me bathe your wounds. That is my purpose in being here."

Walter offered no resistance to the skilful, supple-fingered hands, once so deft with the rapier, which now enabled Brother Louis to be the best infirmarian in the adjoining hospice. The young

man's dexterity, evidently the result of considerable experience, seemed 'to shake Maulny's dis-
belief in him, and it was in a much more serious
tone that he next addressed Loïc: " Do you mean
to say that you followed your master hither? "

" I did, indeed, come hither for love of my
earthly master; but it is for love of the Heavenly
Master that I stay. And here I hope to die, loyal
to them both."

Walter turned his head, with a sudden, impatient movement, which caused the strip of linen to
fall from his companion's hand. " Horrors! can
it be true? The finest piece of mesmerism Fougereuse ever wrought! How could he have had the
heart to change Loïc into a friar! . . . What a
pity! You thought yourself a hero, my lad, and
in reality you were just a simpleton. Better have
buried yourself alive! for it would sooner be over."

"My thanks for your advice!" the novice replied, without irritation. " Would you but remain
quiet, sir knight, instead of bestirring yourself, in
every sense of the word, there might be some
chance of fastening these bandages."

The nurse had regained his authority over the
patient, who mechanically allowed himself to be
tended, while he watched every motion Brother
Louis made. The sight of the young Benedictine
bred wonder, mingled with compassion. Was this
really that same child, full of nerve and pluck, in
love with liberty, dreaming only of battles to be,
and of great blows to strike? the bold, mischiev-

ous stripling, whose vein of humor came to the fore, even in the hour of danger? the Loïc who had defied all the peers at his friend's famous trial?

"Is this the most that Fougereuse could make of you?" The wounded man spoke slowly, casting a rueful glance on the busy, bent head. "To condemn you to this, you so young, so comely, so nobly born, after all your sacrifices for him! Poor boy, why did you not attach yourself to me? for I would have repaid your devotion in a far different manner. Trust me never to have buried, under a monk's habit, the blood of Noménoë! But you are free as yet, Kernis, are you not?"

"Good Lord, good Lord!" exclaimed the other, rising up, and stepping back, with one of his old characteristic gestures. Then he stopped short, and stood for a moment near the bed, silent and motionless. The hanging lamp lit up the brow of one-and-twenty, radiant with youth and purity, already marked austerely with the tonsure; the eyes which still were full of fire, but of fire hallowed and subdued; the face so lofty and yet so meek, whose every feature bespoke a spirit freed from human yoke, and subject to God alone. Before the victorious look of him whom he was commiserating, Maulny's own forehead reddened.

"Good Lord!" the novice said, more gently, "what patience one does need when dealing with you, Walter de Maulny! Father Prior accuses me of lacking it, but I have just swallowed enough to last me. What demon prompts you to this miserable course? Listen, once for all, and set your mind at rest. The blood of Noménoë had to choose either the throne or the cloister! Envy me, or imitate me. but do not wrong me by offering me your pity. It is more glorious to serve Christ Our Lord than to govern a kingdom. Six feet of earth and a shroud: there is man's utmost in this world! Or were it otherwise, I would not, for an empire, exchange my better part. If you knew with what excelling joy and peace God rewards his own! . . . There! be not angry. The wounds are dressed. Let me cover you again."

"Talk not to me of joy or peace, or anything of the sort!" replied Walter excitedly, "nor of hell, nor of death; or may the Devil take you! I will not be preached at!"

"Very well. Have your own way."

All was still for a quarter of an hour, until, the stillness weighing upon the sick man, he began to complain bitterly. "I am thirsty: give me something to drink. No, not that cup; I must have the other. . . . How can you be willing to see me suffer so? You do nothing to help me. . . . I am choking."

"Lean on me. I am going to lift you. Would you like to have me change the pillows?"

"No . . . yes . . . as you will. But I should rather have you drive away these ghosts. I cannot shut my eyes, without feeling them all around me. . . . Drive them away! Talk, shout, sing! Keep me from thinking!"

He was in evident anguish. Loïc was touched; and while he did what he could to relieve Maulny, he began to sing, in a soft clear tenor, an ancient hymn to Our Lady, which ere now had given comfort and pleasure to the fever-stricken under his care. But at its opening measures, Walter sprang up with an oath.

"Blood and thunder, Kernis! Who taught you that? . . . I will not have it. . . . Be quiet, or I "—

"What is the matter? What have I done?"

"Be quiet! Your voice is like *his*, when . . . long ago, we two together . . . sang it at our evening prayers. . . . Curses on *him!* . . . I never can pray any more. . . . I curse you for this life and the next, Guy de Fougereuse!"

"God forgive you, Maulny!" Loïc said solemnly. "You do not know what you are saying."

"I do not, eh?" exclaimed Maulny, shrugging his shoulders. "Own it, young knave! own it: Guy ordered you to sing that, and so work upon my feelings. It was our childish lullaby. A little more, and I should have stumbled into the trap! But I am nobody's dupe, my dear novice."

"I should not wish you to be duped. But you are an ingrate, hostile to those who love you."

"Those who love me!" the wounded knight broke in, with an incredulous laugh. "This child is unique for imagining things. Those who love me! Who are they, I beg you to inform me? Who ever loved me? You, perhaps? Ha, ha!"

"I was not thinking of myself, who am nothing to you, but of nobler hearts which you have broken. Smile not thus, Maulny! Yesterday I saw Isabelle de Villepreux teaching her little ones to pray for you."

A passing regret came over Walter's face; but it flitted away. "Isabelle, poor soul! Why did she come here? I have no grudge against her, for Guy did it all."

"Do not mention his name again, you who never really knew him!"

"Did I never really know Guy de Fougercuse? The charge is amusing: I only wish it were true! Far better for me never to have been born, than to have known that man at all. And I never really knew him? Have you come here to say that to me? Repeat it, if you dare!"

The speaker's eyes were ablaze. Brother Louis did not reply immediately. Bending over, by the light of the lamp on the table, he counted out the drops of the elixir which fell, one by one, from a phial he was holding, into a cup half-full of water. Neither he nor Maulny heard the door open, or saw some one enter with infinite caution, and glide forward, to stand in the shadows, at the head of the bed. The nurse, having finished his task, laid the liquid down, and stood upright, crossing his arms.

"Listen, Walter de Maulny. I have a right to judge Dom John: I who am a witness of his daily life for over a dozen years. No: you never really knew him! Your hate belongs to a phantom which you yourself created in his stead, and called by his name; which you always envied and detested. But he, my master and my Father"—

"That is where you deceive yourself, child," said Maulny, raising himself again. "No one loved Guy better than I did! Do not protest: for it is true. It was in our boyish days. Everybody loved him. If he were in the room, it was useless for another to try to win attention even from a servant, yea, even from a dog! Ah, there was a time when I was led captive, like the rest. Had he willed it, I would have given him the devoted affection of all my heart. With one little word of tenderness, he could have gained me for his friend, and saved me from evil; but he would not take the trouble. He made sport of me, scorned me, defeated me, by preference. Rivals in every field as we were, I had to love or hate him unreservedly. He chose"—

Maulny paused. He stared into the dark with a frightful intensity, as if his last words had had power to call up a spectre. "He chose my hatred. Let him keep it for ever and ever!"

The bed-curtain shook slightly, and a deep sigh came faintly to Loïc's ear. He made the sign of the Cross, as he looked around. "Unhappy one!" he said, approaching the sick man, "have you forgotten that it was Dom John who saved you from Tristram's daggers?"

"Oh, he saved me, I know; he affects the magnanimous. But he must answer for me, all the same, at the Judgment Day. I pawned my soul only that I might get the better of him. . . . Even now, in the very jaws of death, I would sell my salvation to carry out my revenge! to see that imperious Fougereuse humbled, in his turn, as low as I am, and spurned as he spurns me. . . . I am more hungry for that retaliation than I am for Paradise! And now I am losing it. It is all Guy's work. Well may he sing a pæan of victory! . . . Behold what he has made of me! A worm would not take the gift of such a life as I lead, and I die like a reprobate, a reprobate!"

"Oh, let me call Father Andrew!" the novice pleaded. He took a step towards the threshold, but Maulny reached out passionately, and held him fast.

"No. no: I do not wish it. . . . I will not, I tell you! Do not bring back that gray hermit. No priest can absolve me . . . for I must repent, and I will not repent. I regret nothing. . . . Guy has left for me not even the mercy of God in my last hours!"

"He! Why, benighted being that you are, he is invoking that mercy for you, on his knees! You once saw him stand unflinching in sight of disgrace and a shameful public death; but now we of this monastery see him crushed, trembling, unrecogniz-able, because he feels that your immortal soul is in peril! He has ceased to eat or sleep; he lays on himself the hardest penitential exercises; he passes

whole nights in prayers and tears; he is under-
going martyrdom, if only God will snatch you from
ruin! I swear to you, Maulny"—

"Enough! I believe you not. . . . Enough of
your sermons, votary of Saint Fougereuse!"

The sarcasm, so uttered, stung Loïc to the quick.
Under his Benedictine dress there began to beat
furiously, as of old, the heart of the noble page who
loved his master alone, and would sacrifice his life
for him. Louis de Kernis faced the elder man just
as he had faced him in King René's tribunal,
with a look that seared, with an annihilating
gesture.

"Silence, blasphemer! He whom you thus re-
vile may yet perish because of you. It is for you
that he is braving King Louis' demand. To-morrow his head may fall under the executioner's axe;
and to-night your soul may fall into hell! . . . I
have spoken the truth. If I have done wrong in
speaking at all, may Saint Benedict overlook it in
me!"

Walter became absolutely livid, and seized Loïc
again, with all his strength. "If you are in earnest, explain things, Kernis," he said harshly, while
his eyes searched the young face before him. But
Brother Louis turned his head aside, inwardly recognizing and deploring the revolt of his own nature,
and the freshet of angered feeling which had over-
swept the warnings given by the Prior. "Do not
ask me. I have said too much already."

"I must know what you are concealing from

me! . . . Come, no hypocrisy. . . . What was
that about the King? . . . Tristram has found me
out!"

"No, Walter: not Tristram."

"Oliver, the King's other crony? . . . You
answer not. . . . Ah, hell-cat of a barber! He
has scented my track, and loosed his blood-hounds
. . . but they will never get me alive. . . . And
your Prior abandoned me to him; he "—

"Have no fear, messire. Rather did he abandon
himself! Oliver departed, amazed and in great
wrath, haranguing us, at the doors, not to uphold
our fanatic Superior in his rebellion, unless we
meant to make acquaintance with the iron cages
at Loches and Plessis-les-Tours, and reminding us
that the Loire flowed for the benefit of everybody,
and especially of meddling monks! That evening,
Dom John offered to send to the Abbey of Saint-
Aubin any among us who were not willing to suffer persecution for the Church; and he announced
to us his firm resolve to maintain the right of sanctuary, even if he must seal his testimony with his
life-blood. To be sure, no one was disposed to desert him: we would all joyfully follow him to prison
or the grave. Our sole cause of alarm is lest he
should brave them without us! . . . Villepreux
and his Saracens have charge of you; they are
bound to defend a client of Our Lady of Pity. Do
you sleep and take your rest, Sir Walter de Maulny.
For your life is secure, and your revenge is very
near. But if you fear God, turn your attention to

the state of your soul. No man can save that for you, nor spend it, either."

"You have said enough to me," replied Walter, with ever-growing agitation. "Give me my clothing."

"Your clothing! when you have no strength to stand! Maulny! are you determined to kill yourself?" He struggled to keep his companion in the bed, and barely succeeded.

Walter wrestled with him, and tried to break out of the room. "I wish to go from here, to go at once, whether it kills me or not! Do you understand?"

"I understand that you are raving."

"Dare not to repeat that!" shrieked Maulny, in a terrible fit of temper. "It was when I asked sanctuary of your Prior that I was indeed raving! I ought to have known that Fougereuse would not let pass so fine an occasion for playing the hero! . . . Ah, he would die for me, would he? Why? By what warrant? Does he actually think me so mean, so stupid, that I could let him replace me on the scaffold? For what species of coward does he take me? . . . I will not allow it. If the King be set upon finishing his work, well and good: let him finish it! I will not quarrel with him over the miserable fragment of life I yet possess. Let him stab me, behead me, or drown me: it is his right, and I indorse it. See now, you must not hold me back! You do not know Louis of France. My very presence here means death to Guy. Hold

me not back, unless you hate me. . . . Help me,
help me! . . . Ah, my cursed weakness! I cannot . . . do more."

Maulny fell back exhausted, wringing his hands,
weeping with helpless rage. Loïc bathed his brows,
covered with sweat. In a cracked voice, the
wounded knight went on: "Anything . . . rather
than this. Put an end to me, and I will thank you
for it. No? Then call Oliver. Throw me out-of-
doors. . . . The headsman would be so welcome!"

"But what demon has got into you?" Loïc
exclaimed, at his wits' end. "Angels and saints
defend us! The creature has gone mad."

"Ah, there is no pity in you!" Distraught
with grief and passion, Maulny suddenly seized,
with both hands, the bandages which covered his
breast, and tore them off. Brother Louis threw
himself forward, with a cry, to interrupt the patient's action: but a strong touch came between.
A form arose in the shadowy chamber, and there
in the lamplight gleamed a face of mortal pallor:
the face of Dom John de Fougereuse.

Leaning close over the bed, he gathered up and
mastered its occupant, more by his look than by
his embrace, and breathed into him his own great
and quiet force. Walter fought awhile, and violently twisted the monk's wristbands, in the vain
hope of loosening his hold. Then he sighed, his
features relaxed, his head fell back, he lost consciousness; and the blood gushed freely from his
re-opened wound. They made haste to put him

out of danger, not a word being interchanged between the Prior and the novice. From long association, they were accustomed to understand each other, without speech; and the selfsame anxiety now set their hearts beating in unison. Walter seemed perfectly lifeless. The Prior raised him gently; Loïc took prompt measures to staunch the flow of blood, and to renew and carefully fasten the bandages. A generous quantity of cordial was poured, drop by drop, between the discolored lips, where respiration had apparently ceased. A strange, still battle, of some hours' duration, then ensued, where the dying Maulny's rescuers disputed him, inch by inch, with the death which he had invited: an interval of labor, and prayer, and heartbreak, which men who love not God cannot believe in nor comprehend. But at last they triumphed, and the patient opened his eyes, surprised to find himself still in this world. He stared, mutely, at the objects around: at the low-vaulted crypt, the swaying lamp, the table, with its flasks of medicine, the dark bed-curtains, and the ivory crucifix above. Brother Louis tiptoed to his side, with a glass in his hand. Walter knew him; his faculties were returning, albeit confusedly. But whose arm was it which was so strong under him? On whose shoulder was his weary head lying? A mother watching over her sick child could not be more tender than this serviceable stranger! Walter yielded himself to his new nurse's comforting embrace, with absolute confidence. But his memory awoke with a bound.

What if it should be — ? His eyes suddenly met those of Fougereuse, fixed upon him with such genuine concern, such poignant sympathy, that, for the first time, Walter's own hostile spirit was stricken dumb, and disarmed.

"Guy?" he stammered, in a voice which was hardly more than a whisper.

The Prior gently closed his lips. "Hush, imprudent one! Do not try to talk."

Loïc proffered the contents of the glass. Maulny drank obediently, and his torpor began to pass away. He had seen Dom John, he thought, before he fainted; now he was sure of it. It was he who had controlled him so. It was to him that the failure of his attempt to destroy himself was due. And yet Maulny's death would mean the safety of Fougereuse and of his monastery! The patient turned over, and hid his face. Something was going on within, as was evident by the contraction of his hands, and the violent trembling of his whole body. In the depth of that blighted nature, born for better things, a spark of honor still glowed; and the Christian faith of his youth was there too, to trouble, willingly or unwillingly, his defrauded conscience.

"Guy!" He made an effort, and called again. "Guy!" The Prior leaned over, and Walter raised himself a little. "Have me brought to the King. I beg and beseech you! He demands my head: I wish to carry it to him, in person. I tell you it must be done. Zounds! am I a slave? Why did you not let me die?"

"You are here to be protected under the Church's wing, my son. No sacrilegious arm can threaten you, nay, not even your own, without opposition. Lie still, and listen to me. The sanctuary of Our Lady of Pity is the heritage of the unfortunate. You can sleep in peace under its roof."

"Sleep in peace? Who? I? . . . Get me a litter, and horses! Take me hence! . . . Surrender me to King Louis. It is your duty as a vassal."

"My son, I have a prior duty as a priest. I am responsible to God for you, nor can I give you up to another. Spare me this teasing," Dom John added, in tones which were both plaintive and severe.

"Guy, but you are injuring yourself, you know! You are risking your life. No one can foresee what will happen, if you keep me here." Walter spoke in short, breathless phrases. "The King will show you no quarter. I denounced you to him. And now it all rebounds on me. . . . Damnation! Why should you save me? Choose some other revenge, but not that, not that."

"His mind is wandering; he is so weak," murmured the Prior. "Why do you name revenge at all?"

"Because I am talking to you: the man I hated, whom I ruined, whom I would have sent, remorselessly, to the stake. You remember!"

"I do not remember."

"You do not? How is it, then? Are you not Fougereuse? Are you not the baron Guy?"

"Nay," answered the Benedictine, his eyes, with their old, far-seeing power, looking down into Maulny's eyes. "Baron Guy is dead: may the Lord have mercy upon him!" He made the sign of the Cross, as if before a grave, and continued slowly: "Walter de Maulny, that man whom you say you hated, — the heedless lad who hurt you with his light speech, the triumphant rival whose success was your undoing, — he has passed away from this world. Seek him not here! For six years past you have been pursuing a ghost. . . . Do not tremble, my son. The soul which was Baron Guy is no more, now, than a poor friar dedicated to penance, and praying God, by day and night, to forgive the sins of his youth. On the cloister threshold, the passions of this world fade. In the quiet of a cell, at the foot of a Crucifix, faults of our former life which men were far from condemning, faults which they applauded, even, look to us, at last, as they really were and are in the sight of the Eternal Wisdom. Then do we implore Him, with tears, to grant us our purgation here below, that we may see His face in Paradise."

It was a strange scene, at once thrilling and simple. In the stone chamber, solemn as a tomb, under the flickering watch-light, lay the sufferer on the bed, like the dead awakened from his long sleep. All the life left in him glowed in his dark eyes, burning-bright with fever and transient animation. The Prior, wrapped in his ample black cowl, the hood thrown back on his shoulders, his shapely head bare, his face bathed in supernatural peace, his voice peaceful too, but deep and distinct, seemed some blessed visitor come from above to comfort the unhappy. In a dim corner, Brother Louis was on his knees, infinite emotion in his breast. There, a few steps away, was the drama of the everlasting fate of a creature of God, being played between hell and Heaven!

"Blessed be the Merciful Father who brought you hither, Walter, and gave me the supreme opportunity of this good hour at your side!" Dom John resumed. "We have both sinned: against each other, and against Him. But His joy is to forgive, as He has proved to me, my brother. Now, are we two, wrong as we are, going to hold aloof, and refuse to pardon the past? I have reproached myself, many a time, for having treated you with indifference in our boyhood, and even with hardness. I never knew how our little quarrels and competitions weighed on you, Walter, as you say that they did. You might have pledged me loyal friendship, and I wantonly forfeited it; so your hatred began, and grew day by day, until now it looms between you and your Maker. I am to blame; I confess it. I cannot tell you how odious it seems to me now, to have been as vain, as frivolous, as obstinate, as I was at twenty!"

"Father!" Loïc whispered the unheard protest.

Maulny flushed the deepest red, and his head sank lower, despite his will; but he was in no mental condition to answer. The Prior came nearer, with a frank, outstretched hand, and wistful eyes.

" Walter!"

But Walter hid his face, and panted. " I cannot!" He spoke so low that the other could hardly hear him. " I beg you to . . . I cannot."

" Walter, I implore you: my brother of long ago! Have I not come to your death-bed to claim that friendship which, in my folly, I once undervalued? to offer you the same hand which once rejected the grasp of yours? Be generous to me. Forgive me; for the sake of the time and the place."

Nothing can describe the sincerity of these words, into which the Prior put his whole soul. Walter suddenly raised his head from the pillows, and gazed long at his cousin, too stupefied to speak.

" Guy! Have I gone mad, or did you ask my pardon? Yes? And you, ready to die for me, and sacrifice your monastery? My hand in yours? No: it is too deeply stained. Leave me, leave me. . . . But God will bless you for your deed tonight, if " —

He never finished his sentence, for Dom John had taken him in his arms, and gathered him to his bosom, his fair, clear brow against that brow branded with shame, and his hands clasping the hot hands which had wrought for him only persecution and disaster.

"Blush not before me," said the Prior, with deep emotion. "I am a priest, my son: I have the power to absolve you.   If you do really and fully forgive me, let us exchange a kiss of peace, as on the eve of that blessed day when we received, side by side, our First Communion: two little lads under my mother's eyes. You came to me first; do you recall that, Walter?   Now it is my turn: I come to you. And the same Lord awaits us both, in the Sacrament of His Love."

The Prior touched his lips, fraternally, to Maulny's quivering cheek, while the latter, vanquished at last, shook with great sobs. The monk's humility had won over that Satanic pride which, confronted with the mere magnanimity of the gallant gentleman, did but grow fiercer. The hardened cynic wept like a child, pressed to the tender and aching heart of the servant of Christ. Brother Louis rose, and softly uttered an exultant *Te Deum.*

"Dear son, your Saviour calls you," said Dom John, with gentle authority. "You have no cause for fear. I will take your penance on myself; I will answer for you; I would as willingly give my life for yours, as He gave His for us both. But ah, do not refuse Him your soul, which He purchased with His blood."

"Is it not too late?" Maulny murmured.

The Prior stood up with lightning in his eyes: a transformed figure, full of the majesty of his priesthood. "*'Now is the acceptable time, now is*

the day of salvation!' Bid not the Lord to delay!" he exclaimed, in commanding accents. "I
speak in His name. Accuse yourself, O Christian
soul!"

It was indeed the day of salvation. A ray of
Divine Grace shot across the darkness, and darted
into the recesses of that tormented spirit. Maulny
bent his head. " Bless me, Father," he began.

From the heart of the religious a hymn of victory went up to God. Christ had conquered;
hell had lost its trophy! The angels looked down
upon the two best treasures which their King has
on the earth: the meekness of the just man, and
the sorrow of the sinner.

.   .   .   .

King Louis XI. sat in a great dim room of the
castle at Angers. The table near him was covered
with parchments; his elbows rested on the carven
arms of an oaken chair furnished with velvet cush-
ions. He was clad in a surcoat of brown cloth, so
well-worn that any ordinary citizen would have
disdained to wear it. On his head was his famous
cap, fringed with leaden medals of the saints, and
circled with a string of rosary beads. His profile,
sufficiently unlovely, but interesting because of
its individual strangeness, had a waxen pallor.
Dressed in the very fashion of his master, reproducing his every attitude and expression, as much
as a poor copy can reproduce a painting of value,
Oliver le Daim stood before the King, dumbly

awaiting what blame or praise should be allotted to the results of his mission.

"And so, comrade," said his Majesty, breaking in upon his own meditations, "we had a forlorn chase, and missed our quarry in the end, did we? *Pasques-Dieu!* what is it worth, your nickname of Oliver the Devil? I ought to have employed Tristram instead, with his sub-executioners, and his fine thick skull: for he never would have done anything so absurd. You threatened the Prior with violent measures, and yet you come back with empty hands! You should either have said nothing of your intentions, or else put them into immediate action. I would disclaim you, only that so I should be playing into the hands of Maulny, and of my dear cousin of Brittany."

"I did not understand your Majesty's orders in that sense."

"Stuff! Could the King of France afford to give such orders? There are certain services which cannot be prescribed, which a good vassal knows how to discharge, all the same. Does it behoove me, me, the Eldest Son of the Church, wantonly to overturn the sanctuary privilege, and to incur the anathema of the Sovereign Pontiff? May Heaven preserve me from it! But a man like you, a mere pagan, a moral outlaw, would run no great risk in getting himself excommunicated!"

"Another time, sire." the barber had begun, when he was cut short.

"Keep silence, and think of some way to remedy

the mischief done. You allowed a letter from the Prior to reach me: that was the climax of your blundering. I should never have received it. Do you understand me? Am I Julian the Apostate, that such language should be addressed to me? That monk is an adversary not to be despised." He picked up a folded paper which was lying on the table, and read slowly, pausing now and then: "'The Church, sire, is your mother and mine. When she gathers a fugitive to her breast, his retreat is sacred. If the King ask from me what is my own, I shall not refuse him; but divine things are not mine to give. Does he wish my patrimony? Let him take it. Or my life? It should be yielded readily. I would not summon a crowd of defenders to my side; I prefer to die for the integrity of our altars.' . . . It is all in that vein," the monarch continued, crushing the letter. "So much for your foolish behavior! This arrogant nobility is everywhere alike in my provinces: whether under the cowl, or under helmet and breastplate, it is forever seeking some pretext to defy my authority. Well, patience! My lady Democracy will grow like a weed, in the fields of these haughty dreamers. The common people will mow the harvest, and, please God, I shall get the sheaves! And meanwhile, it is better to bend than to break. Where pride canters before, tears and trouble gallop after. We have enemies enough to fight, and rebels enough to tame, without getting into difficulties with Holy Church, whom all

Christians should revere and obey." The King blessed himself piously, mumbling an *Our Father;* then said suddenly: " Robert the Lion: what of him?"

" One little speech, sire. 'Oliver le Daim, you were born a knave, and a knave you will die; and a knave will you be buried, and a knave will you rise again. Go and perform your antics elsewhere!'"

"Really, comrade? That was not ill-put, for a giant of his stamp. . . . Setting aside the Prior and his fast friend, could you make no headway with the monks? In the cloister, as in other places, there are discontented and ambitious spirits. One must make use of these."

"Sire, I tried it. But those men are fanatics. They aspire to nothing but Heaven, and they fear nothing but sin. I turned my batteries especially on one young novice, who seemed to me less confirmed in sanctity; for in him I recognized that wicked little page who used to follow Fougereuse about, like a pet imp. It was all in vain: he is worse than the rest, and romantically devoted to the reverend Father. I am not at all surprised that that man should once have been considered a magician, so great is his power over every one who comes near him."

"Is that so? Did he induce you to go to confession? " asked King Louis, with a mocking smile, and a look which made his favorite minion shiver. " You have the knack of dealing with scamps, but honest folk do seem somewhat beyond you! Send the Devil among the saints, as they say, and you will see him come back disconcerted."

"Indeed, sire," answered the barber, "there are in your Majesty's policy a number of measures which can hardly be the business of the saints!"

"You speak truly, friend le Daim," sighed Louis. "The government of the perverse human race is a hard and trying task. Politics are a sort of infernal stew; often demons, rather than angels, are needed to stir it and cook it. Behold my reason for employing you, Oliver the Bad, and for making you a great lord! But in this emergency, we ought to have here Maulny's wise, level head."

"Sire!" cried Oliver, astounded.

"Oh, be not startled in the least. I was speaking of his head. As to his body, it may very well remain where it is."

The King and his confidant exchanged a meaning glance, which bore out their thoughts. Louis XI. sank again into a revery, pacing up and down the room. Then he said, coming to a halt before his minister: "You have lost the first throw; now I will try the second. I must have that Walter! The Prior will stipulate for his pardon, and I shall strike a bargain with him. One can live, yet live in a dungeon! Have the boats ready. I will go on a pilgrimage to Our Lady of Pity!"

Some few hours later, the boats were gliding gently down the stream between the green meadows, grazing the drooping willow-boughs, and swaying the clusters of blossomy reeds which grow all around the isles of the Loire. They were put ashore at the foot of a hill having a wooded crest, where a slender spire, surmounted by a cross, revealed its delicate lace-like stone traceries through the leafy openings. The bells were ringing their full chime for the evening Angelus, and in the fields hard by, one might watch the laborers suspend their tasks, and fold their hands to pray.

Louis XI. disembarked, separated himself from his escort while passing through the village, and went alone, as an humble stranger, through the monastery gate. He rapped at the door of the hospice, and asked to see Dom John. The King was shown into a plain, bare room, furnished only with a large wooden Crucifix, and a couple of benches. Dom John appeared, very soon, upon the inner threshold.

"Peace be to you!" he greeted his guest, descending the stone steps which led from the hospice parlor to the Priory.

"My hope is all for peace, Father," responded the King, rising.

"Your Majesty in this house!" cried the surprised monk.

"I have come to answer your letter otherwise than in writing: for, *Pasques-Dieu!* it gave me a hunger to make your acquaintance. By all the saints, what apostolic eloquence you spent on me! Saint John Chrysostom would not have disclaimed it. And it touched me; I should be most contrite now, had I deserved it. But you, Father, are quite mistaken. The probable sacrilege, over which you are so very much wrought up, was never contemplated by me! You must accuse Oliver the Bad, and his own folly. I upbraided him roundly, scoundrel that he is, for having attributed to me the criminal intention of violating a sanctuary consecrated to the Virgin Mother of God. Never shall our sweet Lady Saint Mary have such cause to be displeased with me : to that I pledge my word, as a prince and a Christian."

"Heaven hears you, sire," the Prior said gravely, and added not another word. The eyes of the two met, across the silence, and the keen eyes of the King sank before those of the religious, who seemed to be reading his inmost thought.

"You begged me to pardon a wretch," continued the King, "a perjured felon, undeserving of any mercy. He is a kinsman of yours; but I fear, Father, that he has taken advantage of you. Do you know what that man has done for you and for your virtuous community? He stopped at nothing. . . . You do know, you say? Ah, well: your charity is superhuman, sir monk. Following Our Saviour's example, you pray for your murderers. I should like to humor you, and to grant you the only favor you have ever asked, since you became a subject of mine. But pardon Maulny, that vile hypocrite! It would be infamous. I have my duty to perform."

" Perform it, then, sire," interrupted Fougereuse, whose face had taken on an expression of chivalrous indignation, "and be sure that you punish those who are really guilty. This wretch, this perjured felon, had once a heart. If he sank low, and lived dishonorably, the blame must rest with those who were the agents of his fall. The statecraft of princes is a slaughterer of souls! and for every such slaughter, you men of power, you tempters, must give an account to God at the Last Day."

"*Pasques-Dieu!*" The King was white with suppressed fury. " Stop there ! " he cried. " Not a syllable more. You endanger your reverend head."

" It is yours to take; I proffer it to you without remorse. May God have your Majesty in His holy keeping ! "

" You are certainly a strange being," the King went on, after a pause. " I was wrong to feel angry with you. Let us have a truce. I must see Walter. If he be truly repentant, if he will atone for his treacheries by a sincere self-accusation, well and good: '*I will not the death of a sinner!*' Bring me to Maulny, Father Prior. . . . Why should you hesitate ? "

With bowed head and eyes downcast, the Benedictine remained an instant in silent prayer; then he straightened himself, and looked at the King. "Come, sire," he said.

He rose, and Louis followed him, murmuring to

himself: "*Pasques-Dieu!* You will belong to me, once I pardon Maulny."

The usual dimness of the crypt chamber was dispelled by the strange flare of a torch of yellow wax, burning at the bed's foot, and set in an altar candelabrum. Beneath its mournful light, the sick-bed itself seemed more than ever like a catafalque erected in a tomb. The heavy draperies fell all around, their stiff folds resting on the floor. A vague perfume of incense, still floating in the air, testified that the Sacred Host had been borne under those subterranean arches, for the viaticum of a dying Christian. Loïc and Villepreux, one as motionless as the other, stood behind the sputtering torch. Robert started, recognizing who it was that, entering, lingered a moment in the doorway. The Prior made a gesture towards the couch. Louis advanced quickly, passed Villepreux by, without seeming to notice that the latter saluted him on bended knee, and raised the curtain which hid Walter de Maulny from him. He lay on the pilow, emaciated, wan, his lips and eyelids closed, his features stamped with suffering, but also with an austere repose. The fugitive slept so soundly, that neither the sudden echo of footsteps in the quiet room, nor the unwonted rays of the torch, gleaming full in his face, troubled him at all.

"Maulny!" the King called. There was no response, nor even a movement.

Louis leaned over the sleeper, and touched his

hand. It was icy, and he drew back, alarmed. "He is not dead, is he, Father Prior?"

"Sire, Walter de Maulny appeared this morning before the Judgment-seat of God. He has nothing now to expect nor to fear from the justice of this world. He cried to Heaven before he expired. May the Lord grant him absolution and peace!"

The King hardly heard him, as he stood perfectly still, his gaze fixed on the cold dumb figure which would carry to the grave the secrets of Francis of Brittany. Maulny's demise interfered with many new projects, and constituted a very bitter disappointment. "The end came too soon," he said between his teeth. "A few hours later, and " —

"Death is a sovereign who defers not to Kings. . . . Your Majesty will not refuse a *Requiescat,* and holy water, to so old a friend?"

Louis accepted the little branch of evergreen which Dom John offered, and mechanically sprinkled the holy water over the mortal clay. "How did he die? Did he tell you anything? Did he leave any message?"

"He forgave his murderers." Dom John, answering, looked again at the King.

"By Our Lady of Cléry!" exclaimed Louis, determined to let no innuendo reach him. "If you brought that man to repentance and to a forgiving mood, then you, Father, have wrought a miracle which exceeds those of the Prophet Elias!

But the Lord has dealt with Walter: we must talk
of his sins no more. May he rest in peace! if
peace there be, anywhere, for a soul so corroded
with frantic ambition and devouring pride!" The
King removed his cap as he spoke, and hurried
through a conventional prayer. He glanced carelessly at the dead man. What was a corpse to
him? But "Jesus, thou hope of contrite hearts!"
murmured the Prior, as his lips touched, for the
last time, the forehead of his old playfellow. Walter had expired in his arms, receiving his blessing. Men who had ruined him might scorn his
hapless memory, but the priest who had saved
him from despair was faithful to him, in the eye
of Heaven.

Some of the monks arrived to keep watch, until
the burial hour. Louis took the arm of Dom
John, and went out of the crypt, without further
speech.

As the King of France left the Priory, he
pressed affectionately the hands of Fougereuse,
and asked the assistance, in future, of his prayers
and his wise counsels. The royal diplomat wore
a courteous smile, and an air of earnestness. Indeed, he would gladly have bartered Oliver le
Daim and Tristram l'Heremite for a man of the
stamp of Dom John de Fougereuse; and he spared
neither promises nor flatteries. But the monk
maintained his formal respect, and his reserve.

"I wish that I might grant you some favor,
Father, before I go hence," said Louis, with his

most winning affability. "Can you think of nothing to ask?"

"Yes, one thing: oblivion."

Their eyes met again, as on the previous evening. Louis XI. understood that the Prior of Our Lady of Pity sought no dealings with the great ones of this world, and neither sued them nor feared them.

"Oblivion? Not that, Father Prior. But you shall have your own tranquillity of mind, and my profound esteem."

When the King returned to the castle, le Daim was awaiting him. "Oliver," he said, "I have learned the explanation of an enigma. Whether he be a great statesman or a great saint, that Fougereuse is a master. I never saw one like him! But unluckily, he is now the man of God, and naught else. We shall have to let him alone."

"And Maulny?"

"He died before I arrived, and he died with the Last Sacraments. Do not talk about him. He cheated, up to the very end. He could do nothing that was loyal, first or last. Even his dying was so inconvenient for me, so inopportune!"

.   .   .   .

"'*If Thou, O Lord, will mark iniquities, Lord, who shall stand it?*'" murmured Dom John, prostrate at Maulny's grave. "'*For with thee there is merciful forgiveness; and by reason of Thy law I have waited for Thee, O Lord!*'"

Brother Louis and Villepreux, kneeling by the stone cross, deciphered the new-cut inscription:

HERE LIES
IN HOPE OF THE RESURRECTION

WALTER FOULQUES DE MAULNY

SON OF JULIAN DE MAULNY AND OF BLANCHE DE
FOUGEREUSE WHO IN THIS MONASTERY
PASSED AWAY AT PEACE WITH GOD

ON THE XXX DAY OF APRIL, A.D. MCCCLXXVI.

Pray for him Mother of Sorrows.
Pray for him O Penitent Thief.

And a little below, was yet another line:

Hodie mecum in Paradiso.

THE END.